About the Author

From the magical fjords and mountains of Norway to the mythical highlands of Scotland, and down under to the mystical red sands of Australia, Carina Steinbakk has gathered the inspiration for her first novel, *Flames of Eader*. Her wild imagination, sprinkled with life experiences, and her engineering background sheds a colourful yet critical light on Earth's wayward yet extraordinary ways in this twilight tale. She is also highly particular about her taste in chocolate and pet doggies, and believes in unicorns.

Flames of Eader

Carina Steinbakk

Flames of Eader

Olympia Publishers
London

www.olympiapublishers.com
OLYMPIA PAPERBACK EDITION

A CIP catalogue record for this title is
available from the British Library.

ISBN: 978-1-80074-676-3

This is a work of fiction.
Names, characters, places and incidents originate from the writer's
imagination. Any resemblance to actual persons, living or dead, is
purely coincidental.

First Published in 2023

Olympia Publishers
Tallis House
2 Tallis Street
London
EC4Y 0AB

Printed in Great Britain

Dedication

To my family

Prologue

Grey

Have you ever thought about why the world keeps spinning? I mean, with everything that is happening in this very moment, why are we still revolving around the sun? How is everything connected, or is it? Many a philosopher and drunken bar fly might have tried to answer this question. And found the answer to be God, love, or just bullocks? I will tell you the answer, however, and it is very simple. Namely energy, and some luck. Energy is an easy one to understand. We all need energy, as we can be low on energy, use energy, crave energy, exert energy, or eat energy bars. In one form or another, energy is what makes everything work. What is it really though? One theory states that energy is constant, that it cannot be destroyed, only change its form, say, from kinetic energy in a turbine to heat and electricity through a generator, powering a city or heating up your home. Some say it is a person's aura, spiritual energy, or love. Some say it is liquid gold, others say it is golden rays from the sun, the light in the room or the energy a smile provides.

Well. They are not wrong, but it is however a tad more complicated. You see, energy is magic, and this is where the luck comes in. And no, this is not about boy wizards or bibbidi-bobbidi-boo; this is about real magic. Many books and movies talk about it as science or a mythical force, or even the proverbial capital F – force. It is actually much easier than this. It is about life. It is about death. And the shadows that walk between.

Okay, I feel like I lost you. Let's just look at it like this. You live in a city, right? Or a town? Well, either or, you live on planet Earth, as you haven't got much choice in the matter, which in itself is bloody close to magic. Like, if you knew the itsy bitsy margins for there even being life on this rock. Geez. Anyway, do you like it? Do you appreciate breathing? Do you value being alive? Good. Me too. Most of us do. We have it good. We have comic books, chocolate, and strawberries. Movies and music, good friends, and most of us are free to do as we please. Even though yes, we have had wars won with lives lost, and some still being waged against cruelty, injustice and ignorance. Technology did bring about the rise of the reality stars royalty and we still argue about who wrote which book on how we humans got here. Spoiler alert – it is all propaganda. Though, the different deities from various pantheons have power in that people believe in them. Believing really is seeing, and seeing means leaning into forces of light or dark. Okay, that just got very complicated, real fast, so let's simplify things.

Overall the world is okay, only a bit askew. Not that this misalignment is making any big headlines and if they are, it is only until the fifteen minutes blow over, making it old news. Instead, we are diving into our social media bubbles, with the swipes on dating apps and the hunting of pixelated monsters. Guess what? The world is fucked, and we, the people, are blindfolding ourselves, and therefore part of what is fucking it up. Not even a world pandemic seems to be getting in the way of it. However, I am seriously getting ahead of myself, and may be letting some of my bitterness seep into this. You see, people, most of you are stupid. I know you aren't trying to be, and I am not saying that to be an asshole. Stupid people will just go around in your perfect little world, ignoring what is important. And this is what is pissing me off. This does bring into question 'what is really important?' I would say the fate of the world? Having oxygen to breathe? They both qualify. So this is where the stupid part comes in. If these things are so important, why do we keep pretending we do not care? Or better yet, as the world is a complicated organism with so many moving parts, it is hard to know what to focus on and not. I am not saying you are a lost cause. More like ignorant sacks of meat not able to comprehend the big picture, which is why I am here. To tell you, this is not the time to swipe right. Or left. Or to keep scrolling down your feed. It is time to widen your horizon from a smart phone to the actual horizon. That is why I have come to throw some knowledge your way. And some of you readers might already know this.

The world is awesome. But to stay awesome, it has certain conditions. And needless to say, we haven't been following the instruction manual. Like 'Do not suffocate all life with excessive pollution', or 'Do not kill people just because you don't like their religion' and so on. We are not big on sharing, or caring about what we do not understand. So, we are screwed.

Okay, fine, maybe not entirely screwed. There are those who are trying to turn things around, but against overwhelming ignorance and greed, that shit isn't easy to do.

Let's start at the beginning. Not the beginning of all, because we ain't got that kind of time, but at the start of my story. I promise I will get back to the energy thing, and that it will be good. Plus, not judging, I was one of you. A stupid one. A gamer. A super nerd. I was part of the masses. Loving to ignore the dying of the world. Hell, there I go again. Anyway. Back to my start.

It is almost hard to remember, even though it was not that

long ago. Lucky world. It really should not be this lucky. It is like humans are the fortunate winners in every lottery, always having the odds in their favour. There were the World Wars, then the near-nuclear apocalypse during the Cold War, and of course, some dumbass being elected president, followed by a pandemic in the near future. It is like humans are stumbling along a tightrope over the ever so dark abyss, a tightrope they have soaked in gasoline, and each raindrop falling around their bobbing heads is made of fire. Who are you gonna call? Well, not me, but I am the best thing you got at the moment. I am the solution. No, I am not the chosen one, or the saviour. I do not have a lightning shaped scar, or a burning bush. On the contrary, I am just the fire extinguisher. And why am I the solution you ask? Because I am different. One of a kind. Super special. No. I just decided one day to take a walk.

Chapter 1

Grey

Taking a walk outside, more specifically. Voluntarily. It is not like I have that much else to do. My last assignment is done, the laundry is brought closer to the laundry basket, and I finished with my favourite wolf show, season 3B (Stiles is really good in this one). So, quite out of character, I have decided to take a walk. Even put on my sportier, less worn-out Chucks, the red ones. With the shaggy hair and the awesome 'merc with the mouth' grey Taco Tuesday T-shirt. Its colour matching my name and mood, with a black hoodie, and ripped jeans, I even look kind of normal. Pitch black, straight, messy hair, which seriously needs to be cut, pale skin and a few handsome features, such as big royal blue eyes, with a hue of purple in them, high cheekbones, and square jaw, not that I really care about that. I never got close enough to other people to really show my medium level handsomeness to anyone. Bottom line, I am taking my pale face outside for a walk. I walk down the stairs from my room on the second floor of my dark blue, two-storey townhouse. I am really proud to call it my own, and yes, thanks to my Lizzie and some hard work, it is totally all mine. It has shutters on the windows, with black wrought iron guardrails on the outside, and large oak trees in the front and back of it. My neighbour is this nice old lady with three cats, and too deaf to hear my loud music. The rest of the neighbourhood is okay. Very normal and suburban-like, with minivans and a newspaper guy missing my doorstep every morning. The only exception might be the hot angry girl across the street, who is way too sporty and with a huge dog. She always seems to glare at me from her porch, with arms crossed and hip cocked when I venture outside. She had moved in after the redhead left, who used to hang out in the porch swing all day, knitting and watching the goings on.

I lock my door and trot down the stairs, putting my hands in my pockets in the chilly October air. Heading down the block, then another one, I pass house after identical house, with their SUVs, more minivans and garden swings. I can see some people eating dinner while watching TV, while others are coming home from football practice. Feeling the familiar hollow pain in my chest, I pull up my hood, cross the street, and walk into the forest beyond the suburban bubble. I have my Bluetooth headset in, playing my Favourites playlist. Not quite one with nature, but at least putting my own spin on it. The trees start to crowd me after a while as I move deeper into the darkening forest. I keep walking, finding my own way through the thicket. As the sun suddenly decides to wander off, one Patrick Stump sings about what someone did in the dark and I enter a clearing. Little do I know that this is when and where everything changes.

The clearing is large, with massive oak trees surrounding it. I stop, pausing the vocalist from telling everyone that he is lighting it up and take a deep breath. The wind is running through the leaves, making music by playing nature's own wind chimes. It rustles the long grass around my feet as it trickles through the clearing, while the dusk is quietly flowing in around me, waiting for the night-time sounds to set in. It is like everything is holding its breath. I feel like I put the mute button on nature, which is a mix of awesome and terrifying. Shadows begin peeking out from the surrounding trees as I look around, wondering what the hell I am really doing here. I should be home, watching Stiles's epic performance. Why am I here? I have never been here before, and I do not really do nature, other than the various desktop images on my computer. All I know is that I really needed a walk. A sudden rustle makes me flinch and turn around. Probably just the wind. Or maybe not. But who cares? I am going home. At least, that is I am thinking, before the shadows start to speak.

"Finally ah fun ye," the whisper says, barely making a sound over the rushing of the tall grass all around me. It is gravelly and has a weird accent, making my skin crawl.

"What the hell? Who said that?" My voice, which is usually pretty much deadpanned and deep, is suddenly on alert, one octave higher than my ego would have liked it to be.

With a deep sigh, the clearing answers, "Ay have bin searching fur ye fur a lang time, Grey, an' now yer comin' wi' me. The time haes finally come." This might've been cool, but I am too old for this shit now, and know better.

The headless voice continues to yammer on, and I spin around in the clearing, trying to find the source of it. "Time for what? Time for you to stop stalking people?" Being challenged by a freaking shadow voice is more irritating than scary, and my natural sarcastic side is now taking over. This is not real. This is more like a movie scene. And I want to shout CUT! or turn off this TV right about now, or perhaps nominate it for a Razzie.

"There is nae time fur bullshit. Yi'll need tae come wi' me."

Shadows are creeping in from all sides, making no sense to me at all. Definitely not cool. The eerie voice even swears, in that weird accent, nonetheless. Nature is overrated, I decide, and make a run for it. As it turns out, I am not very good at running, probably should have practiced more. Stumbling through the woods, an eerie sound follows me. It is a whistling sound and ends with me being hit with something pointy. Right in the middle of the back.

Sinking to the forest floor, among the moss, roots, and creepy crawlies, the last sound I hear is what Fall Out Boy's very insightful song has to say about this darkness thing. Could probably give them some input on that, I think as my face slams into the soggy ground.

Chapter 2

Grey

The worst thing about nature? It is wet. Just so wet. Seriously, it gets in everywhere. I wake up shivering and overall soaked and pissed off. Every speech from PE teachers and Discovery Channel shows had told me that nature was awesome. Well it is not. At least not when it is firing pointy things at you.

"So much for the healing powers of nature, Lizzie," I say in a supressed voice, hoisting myself up. Looking around, I realise I am not where I fell, though there is not much to see. I am still wearing my red Chucks, now dark grey Mexican food T-shirt, and I am sitting on something resembling a cot. Not much else here to help pinpoint where I am or what happened. Everything is quiet and my tech is gone. It would probably be waterlogged now anyway, but still, being without my music is like being in a world without oxygen, without light, witho—

"Grey, we are waiting for you." Different voice this time, but the same annoyingly interrupting and all-knowing tone as the last one. Well, I am not going anywhere. Not because I am scared, because I am, totally. But no stupid ass intangible voice is gonna get to know that. So, I lounge on the cot, thinking. Where the hell am I? I have both arms and legs, all fingers and toes. I even pinch myself. I am awake. Damn. What could I remember? Everything. My whole goddamn life. All twenty-six years of it. So, overall, a mid-twenties nerd, caught out in a forest by a weird-ass voice, sure. Doesn't sound surreal at all.

"Seriously, get your ass out here." The voice is more human now. "We ain't got all day." OK, the voice is a *she*. Must be. Too sassy not to be. I am right. The source of the voice is not waiting any more. The flaps of the tent fly open, showing a silhouette of a tall person wearing a hood, which is about all the details I get before she grabs my shirt at the shoulders and drags me through the slit of the tent and outside, into the light.

Light might be an understatement. It isn't light, it is more like a glow. It is like the air itself is bathing in colour and it has decided to take on a hue of gold. It looks like it is engulfed in a golden fog, which makes absolutely no sense to me. All I can do is blink, gape and more or less just look stupid. Which is what I am in this context, so that is fine. I'll admit it. This was above my level of clearance. Glowing air, bossy women and talking shadows. I am basically in a twisted Disney movie. I really should be more freaked out. There are people standing about in the glow, staring at me. The staring is not very Disney-like at all. They are glaring. Disney is cosy, warm, and fuzzy, this is more nails on a blackboard situation. The people are dressed in cloaks and very woodsy clothes, most are women, and all are armed. Some with knives, others with crossbows. Everyone with shielded eyes under their cowls. Bottom line, this is getting too crowded for me. Let's just get that straight right now. I may have some genetically favourable traits, and hey, these women are hot, but no. It is too much. Surrounded by weird light, armed women, and unknown surroundings, not even sarcasm will do the trick.

"Who the hell are you people? And what do you want with me?" I am trying to sound confident but am busted by the twitchy shuffling of my feet on the mossy ground, and my eyes shifting to find an out.

"We are the Guardians, and you, you are late, and quite lucky we found you in time," says the one who had so gracefully collected me from inside the tent. She has her arms crossed and hip cocked, looking very familiar, but I cannot see her face, only the smirk her shadowed mouth is making. She turns and starts walking, and with a forceful nudge, I am persuaded to follow her. The light follows them as well, though suddenly dimming, then coming back in force, partly concealing the surroundings. These surroundings are basically just a forest. If a forest could have wide, impossibly tall trees and a ground so soft, it basically gives your feet a hug every step, or shifty shuffle, your feet make. The place has that earthy smell, musky and fresh, like right after it has rained. The air is fresh, but it is gloomy, and brisk.

The glowing, almost tangible light and the greenery surrounding me makes me feel like home, a feeling which has no reference as the closest I had been to nature was like fifteen minutes ago, or however long I have been here. Shaking it off, I move on, trotting after the billowing cloak of the hooded woman, wondering if this what was it felt like receiving a letter to Hogwarts; a very pointy, poorly delivered letter involving kidnapping that is. I know I should be feeling more frightened, angry, or even just a little miffed due to the circumstances, but it all feels just too familiar for that. I do however have questions.

"So, you are guardians. Of what? The galaxy?" The joke is lame and seriously obvious, and receives nothing but stark silence from my tour guide. "Hey! Would appreciate some feedback if you don't mind? I am the kidnapped victim here, after all."

At this, the woman scoffs, but continues on. I do usually prefer being ignored, but this time it is not appreciated, and especially when it is combined with that condescending attitude. So I stop. This makes me aware of the fact that we are alone, the rest of the group having moved on past us, along with the light, leaving me in growing darkness.

"You can stay all you want, but you won't like what joins you in your solace," the woman shouts in the distance, her words audibly twisting in a hidden smirk. I hold my ground. Like, for a whole five seconds until I can barely see the floating lights, and then I sprint after my silent guide, cursing for not having practiced more physical activity. Tripping over the uneven, moss-covered ground, I gracelessly catch up with my captor who is talking to another hooded figure, staring needles into their backs. I silently wish for a magic wand or a more cake-baking, friendly guide. I guess this isn't that kind of story.

"If I'd known you needed sugar to make this all better, I would have brought you some." The sarcasm is dripping from the comment coming from the second cloaked person, almost making me smile.

"Excuse me?"

"Lay, don't!" the first one exclaims. The sarcastic voice persists, however.

"Not everyone gets to eat cake, you know, and the sugar isn't good for you anyway." It takes a second, but then it suddenly dawns on me.

"Are you freaking reading my mind? 'Cuz that would be a serious invasion of privacy."

At this the second cloaked woman stops, does a one-eighty, showing a mischievous expression below her cowl. "Well, let's just say accepting the terms and conditions without reading them might not always be the smartest move." Seeing my astonished look, she winks, shrugs, and sets off again. I am stunned, wondering which of the hundreds of unread terms and conditions mentioned unwanted mindreading in their fine print.

Chapter 3

Grey

Turns out, the reading of minds is just one of the amazing things this place has. There is the floating, tangible light, the mindreading, and the coffee. No shitting you here, real coffee, which in itself is magic. This reboots my reasoning powers. Floating lights and mindreading. Sure – probably tricks, but anyway. They do however have coffee. A very human and reassuring thing. Sitting with this cup in my hand, I start to actually turn my brain on. Okay. I am in the forest right next to my neighbourhood. Normal forest in a normal part of the world. Then, weirdness and more weirdness. But coffee brings it all around. There is a level of normalcy here. Therefore, I am calm. I have coffee. The warm feeling in my hands, the smell of comfort and tranquillity this golden-brown liquid magically brings forth out of confusion and darkness. Ah, perfection. We have arrived at our destination, or at least I assume as we have stopped and are sitting around a fire, with coffee, of course in silence, as people here do not like to share. I would give my vintage Camaro right now just to know what the hell was going on. But I am sipping coffee, reassuring myself that the world is still the world as there is coffee. Did I mention the coffee?

The smirking cloaked woman is talking. She disappeared the minute we arrived at the camp as I was ushered to this fireplace and given coffee, which did not produce any complaints. With her back I am a bit stressed. Coffee is good. The status quo is restored, but now, it turns out, the now uncloaked lady is hot. Of course she is. It is so cliché. Without her cloak I can see her tan skin, not the kind you get from a solarium, but the kind of tan you get from just being outdoors, meaning the exact opposite of me. She has auburn hair with green, almond shape eyes. Tall, fit, well damn. I just stare. The reason for this is not her looks. Okay, not only her looks. It is more because this woman now standing there, again with her arms crossed, hip cocked and glaring at me as usual is my neighbour, miss Darby Teine. Who knew she would look so good in tight fitting brown leather pants?

"Well hey to you too, Darby," I say, not even trying to disguise the sarcasm. Why would I? It isn't like we are good friends or anything, just the typical I-know-who-you-are-and-see-you-because-we-share-the-same-street-address relationship.

"Grey, we don't have time for this. Yes, sorry for not holding your hand and sugar coating this," Darby says while rolling her eyes.

"Sugar coating? You haven't told me squat!"

Darby frowns, making a small crinkle above her nose. It is actually adorable, making me hate her more. Taking a deliberate breath, she looks at me. "You will know everything in time. Right now you will just need to trust me. Or well, not really, you don't have much of a choice in the matter. Now shut up and power up." This makes me at least shut up. Power up? Huh? Like, 1-Up? It isn't like I am Super Mario or something.

"What do you mean 'power up'?" I even make air quotes with my fingers.

With a frustrated sigh, she just stares at me with a 'you are so dumb and useless' kind of look. Well, this is fun. I turn back to my coffee, which is now cold, trying to ignore her.

"Seriously, tell me. Where am I? What do you want with me? And for the love of all Marvel comics, is there any more coffee?" When I look up, I realise I am talking to air, as Darby is not here anymore.

Shaking my head as I look at where her irritatingly adorable wrinkle would have been, I start to notice more about the place I am in. Yes, there is normal stuff, such as fire, coffee, oxygen, and trees. There are, however, also the previously mentioned floating lights, less now though, under a kind of purple sky, which could be a trick of the light or maybe hallucinogens they put in my coffee. But weirdest of all would have to be the person bringing me more coffee. And I am not complaining. It is just that the person is not a person, more like a Tinkerbell. Seriously. It is a fairy. Or pixie? I am not quite sure on the difference. She has short, pointy black hair, pointy cheekbones, some kind of flower tattoo running all the way up and down her legs. She is wearing a dark blue dress with leather sleeves. And oh yes, she has wings. I have to admit, they are cool. Big, black, pointy wings, shimmering in the light from the fire. A very pointy pixie.

"Actually, you were right the first time, Grey, I am a fairy. A combat fairy to be exact, but I won't bore you with the details."

OK, so she is a mindreading fairy.

"Yes I am," the fairy declares.

Damn it!

At this she just smirks, pouring me more coffee, heating up the cold leftovers in my cup.

"How are you… never mind. Now, details. Please! And, eh… sorry?" She puts the coffee down and motions for me to scoot over on the log I am sitting on, and I happily oblige. Making herself comfortable, her wings laid down, she smiles at me.

"Well, let me start with this. We arrived at a scouting camp, which is where you woke up in our interrogation tent. We are now at the military base of Manawa, in Eader. Which roughly translates to…"

"…the Between." Wait what? I shake my head, a little surprised over this little fun fact I just served up. "How did I know that? What language is it? I do not remember ever seeing that on any map."

Clearly, I did something wrong, because now she looks kind of sad, her large green eyes turning away. "You did nothing wrong. It is just complicated. I do not have all the answers you seek, and the ones I do have are not for me to tell you. But I will tell you this – the more you seek, the more you shall find, because that is your purpose."

"How very… straight forward of you. Thanks."

I try to hide my disappointment, but she does not have to be a mind reader to detect it and laughs. It sounds like Christmas with a dash of Terminator, hauntingly merry, making me smile. I love it.

"I understand you are frustrated right now, and I wish I could be of more help. But, got to go. We will see each other real soon!"

She gets up, and reaches for my hand. I take it.

"I am Laoch-Mór by the way, but everyone just calls me Lay."

Before I can respond I hear raised voices coming from the tents, and see Darby standing in the middle of a group of shouting creatures, the loudest one in a billowing red cloak. Lay gets up, and lightly lifts off the ground with her wings brushing my face. "Oh, sorry! Just… wait here! Do not move, I will be right back. It isn't safe for you, I will explain soon!" And with that she is gone. Not just poof gone, because hey, that would be too weird, right? No, she flies away, totally normal, taking the coffee pot with her. Which blows, since now my coffee is cold again. I realise this must be one of the other hooded figures who brought me here. At least she is more fun than Darby, which really isn't a hard competition to win at the moment.

Chapter 4

Grey

I try to sum things up in my head, but it is melting my brain. Coffee serving fairy, floating lights, a slowly building hate for my hot, irritating neighbour. Sure thing.

Well, to hell with this. I get up, deciding to go investigate my new surroundings. I feel kind of woozy, probably got up too fast or have had way too much fresh air, so I take a minute, just scoping out where I should start. I could try and make a run for it. Again. Where though I wouldn't know, and I am too curious to be honest. You didn't get as good as me at video games without a healthy curiosity, and yes, a whole lot of downtime.

Most obvious route is towards where the sound of something is coming from. More specifically, towards the sound of people, or maybe fairies talking and by the sound of it, quite agitatedly. But no. I need information, and by the looks of things, I am not gonna get it from anyone by asking. So I might as well snoop. I smile deviously at the thought, and sneak off into the woods.

I am a decent woods-sneaker. By this I mean, no one noticed me go, and at the moment I am alone. In the dark forest. At least I have a bit of light. Some of the floaty, moving light substance thing is off to my right, lighting my way. I need to get a better name for that thing. Well, I did just meet a fairy, so how about Fairy Dust. Well, just Dust. So, I have Dust and a plan. Not bad. I try to keep the clearing to my immediate left, but to avoid being detected I slip a bit further in to the dark, passing the Dust, which does not seem to like to be touched, as it parts to let me through. As if I have offended it by not asking permission first to pass through it, it floats back towards the clearing and the fireplace.

When the Dust leaves, the dark rushes in, and I take a moment to let my eyes adjust. They barely do. Looking up, there is not much light coming from the sky. I can see no moon or stars, just a faint glow coming off of that purple, shimmering backdrop. Shrugging, I start to move again, this time a tad more slowly, not wanting to alert anyone of my presence by face-planting into the forest floor. Not that I think the feet-hugging moss would be that noisy.

On that note, I fall.

Actually, it is more of a tumble roll. After about a hundred metres walking in the dark after the Dust left, my foot found nothing but air and being the graceful gamer that I am, I plunge into nothingness. Nothing might be an overstatement as the rocks I roll over do not feel like nothing. After what seems like forever, my journey down the hill is stopped by what feels like a fallen tree. Let me just tell you this, there is no moss hugging me down here. My body does not want to listen to me as I try to get up, and I can feel that something bad has happened to my ribs, as breathing and whining about not being able to breathe hurts a lot. I make it off the ground and sit up against the dead tree, trying to get my bearings. I can't. Now there is definitely no light. I can't even see my own hand as I hold it in front of my face.

"Well that was stupid," I say to myself, as I stagger to my feet and start moving back the way I rolled down, my angry ribs telling me I am a moron.

"Aye laddie, indeed 'twas, bit 'twas gey entertaining."

I come to a full stop, which makes my ribs repeat the

message, underlining the moron part with a deafening jolt of pain on my right side.

I grit my teeth, and look around again. But there is still just utter darkness. I hear rustling behind me, like small rocks rolling over bigger rocks.

"OK, bogeyman, who are you?"

This prompts a laugh, and there is nothing Christmas-y about it. It is all The Shining, all the way.

"Bogeyman 'ey? Well nae quite, but aye nae far off." The scratchy voice drags the words out in a weird British accent, no, Scottish? I'm not sure. I am sure I have heard it before though.

"Well, then who are you?" I keep my eyes moving, trying to catch movement in the blackness, all the while moving slowly back towards where I think the clearing is, though it is getting harder to tell.

"Yer the wee hen that never layed away, aren't ye? Don't ye know, Grey? Have ye forgotten me already?" Then something clicks. The clearing. That creepy voice telling me it was time or whatever, but then Darby and her gang got there. How is he here? He is really hard to understand with the accent and odd wording. I forget all about moving. He knows my name too. How? No answer comes, so I guess he is no mind reader like Lay. Lay! Maybe she can help me?

I try calling her name in my head, first just saying it, then shouting it. Nothing.

"What? Are ye ignoring me?" There is an edge to the voice now, coming from closer nearby.

"No, of course not. Hard to ignore such a lovely voice. It is like bloody pigs in purgatory." I am kind of proud at that calm delivery, with it getting harder to catch my breath and my heart is about to break free from behind the bars of my broken rib cage.

"Aye got that sarcastic sense of laugh ah see. Well, ah could never seem tae get ye tae shoogle that." Shoogle? Hah! The voice is definitely closer now, and I feel like I am getting colder. Not that my T-shirt encourages a lot of heat, but it is definitely colder. Where is my hoodie anyway?

"I am glad ah will get another chance though, ah have missed ye, ye know." Suddenly, something grabs my arm. I didn't see it coming and I can't see it now, but I can sure as hell feel it. Like knives are digging into my skin, and with them like all my energy is dissipating. My knees buckle, slamming into the rocky ground. My ribs are all but forgotten as all I can think about is how alone I am. All that is holding me up now is that hand, and the scraping voice is now laughing. I look up as I can see something where my arm should be. There is a white flowing light, travelling from me and into what can only be described as a man. At least the silhouette of one.

"Lay, please, help me," I whisper.

"Haud yer wheesht, wee laddie. Na one can help ye now! Finally, it's off tae be mine!" The silhouette-man laughs, and as my eyesight dims, I can feel him next to my ear, pulling me closer so he can whisper into my ear. "Ye knew 'twas inevitable, Grey, ye were never off tae escape this. Just let it go, all off it." Despite whatever he's doing to me, I still have no idea what he is saying.

"Like hell he will!" Lay with a wall of Dust behind her comes shooting down towards me, and I can sense the hand letting go of my arm and my head hitting the rocks as I fall backwards. From this angle through half-open eyes I can see that I had managed to fall into a ravine of some sort, filled with dead trees. It looks to be shaped as a bowl. The Dust is floating all around and Lay is screaming something in some language I can't understand and suddenly the Dust is congregating around her.

The dark voice laughs and says, "Ye know ah will find him again; ye cannae protect him forever." Yeah, pigs in purgatory sucks, I think, really starting to hate that voice. The laugh disappears and I can hear the Scottish pigs scream in frustration. Some of the chill dissipates and Lay is bending down beside me.

"Pigs? But at least that heinous pig is gone for now. Oh, Grey, why did you sneak off like that?"

I try to sit up, but find that this time I really can't. A very unmanly sound escapes my lips, though nothing that could have been avoided as my entire chest area now feels like it is on fire, and I can hardly breathe.

"Grey? Grey, look at me. Ah, shit!"

She puts two fingers in her mouth and whistles, or it sounds more like a foghorn, and after like twenty seconds four more fairies arrive. Men this time, all as pointy, with the same hair, brown leather get-ups and black wings, looks like some uniform or what not. Not that I care right now.

"Soldiers, hurry, we need to get him back to Darby and Thiam. Now!"

The four Guardians gather around me and lift me up, which I wish they wouldn't have. The pain is unbearable, it shoots up from my chest into my head, making me scream.

"Oh no! Grey, it will be all right. Just stay with me!"

Too late for that, I think, as I slip into darkness.

Chapter 5

Darby

"What the hell happened?" My voice is dangerously close to blowing up. I step away for one bloody second, and my freaking loser neighbour went and got himself caught by... I let the thought die out. Well, Lay got there in time. I glance over at Grey. He is laying on the cot in the farthest corner of the med tent with the head nurse taking his pulse. It was close, you can tell as his skin tone now matches his name.

I turn around, setting my shoulders and staring at Lay, daring her to read my mind. "Darby, I am sorry. I didn't tell him to leave the safety of the clearing and go into the forest, maybe you should have told him..." The sentence is left hanging as she reads the look on my face, no mindreading needed.

"You are dismissed." A dismayed nod from Lay lets me know she understands, and she exits the tent. What was I supposed to do? Tell Grey the truth? He will have to know in the end, and it will be ugly. Right now, I have a mission, and all that matters is that it succeeds.

For that to happen Grey needs to be on board, or more importantly, he needs to be alive. He is such an idiot. Then again, he didn't know. Because I didn't tell him. Ah, damn Lay for getting under my skin like that. From the corner I hear moans coming from Grey's cot. Good, he is awake.

And the nurse is calling for the doctor. Not good.

"What is wrong with him, what happened?"

The nurse shakes her head but decides to divulge what she knows after she sees who's asking.

"He has a high fever and some internal injury we have not yet pinpointed. We are not sure what was done to him yet." Looking down at him, her statements seem blatantly obvious. Grey is covered in a sheet from the waist down, shivering uncontrollably and his entire chest is either covered with bruises or completely black, only wearing a medallion around his neck.

"Darby, is that you?"

I look down at him, and feel something flutter in my stomach, watching him lying there now. He sounds and looks so defenceless, so vulnerable. And honestly, quite ripped to be a couch-dwelling gamer. Where did that thought come from?

"Shh, stay calm. You went where you weren't supposed to go, and you got yourself hurt." I feel kind of bad saying it, but it's true, and I am pissed off. Mainly at myself.

"The Dust saved me. And... I saw someone..." His raspy voice doesn't get out any more syllables as he falls still. Totally still.

"What happened? Why isn't he moving?" This time the nurse doesn't care who I am.

"You have to move. It seems he lost more than we thought."

I know what that means. "Well, help him! Give him some of mine if necessary!"

Hurried steps come up behind me, and after the doctor checks Grey's vitals or more lack thereof, he gives me a nod and points to the cot next to Grey.

"He will need surgery to patch up the worst of the damage, but that won't matter if we don't replace some of what was taken." With me seated on the cot, the doctor places one hand on me and the other on Grey. I can see the light streaming from my arm and after passing through the doctor, into Grey. Healing powers at its best. When I start to get dizzy, I ease down on the cot, but the doctor quickly releases his grip.

"That is enough for now. He will be able to replace some of it himself if he pulls through."

I nod and watch them carry Grey away into surgery, his skin looking a bit rosier. Closing my eyes for a second, I try to not feel too guilty. I didn't decide this. But Grey didn't choose this either, and it was my responsibility to keep him safe.

After recovering some of my strength, I move out into the clearing, and I see that the darkness has slipped away as more of our... what was it Grey had called it, Dust? has gathered around the clearing, probably on Lay's orders. We simply call it light, as it is light sentient light particles which functions as our source of illumination and our first line of defence against the Darkness. Though I guess Dust works too. I move away from the rest of the people and walk over to sit down at the log where I left Grey, and seeing where he left his half-drunk coffee cup I stare into the fire, thinking back to the first time I saw him, well the second time really. Not that he was that easy to spot, to be honest. Seemed like he only came out at night, paying for the pizza he ordered or going to the cinema. Such a nerd. Not that I was staring or stalking him or anything. It was my job to keep an eye on him. So four years ago I had moved in next door. The house was OK, typical suburban schtick, with a white picket fence, newspaper delivery each morning and that too nosy neighbour lady with three cats. Not that I should judge. It hadn't been all bad. Grey was relatively easy to track, which meant I had had a lot of free time. So, I had gone for runs, always making sure it was during the day when the Batcave – at least that was what I started calling

Grey's house after I saw *The Dark Knight* – showed no signs of activity, read my favourite books, gotten the hang of the technology, even tried out Netflix. It soon got old though. I was used to having more responsibility, more to do, and more friends. The extent of my interaction with people was my companion, Lika, my Samoyed dog, who mostly complained about the food being better in Eader and her favourite show getting cancelled. Dogs like Marvel shows, go figure! My thoughts were interrupted by a commotion behind me.

"What do you mean 'it was my fault'?" Lay is facing off with Decipiér, head of the council. Although he towers over her with his large silver wings and red cloak, Lay was not backing down. "I did everything I could to help him, and you know it. Where were you, you…"

I step in before she can go where there would be no option of retreat. "I think there is enough blame to go around and there will be no point in, well, pointing fingers. Grey is safe for now and in surgery, and all we can do now is learn from what happened."

Decipiér wrinkles his nose, which is kind of unnecessary as his whole face is one big crinkle. "Quite right, madam, you are absolutely right. There is a lot of blame to go around, and I will make sure it gets dealt out according to guilt." With a stern look at both of us, he whips his cloak around and strides off towards the council tents.

Hate that guy, the pompous tall…

"Yeah, me too," Lay interjects, before catching herself. "I am sorry Darby, momentary slip."

"No bother, Lay, just watch your step with that one."

Lay smiles and nods, something glinting in her eyes, but it's gone as soon as I notice it. The med-tent flap rustles and the doctor, Thiam the Healer, steps out, looking worn. "How is he?" Lay and I say, almost in unison.

"He is alive. A rib had punctured a lung and he had severe internal bleeding. But thanks to your rapid response, Lay, and your donation, madam, he will be fine. All he needs now is rest."

The fairy gives me a look after the doctor mentions the donation, but I don't care. Grey is going to be okay. The mission is still safe.

"Saved in the nick of time," Lay whispers, smiling briefly to herself.

"Grey said he was saved by Dust actually." I turn and leave for my tent, leaving Lay looking more than a little puzzled.

Chapter 6

Grey

I wish I was the guy on my shirt. He would've totally handled this like a boss.

"Where is Wade?" I croak, sounding too much like the Bogeyman. And with that it all comes rushing back. The darkness, the voice, the unforgiving rocks, and that cold, sinking, draining feeling... I shudder.

Before I can muster the courage to see if my eyelids hurt, I hear rustling tent flaps and footsteps beside me. Turns out my eyelids are fine as I look up at Darby.

"Excuse me? Who's Wade?"

I roll my eyes and start reaching for the glass of water standing on the table next to my pillow. Turns out my arms and torso do hurt, like a lot. I sink back down, squeezing my eyes shut and waiting for the pain to subside. "Yeah, it's a comic book thing. You wouldn't get it." Darby scoffs, and clears her throat, which after I open my eyes again, seems to indicate her holding out the water for me.

I take a sip and it feels great.

"Oh, I get it. I just never liked those comic book things, my dog did though. Loves that dark knight."

I am too stunned to say anything at first, but then quickly recover. "Your dog? Really?"

"Lika likes it a lot," she says and actually smiles. Must be from my profoundly stunned expression.

"Well alrighty then! Anyway, I was looking for my shirt, you know, the one with the lame comic book dude on it?"

Darby raises an eyebrow at this and throws me something from the end of my bed. "Glad to see your humour survived. Sorry, shirt didn't make it though, didn't have the regenerative power of its imaged anti-hero, so you'll have to stick with this." She strolls off, and out of the tent.

"Hah! Not so lame are they then?" I shout, half annoyed, half impressed.

The humour comment does jog another not-so-pleasant memory though, and I am getting very annoyed with the 'above your pay-grade' attitude of the people I have met. Even the eerie forest dude had been speaking in freaking codes. He had however said something that is creeping me out; he said that he had met me before. Like he knew me, really knew me. And by the way, who doesn't like my sense of humour? It is awesome.

The flaps of the tent rustle again, and this time it is Lay who's come to visit.

"Heard you were up! Ah, and I see you got my present. Well not present, I got it from the supply tent. Hope you like the colour, and that it fits, had to guess your size." She blushes, seeming flustered. Not that I know her that well, but this vomiting of words seems out of character. Before I can comment on it, she starts up again.

"I am so sorry, Grey, I should've been there, I should've..."

Before she can really get going, I hold up my hand. The one without a weird outline of a creepy handprint on it. It did however require some effort, and my groan kind of counteracts what I want to convey to Lay. She looks miserable.

"It is me who should say sorry, and thank you. For saving

me."

Lay blushes. "Told you I was a combat fairy, and I was just lucky that I found you in time after you called me."

"So it worked!" She heard me! I am stoked. Still wanting to reassure her, I keep going. "Anyway, it wasn't your fault. I was bored and I wanted information, so I went seeking." Again, poor choice of words.

She shoots up from her seat at the end of my bed. "But it was I who told you to seek! Not that I meant like that, or there. But now look at you! You nearly died, Grey!"

I try not to look too shaken up by her rant, but in truth I am kind of surprised. Almost died? I didn't realise how close I had come, not that I know what exactly has happened yet.

"Again, not your fault. I would however like to know what happened to me? That is, after being an idiot, stumbling into that ill-placed ravine."

"And know you shall," says a voice from the other side of the tent. It is Darby, back again, and this time with reinforcements in the shape of a tall, square-jawed man, oddly resembling a black Aragorn. Wow, I really need to update my reference sources. Together they approach Lay and me, and without further ado, strong-jawline-guy puts his hands on my chest and shuts his eyes. I am about to firmly object before I feel a weird heat spreading from where he is touching me, then pain. So much pain. I try to push him off, but I have no strength. Lay and Darby take a step back, but none of them move to help.

I must black out for a second, for suddenly the warm-hand-dude has vanished, leaving me alone with the traitor duo.

"What the hell was that?" I say as I sit up, looking at the two girls accusingly. They both just smile, Darby raising that annoying eyebrow.

Wait. I sat up. By myself. No pain. Looking down, even the bruises are gone, I feel OK, though the hand mark is still there.

"You're welcome, now put some clothes on and come with me."

Suddenly I become very aware of being half naked in front of two very attractive girls and scramble to find that new shirt Lay brought for me. It is long, grey (how fitting), with a hood and long sleeves. I give Lay a thumbs up, who smiles, and together we walk to a smaller tent. It is still dark outside, and on the way Darby explains that Thiam, Mr Hot-hands, is a fairy-healer, not that I had spotted his wings in the heat of the healing, pun intended. Suddenly she is just a fountain of information, and partly I wonder why, but decide not to go into it now.

"Why didn't Thiam heal me earlier, if it was as Lay said, with me almost dying and all? Punishing me for taking a walk, were we?"

Darby, who doesn't seem to notice the clear irritation dripping from my words, only shrugs, while picking her way through rows of tents, nodding to passing fairies, people and other creatures I make a note to ask about later. "It doesn't work like that. Healing, like all other powers, demands energy, too much and the healer will die."

A shiver runs through me, and I follow the two girls in silence.

"Okay, there was no coincidence me moving in next to you. I was assigned to look after you, taking over might be more appropriate but yes, my mission was protecting you." We arrive at the smaller, more cluttered tent, with a desk, a cot and clothes strewn everywhere. I feel right at home.

"Take over for who? Protect me from what?" I sit down, feeling relieved that I am finally getting answers, which in this case clearly means giving me more questions.

Darby holds up her hand, stopping me. "If you continue to interrupt me, I will never get through this. But okay. I took over from Hannah Axelrod. Remember the super-sporty redhead in number eighteen?" I nod. "Well, she got reassigned after getting too bored which resulted in her losing her focus. You aren't, shall we say, very challenging. As for the protection part, I am getting to that. Now shut up."

I was about to comment on the boring part, but instead I lean back in my chair, cross my arms and look at her, locking down on the forty-two questions lurking beneath the surface.

"The protection detail has been constant since you were relocated to Earth when you were nine. And before you ask, no you are not an alien, and no, I am not at liberty to say why you had to move. All I can say is that you were important, your life was in danger, and you had to be relocated."

The moment she says 'moved to Earth', all my forty-two questions take a hike. Mind. *Blown*. It is no secret that my family history is a bit shady, but damn. This is a lot. Not just that, some stranger has been watching me for the last sixteen years. At least I knew they didn't care much for the quality of survival, that was for sure.

"You okay, Grey? You look pale." It was Lay who voiced her concerns from my right, gently touching my arm.

"Who me? Oh, sure. Just a bit hungry, that is all." Truth is, I am angry more than anything else. Shocked, sure. But maybe all the movies and books have made me desensitised to weird shit. The worst part is how they have let me believe I was alone. Never reaching out. Not even when I… Never mind.

At the mention of food, Lay jumps up and runs out, saying something on being right back with snacks. Being lost in my own thoughts, I don't stop her. I feel bad. Clearly not as bad as she does, but I wish she would stop making a fuss.

Darby is eyeing me closely from across her desk. "Shall I continue?" I give her a slight nod, all sass gone for the moment. "Don't let this go to your head but, Grey, as I already said, you are important. Or let me rephrase this, you will be important, and in addition you have special gifts few others have."

"Is this the point where you tell me I got accepted to Hogwarts? 'Cause I feel like you buried the lead in that case. Or no, this is my origin story, isn't it? The Chosen One!"

Darby leans back in her chair, both eyebrows raised this time. "You are such a nerd. Or is it geek?"

"Thank you, I'll take both!"

Darby sighs, and I motion for her to continue.

"No, I am sorry, it is not as grand as that, and I do believe you are a bit old for a Hogwarts letter? Missing the mark by, oh, fifteen years?"

I can't do anything else but shrug, secretly acknowledging her light nerdiness.

"Now, about your attack. First of all, I want to say that I am sorry for not being clearer about how stupid it would be for anyone to venture out into the forest alone, especially tourists."

How does she manage to apologise while simultaneously blaming me for everything? It's like a reversed two-for-one special. Before I can voice this thought however, she goes on. "Secondly, you were ambushed because of the danger you represent for the forces we are fighting, and this specific representative you have met before."

This time I have to hold up my hand. "If you tell me this guy is my father, I will literally punch you." This time Darby actually laughs. It sounded like hard summer rain and those first glittering

41

rays of sunshine that come after, all wrapped into one. Which was a totally weird thing to be thinking really.

"You couldn't have touched me if you tried, tough guy. And no, no need to start fearing the Dark side, Luke."

Her smile isn't mocking, just highly amused. Again, nerd alert. She is giving me a run for my money. Okay, maybe not.

"Then who is he, and what does he want with me?"

"It is not that easy to explain, or rather, it is really complicated, and we do not have all the answers yet." Here we go again, giving me the run around.

"She isn't, Grey, she is telling the truth." It's Lay, returning with a plate with something green on it. Yay, my favourite-coloured food. "Well, it is all we have for you at the moment, and you need your strength."

This mind reading thing is getting annoying. Lay doesn't comment on this.

"At least tell me who this 'we' are. And what this place is." I make a point out of placing the plate on the desk, earning a stern look from Lay.

Darby takes a deep breath, pushes her chair back and starts pacing behind her desk. "That is easier to explain, though maybe not as simple to understand. It requires a certain mind-set, but I will try as best as I can." Challenge freaking accepted. I am tired of these people underestimating me.

Darby lays a piece of paper on her desk after pushing the previous content onto the floor, earning her an approving nod from yours truly. My kind of tidying up.

Drawing a circle, she starts to talk. "Okay, so this is Earth, right? Nothing new there. Exists in space, the Milky Way and all that. The thing is though, Earth is the only known planet we know that has existing life."

I feel like she is choosing her words very carefully, even the way she says planet sounds calculated.

"The fact that it can sustain life is incredible in itself, but I won't go into the details. Let's just say there are a lot of factors involved."

This was offensive. Really? I'm getting an elementary school science lesson? "Listen here, sweetie, what you are referring to is called the 'green zone' and is due to our relative distance to the Sun, allowing for the right temperature interval where water won't freeze or boil away, thereby permitting life to flourish." I might have gone too far with the 'sweetie' comment, and the look on Darby's face confirms this.

"Okay, science nerd, gold star. Are you done?"

I can tell she was surprised that I knew this, but right now I am jumping around up in my head. Gold star!

"Point is, these factors alone should've been enough for humans to live peacefully and safely here for a long time. As luck would have it, it didn't work out like that." During her explanation I am starting to notice small details, like Lay's strained look as Darby says that last sentence, and the dark circles under Darby's eyes. She looks exhausted.

She draws another circle around the one representing Earth on her piece of paper. "This is Eader, where we are now. Your movies might call it a parallel universe, but it is not. It is not really a world, more like a fence, an extra layer, or a defensive barrier. Just like the ozone layer protects against the harmful radiation from the Sun, Eader defends against Darkness. And yes, the darkness that comes after the Sun goes down counts. However, mainly, the Darkness endangers the very existence of any source of energy on Earth. Yes, actual energy sources, oil, gas, even the Sun itself. But also, you know that good feeling music gives you when just the right song comes on?"

I nod, trying to come up with some form of a witty retort despite my brain having a total meltdown.

"Well, that good feeling is due to this light energy. Same as when someone you care about gives you a hug. A stranger holding the elevator door for you. The list goes on. Some call it food for the soul. Religion is often brought in here, and no, it is not about any god, though how humans need to interpret it is fine, and we don't get mixed up in it.

"The point is, all the different things humans call it, the explanations they want to give it, or how they try to understand does not matter. It is all the same thing, and it has been here forever. Science has come the closest, such as the first law of thermodynamics—"

"—Which is an application of the conservation of energy principle, where energy cannot be created or destroyed, only change form, and the total energy of a system will equal heat added to and work done by a system." Now Darby doesn't even attempt to hide her impressed look.

"Cards on the table. How did you know that?" She is still standing behind the desk, arms crossed, and I swear that crinkle on her nose just got cuter.

"What? I thought you knew everything about me?" Putting on the most innocent facial expression I have, I start eating the greenery on the desk. It isn't half bad actually, at least it doesn't taste like kale.

Narrowing her eyes, she sits back down, scooting her chair closer to the desk and carries on. "Just for the record, we weren't spying on you, Grey. Just making sure you were breathing. What you did with your life was up to you."

Clearly, I think sarcastically, hoping Lay isn't listening in.

"Moving on, what I have told you so far is the big picture. The Darkness is also the most likely suspects, such as pollution, night, and death. But also bullying, war, killing. Examples would be politicians taking a bribe, a husband beating his wife, stoning in the name of religion, racism, the list is long and depressing. All things that makes us angry, hate, scared.

"And I know, it is kind of cliché. Dark threatening light, black hat versus the white. One way to look at it would be that the Earth's light energy is being hunted by this Darkness and its minions. What for, we don't know. There needs to be a balance between the two, and Eader is, and has been the guard between the two since it all began, maintaining this balance. Without Eader, the Darkness would flood the Earth and we could kiss the 'Green Zone' goodbye. We who live here are Eader's Guardians." She twirls her wrist, pointing in a circle, indicating the camp we are in. I start to nod slowly.

The thing is, having an imagination as flexible as mine, the things she is saying aren't a stretch. Combining my education, cynicism, and extensive database of fantasy knowledge, it is not that farfetched. Still, this is happening. For real. To me. So I let it sink in for a while.

This silence is misunderstood as shock, as Lay puts a supportive hand on my arm, and Darby smiles reassuringly at me. I liked it better when her eyebrows were pissing me off.

So not to give them the pleasure of stumping me, I ask instead, "Where do I fit into this war between hugging and pollution?"

Chapter 7

Darby

Grey seems to be taking the news of him not being from Earth quite well. I am starting to realise he maybe isn't as daft as I had painted him to be. Maybe.

"That is not for Darby to disclose, nor was any of it." The voice is coming from outside the tent, but soon after Decipiér is striding in, his red cloak billowing around his large frame, wings dragging on the ground behind him.

"I do wish you had come to me first before doing this, Darby, we did have a plan you know." His pompous demeanour is bugging me, as always.

"Who are you to tell me about the plan? I was the one who made it! And that is madam to you, Councillor." Reminding him that I outrank him isn't the worst idea.

"Yes, you were, *madam*, but need I remind you that all plans also need to be approved by *me*, I mean, the council?" I know exactly what he is getting at and it is infuriating. Pretentious little council fairy.

The way he emphasises his words is really making it hard to not get angry. Even Grey raises an eyebrow.

I look meaningfully at Lay and Grey, and send a message along to Lay. They both get it and excuse themselves, but not before Decipiér gets a word in. "Yes, that might be best," he says, clearly having missed the communication between us. "Madam and I will need to talk in private. And, Grey, don't wander off again now." The look on Grey's face makes me smile, it is a nice mixture of 'who do you think you are' and 'I do not really care who you are'. As they leave, I wish I can go with them.

"So Decipiér, what can I help you with? It seems like you were waiting outside my tent for quite some time?" If the indication of him eavesdropping on us offends him, he gives no sign.

"General, I did not mean to interrupt your little club meeting, but you were overstepping." Having my authority challenged never gets old, especially me being a woman. Stupid old man.

Walking around the desk, seating myself on the edge, facing Decipiér, I wonder how I got here. Sure, I didn't have much choice as I was born into it, but damn.

"There is no reason why he should not know at least where we have brought him. I did not divulge more than necessary. He was almost killed, might as well know why. Anyway, there is much more information left for you to keep from him, don't worry. You know very well how much this means to me, so stay out of my way, old man." I stride off, leaving the seething councillor to fume by himself.

As much as that feels awesome, I might be taking it a step too far. Whatever. He had it coming, and he is wrong. Grey needed to know. Outside by the fire pit, I find Grey and Lay. It is a tad lighter outside as the woods are teeming with Dust.

"Speaking of which, Grey would like to know more about Eader!" Lay shouts as I approach. I send her a pulse, making her wince. "Sorry, Darby, my bad."

"Wait, what was that?" Grey looks curious, sitting on the same log where I had left him the previous night.

"So you caught that, huh? Oh, Lay isn't the only one with a

few tricks up her sleeve. I am able to, let's say, shock people into place."

Lay sticks out her tongue and I am tempted to repeat the gesture, but I catch myself. I need to stay on mission.

Seating myself opposite Grey by the fire pit, I fold my arms and dig my heels into the ground. "Eader is as I said a protective wall of sorts, but as you probably have gathered it is not like it is made of bricks."

At this, Grey harrumphs, quickly catching himself and clearing his throat. "Must have swallowed a bug."

"First of all, I can start by telling you Eader does not have any bugs," I say, sending Grey a meaningful look, "or animals. It is not a world in the sense that it inhabits a civilisation or fauna. It is more like border control." Grey is holding his hand up. Choosing to ignore it for now, I go on. "We do have the illuminating light particles, or as you have nicknamed it, Dust. It is our source of light, as Earth's Sun does not reach us as well, but I will get back to that." Grey lowers his hand, eyes round. "Eader is as big as it needs to be, in a sense that it has no start or end. There is no map."

This time Grey forgoes the hand in the air. "Sorry, you are guarding a border which has no map? And as for the fauna; trees don't count?" He points to the surrounding forest with his right hand, and with the left he gestures something that can only mean he is dropping a microphone.

"Your observations are as appreciated as ever, Grey, but if you would let me finish you will understand." I get up, and start pacing around the fire, the other two following me with their eyes, well, Grey actually rolling his eyes, but whatever.

"So, as I was saying, yes, Eader has no map. It does not need one, as it does not exist." A hand shoots up in my peripheral view, but I quickly continue. "By that I mean, it is a gateway. Nothing will grow here, the trees you see are funnelling energy, maintaining the balance, and are elements of magic, as there is no sun and if you walk out of this clearing in a straight line, you will at a certain point end up back here. Yes, you might fall down a ravine and take a break there" – Grey makes a very ungentlemanly comment at this – "but you will end up back here. Can you guess why?" I point sarcastically at a very annoyed Grey – annoyed, but willing to take the bait.

"So it's like a riddle? Okay, you can walk and walk, but always end up at the same place, no matter what direction you take? Wait, what? But that would mean…"

"Yes, exactly. Eader is shaped as a globe, actually, it is the inverted Earth, though, much smaller proportions. Or, just scrunched together, yet encapsulating it. There are an immeasurable amount of access points, and they are all fitted together to make up Eader. The reason why we cannot map it is that the amount and location of the access points change."

Anticipating Grey's eager hand, I grab it and lower it gently to his side.

"I am getting to it. This is connected to how you actually get here. As we are Guardians of the light, we can travel here through the light, portals made up of positive energy, no matter what form it takes, though the concentration needs to be high enough. It is not like any euphoric human being can pass through though, or a high turbo engine suddenly drops from the sky; there are certain safeguards. Likewise, the Darkness uses negative energy to penetrate Eader, and then to travel via here to Earth. Though there are also sources of negative energy, or magic, on Earth, increasingly so since the industrial revolution. And, as all these sources are highly inconsistent, Eader's dimensions change, though it is more stable the better the balance between light and dark becomes. The only thing constant, however, is this clearing and our capital."

Grey is rubbing his temples and glancing over at Lay, who has stayed very silent through the whole presentation. Then he sighs. "So, a globe-shaped barrier, defending against evil, no, sorry, negative energy, and can change size whenever. Got it. And the plants?"

"Yes, the trees are fauna as you might call it, and we do have moss as well, as the only undergrowth. However, can you tell me what kind of trees they are? Or guess how tall they are?"

Grey rolls his eyes, then gets up and takes a good look at the nearest cluster of trees. "Redwoods maybe? But they couldn't all be. It is hard to make out the top of any of them."

"There is no end to them. You can look at them as support beams for the border, keeping each side at bay. When the Eader weakens, so do they. Besides this, they provide shelter and structural support." I just get a blank stare in response to this information, and as if he just chooses to overlook this particular input, he launches into the next questions.

"What about the Fairies? And you? Are you human? More importantly, am I? Are we superheroes, 'cause I call dibs on naming myself!"

I could see him struggling to wrap his mind around it, only amplifying it by using humour. His own personal Eader I guess. Whatever works.

"Lay, you want to answer this?" Lay looks up, seemingly surprised to hear her name.

"Huh? Oh, sure!" Spreading her wings, she floats up and lands opposite the campfire as I situate myself next to Grey. "So, I'll start with the history, as it will make more sense that way.

You have heard us use weird names and words, you even understood one of them, remember?" Which must've been a rhetorical question as she dives into the explanation. "Well, that was of course Scottish Gaelic. Oh, don't you sass at me, Grey, remember I can hear you."

I glanced over at Grey, noting a slightly guilty look on his face.

"Okay, so not obviously. But yes, Scottish Gaelic. We also use Latin, native American languages, Maori, other ancient languages, names and much more. The reason for this is that the individuals selected to guard Eader were from all over, from every continent, both new and ancient cultures – that is, for the initial selection, at the beginning of it all. Now, the council, by use of scouts, would make selections from Earth – sometimes meaning kids from previous Guardians as well. In addition, and this is the good part, the Eader gifted us with four special Guardians, or Gatekeepers." At this, she draws herself up a bit. "As the Eader is fuelled on, well, energy from all in existence, these Guardians took many different shapes. Remember how Darby told you that light energy could be good feelings, something positive?"

I see Grey nodding slowly, half-expecting him to tip over.

"Good. This positivity seeps into music, books, paintings, photos, in all art really. As well as actions and more tangible sources of energy, such as technology. As far as we can see, Eader takes inspiration from this, and the Gatekeepers are shaped accordingly. People of Eader are people touched by the twilight of Eader – when arriving in Eader, their recessive genes are activated – effects of which are signs of their ancestry, such as fairy, troll etc., or simply a skill – potions, sword fighting and so on, but most importantly the underlying ability to use magic."

"Whoa, sucks finding out you are a troll," Grey exclaims.

"Yeah, for many it can be quite a shock. We do however have a very good integration department that helps people with the transition. There are also many inactivated Eadorians living on Earth, having chosen a normal life, or simply do not know about their heritage, while others live here, working together to protect Earth."

Grey seems to be thinking this over, then nodding, as if it all makes perfect sense.

"Anyway, that is why I look like a fairy, we have dwarf-like people as well as nymphs, Valkyries, brownies, satyrs, once there was a unicorn and I think we even had a Pippi Longstockings. My ancestor was a fairy born from the original Eader four," Lay finishes proudly.

"Hold up! Unicorns? I feel like I entered Narnia right now." So he doesn't pass out, but Grey is starting to look flustered.

"Not Narnia, but that too was a separate universe I suppose, though this is much more real I'm afraid." I mean it as comfort, but I'm not very good at that. Comforting. It seems unnecessary. Woman up or don't, don't whine about it. That is at least my motto.

"But seriously, Pippi? Anyway, you said dwarves and fairies. What am I though, and Darby? Human, right?" Grey was sounding hopeful.

"So, that is where it becomes really interesting…" Lay starts, but Darby cuts her off.

"We can get back to that. The more important part is the counterpart to this. As the Eader takes inspiration from positive things, can you imagine what is spewed out on the dark side? More appear each cycle."

Even I shudder at the thought.

"So you are saying there can be Hitler-copies walking around out there?" Grey looks incredulous.

Lay steps in. "Nah, it doesn't copy specific humans, just types, or fictional imprints. As well as species or races if you will." This seems to relax Grey a bit. Though he doesn't stay silent for long.

"So, Voldemort then? Wait. When you said cycle... you meant year, right?"

"Actually, no." This is the one question I haven't been looking forward to answering really. "You see, time works differently here. It is more like a waiting area. You can kind of look at it as Eader is getting pressure from two sides, dark and light. As a result, time is squeezed to an almost standstill."

Grey looks annoyed, and proves this by saying very annoying words, "Okay, I know you aren't very scientifically minded, but you cannot squeeze time. Time is not squeezable!" Grey is on his feet now. He looks really upset. "Time is measured on account of the Sun's movements and will be constant, so like, this is a different time zone. That is what you are saying, right?"

I grab Grey's shoulders, wait for him to look me in the eyes, and speak calmly. "Look up, Grey, have you seen the Sun? Or the moon?"

Shaking off my hands it is Grey's turn to start pacing. "This means... Wow. Shit. Okay." I follow him with my eyes from where I stand. Even Lay looks half amused. "But you said I came to Earth when I was nine. Nine years, right?"

Chapter 8

Grey

Holy chimichangas! This place stops time! "Let me just repeat that. I was nine when I left here. How does that work in, eh, Eader cycles?"

This is not cool. Sure, I can handle the unicorns and the globe-shaped alternate universe I am currently visiting. And, oh yeah, some weird source of energy creates magic warriors. No biggy. I am storing all this for later processing. Because right now I'm running out of CPU.

"Bro, you need to chill out." The voice is coming from my left, and the source of it is this tall, murky blonde-haired kid. Well, me calling him a kid might not be right, he is at least one head taller than me, and with that time relativity thing here who knows how old he is. By the looks of it, he also knows his way around a sword, at least by the way he is swinging his, and he is giving me this funny, almost piercing look. He is wearing tactical gear, all black, with a sleeveless shirt and combat boots. Even accessorised with a silver bullet hanging on a silver chain around his neck.

"Name's Stone. Callan Stone." He chuckles as he stops outside the sitting area of the fire pit, looking the three of us over, his sword placed carelessly across his shoulders. "Did I miss anything?"

"No, but you are early." Darby looks annoyed. "I still have

details to go over with Grey."

"Too easy," he says in way of acknowledging the delay, then shrugs and puts down his sword, sitting down on the log furthest away to wait.

A quiet sigh escapes Darby, but she turns back to me. But before she can continue, I turn to Callan. "So, what are you? Warlock? Vampire?"

"Nah, just pure awesomeness," he says, nodding as if agreeing wholeheartedly with himself.

"So, just a humble human then?" I raise an eyebrow. Who is this dude? Callan just smiles.

"Spotty dog, my friend."

I snort. Seriously.

Another sigh, more audible this time, tells me that Darby is running out of patience.

"Sorry," I mutter and shrug.

Ignoring this, Darby continues, "Well, now that that is settled... it is actually easier to just show you the numbers in order for me to translate how time works." She starts drawing again, this time in the sand. "One day on Earth takes about 50.5 hours here, making one Earth year..."

"Are you kidding me right now?" I jump up, yet again. This is too much. She can't be serious.

"2.1 years! If that is true... I spent almost nineteen years here? But... how? Why don't I remember it?" I feel sick... Lay must sense this, or just read my jumbled, freaked out mind, because she coaxes me down on the log again.

"It is okay, Darby will explain. But I can say that time is experienced slower here yes, but a day here will relatively take the same amount of time on Earth. Meaning, we share the same calendar. We just have more time per day, that is all." Nope, not helping.

Darby, however, is less inclined to sugar coat. "As much as I am impressed by your math skills, if you would just let me continue…" I just stare into the dying embers of the fire. How old am I? Why don't I look older? Or more importantly, as shitty as my life has been up till now, it seems like I am missing a huge part of it. As if being adopted hadn't already caused a lack of roots.

"The reason why you cannot remember your time here I do not know. All I know is that, as I said before, you are special, and we need to protect you.

"Lay told you how, initially, the Eader gave us four Guardians, pure ones, or Gatekeepers, or Fiors as they are called. There are always four. There has however not been a new Fior in over twenty-five years, Grey. Now there are only two left, and you were the last one to be born."

And there it is – with the extra nine Eader year conversion, I am not only a very young looking thirty-five-year-old and I am not even human. I am the spawn of some energy spouting sperm bank.

Looking up from the orange glows in the pit I notice how it is suddenly very quiet. Looking around, three pairs of eyes are staring at me.

Meeting Darby's eyes last, she asks, "You okay? You are being uncharacteristically quiet."

I am not okay, but I have had enough of everything right now. I stand up and mumble something about how my head hurts.

Callan stands up with me, jokingly saying, "Let me show you to your room, oh special one." This really isn't the time, and if he senses that or not, I don't know. Maybe he isn't so cool after all. Let's just say that the jury is still out. I nod to Darby and Lay, both looking worried, or at least Lay is.

Callan has already left the clearing and is halfway back to where the med tent is. I walk after him, in no hurry to catch up. Lucky for me, he slows down, giving me no choice. "So, what can you do, newbie? You must forgive my manners, there just hasn't been anyone new like you here as long as I can remember. That is, for fifteen of your years."

Is this what I sound like, nerd diarrhoea mixed with annoying questions? Of course not. I at least have a filter. I think. "Wait, you are only fifteen?"

Callan laughs, skipping over a fallen tree branch. "As you just heard, it is a bit more complicated. I was selected to be a Guardian when I was five, so I have lived here for ten Earth years, making me..."

"My age. Or at least, kind of?" I was used to tough math, but this was just ridiculous. "Do we age differently? Because you don't look like a fifteen-year-old at all, and I look your age, but apparently that is not the case." Callan's face reflects the pained expression on mine. I stumble after him, not really paying attention to where we are going, as Callan bursts out while throwing his hands in the air.

"I think the word you are looking for is mind-blown! And to answer your question, the mix of the time tempo difference and energy interference makes ageing a bit of a... hard thing to measure. Time doesn't really move, so the body more or less stays the same when you are here. That being said, just imagine how old Decipiér is! You met him, right? So, I guess anything is possible in your case. We don't know what sort you are yet. Ah, but here we are!"

The nonchalant change of subject was dizzying.

'Hey, you are an ageless, unknown entity, and here is your

room.' Nothing upsetting about that. Yeah, the jury might have an unfavourable ruling on this guy. I have never really liked people anyway, and this guy is starting to prove my point. The abrupt change does however bring me out of my stupor, and I notice that this place is way bigger than I thought. As all I knew until now was the clearing, the Freaky Forest, the med tent and Darby's tent, all situated at the edge of the clearing, it had seemed small, intimate, really non-threatening.

I can now take that back. We are standing at the bottom of a hill, clearly having just come down it, and spread out in front of me is a city. A real city. No tents. The houses are built from a mixture of stone and wood, no surprises there, and they are everything from two-storey apartment buildings to mansions, and a castle in the heart of the city situated on a small hill, some cottages hanging in the monstrous trees left standing, and everything is in different, earthy tones. The architecture is dizzying, with everything from gothic towers with pointed arches, flying buttresses, ornate decorations, and gargoyles, to Japanese style houses, complete with shojis, tiled sloping roofs and flaring corners. To my right I see Scandinavian styled timber buildings with notched corners, while to my left there are buildings with Spanish archways and arcades, with painted tiles and circular towers complemented by ornate iron work. Their neighbour lives in something between a hobbit hole, Viking longhouse and an Icelandic turf house, and next to that, further down the path, a Victorian mansion with turrets, porches, balustrade stairway and bay windows. In addition to all of this, there are the more modern townhouse and classic mansion styles, with the occasional surf-style beach hut in between. Simply surrealistic, yet utterly amazing.

It looks like someplace magical, all gathered in a shallow

valley, with the floating Dust frosting the view.

"Yeah, like a rainbow threw up, isn't it?" Yep, this guy is an oaf. "The big one in the middle is the town hall, where the council resides. We have what you would expect really. You can get decent food, clothing, utilities, weapons, beer, and we even have Wi-Fi – the password changes once a week, but I'll hook you up. I wouldn't try the local beer though. Anyway, welcome to the heart of Eader, Manawa."

I must be gaping, because I feel a finger under my chin, nudging it up. I brush away Callan's hand, and take it all in again. The half-normalcy of it all helps calm my mind. Tree houses, bar, town hall. Normal things.

"This is you. Hope you have a good nap, and we can go for a beer later, imported of course!" Callan points at a house at the edge of the city, right where we are standing. House is maybe an understatement. It is a dark blue villa, same shade as my house. It has two floors, big oak double-doors, and massive windows. Even a porch running all the way around it. As there are no streets, saying it has a garden would be lying, as its immediate surroundings are made up by the forest floor, but it does have two big trees on each side of the oak door. Cosy, I think as I step towards the door.

"Do I need a key or what?" But there is no answer, Callan is gone, and I am alone. Finally.

Why is this my house? It is too big for one person that is for sure, and, as it turns out, I do need a key. The door is locked. The door itself is massive, with intricate markings of what looks like exploding lights and leaves caught in a tornado. In the middle of the tornado on the left door is a handprint, a bit deeper into the wood. It looks weird. I feel like there should be words above the door, a riddle or code to let me in. Instead, I put my hand in the handprint, and immediately I regret it. I feel a tug inside my chest, sucking the breath out of me. I can't rip my hand from the door because it is of course stuck. Damn it! Me and my 'got-to-touch' habit. Bad Grey!

After a few seconds I open my eyes and am standing with my burning palm facing away from me, arm outstretched, and I can't see the door any more. Actually, I can't see anything except a faint glow coming from my right. I am inside the house! Good Grey!

The dim glow is all I can see, and as I move over to it, the light intensifies. The glow outlines another handprint. Great. Turns out new habits just like old ones will die hard, and I place my hand over it. This time all that happens is that the light turns on. Or actually, it is more like it floods in. I am in a hallway of some sort, with four doors, two on each side, and a staircase at the end. Pretty standard stuff. The first door on the right swings into a spotless kitchen, and I dive into the fridge, which is heartily stocked with, guess what, normal food. Grabbing a can of coke, I swing back out and try the next door. This one must be to the cellar, as the light from the hall is swallowed up by darkness, only showing a couple of steps of stairs. I can't see any light switch handprint, and no Dust to help, so I leave this one for later. The first door on the left side leads into a comfy sitting area, with windows facing out towards the city. There are bookshelves laden with all sorts of books and magazines, and even a TV. Wondering about the reception possibilities here in Eader, I wander out into the hallway again, and check the last door, turning out to be my least favourite room – the laundry room. This room is also spotless, with folded linens and towels. Well, I will not frequent this room.

Running upstairs, the staircase made from a hollowed-out

tree trunk I might add, and the gist is the same up here – four doors, though here each door has a handprint next to it. Doing the same round as before, I test the first door on my right. Already nearing the handprint, I feel that something is wrong, and this is confirmed when a small jolt is sent up my arm. At the same time the faint blue hue around the handprint switches to red. Access denied, I think.

"That is not very nice!" My voice echoes in the large space, but I feel better, sending a nasty look at the lock, which is now switching back slowly to blue, passing through stages of purple. "Let's see what you can do then, shall we?"

The second door on the right doesn't answer, but does deliver a nasty bite as well. Shaking my hand, I end up with the same response with the first door on the left. "Let's break tradition with fourth time is the charm!" I mutter. Success! The same tug in my chest and sucking feeling in my chest and I am in the new room, my room, I guess. My eyes are immediately drawn to the window, a massive panoramic view, showing the city and the town hall castle dominating the middle. But from this height I can see further, to the forest surrounding Manawa, and beyond. It is like Darby said. It is an inverted dome. Not that it is like I can see the whole picture, due to the dim lighting mostly – but I do see how the edges curve slightly up, like you would on a horizon on Earth, only opposite. If the Flat Earth Society could see this. Ripping my eyes from this mesmerizing view, I check out the rest of my room. The bed is super king-size, at least by the looks of it, and is placed on a rise in the middle of the longest wall. A small door leads into a bathroom, with shower, sink and toilet, nothing fancy, which suits me perfectly. The rest of my room consists of a closet with different variations of clothing, some normal looking, others very much like Darby and Lay were wearing, though more in my preferred colour scheme, black. I do see a major flaw though. There is no computer, no TV, no gaming console in here. Nothing.

"What the hell do people do around here?" At least there was the one downstairs. I step up to the bed and throw myself across it, and I am suddenly reminded of why I wanted to be alone in the first place.

Chapter 9

Darby

I find Callan standing outside Fior Mansion. "Where is Grey, Lieutenant?"

Callan snaps to attention and salutes me lazily. "Didn't see you there, General. To be honest, I am really not sure. One second I was showing him the sights and inviting him for a beer, and the next he was gone."

Raising my eyebrows, I look at the mansion. I am not really surprised, as no one could get near the place. As if to prove this, Callan takes a step closer, raising his arm. A low buzz starts up, and only intensifies as he takes another step.

"I wouldn't do that if I were you." Callan has never been my favourite lieutenant, and I would not keep him around if it wasn't for his superior fighting skills and strategic knowledge.

"Thank you for that, I am very aware of the consequences." His snark doesn't really help either, I note.

"We will just have to give him the time he needs; it has been a long day for him." It has been a long day for everyone, and mine is just getting longer. "Come with me, we have a meeting with the council."

"Oh joy!"

I give no reaction to this, though it is close to subordination. He is merely saying what I am already feeling.

We walk through the city towards the castle, feeling our

surroundings change. There isn't much of a class system here, as the entire population more or less works for the same purpose. All sixty-thousand-four-hundred-and-two, or I guess three now, working together to protect Earth. The Guardians and Special Forces are the more direct fighters, but there is the supportive network as well: cooks, cleaners, tailors, blacksmiths and swordsmiths, potion makers and healers. The list goes on. It is a grand operation. I am always amazed over the commitment and talent people here have. Even though the work we do does not require a large force, it does require power and courage, and none of it could happen without everybody here. Even the council. I really do not like politics, and bureaucracy is seriously the worst thing ever. They are the ones who create the air of superiority above everyone else, and if you ask me, in a war against Darkness, it seemed like some of it lived right in the middle of Eader. But no one asks me. It is however a necessary evil to keep everything running smoothly in the city. And speaking of evil, Decipiér meets us at the door. I never liked the Castle, it is like the Beast's castle, before Belle broke the spell and without the charming talking furniture. Giving me his most winning smile, which just gives me the creeps, he leads us into the main chambers, where the rest of the council is waiting.

"Here we are, step right in." Decipiér is being way too nice, or at least he is trying to be. Callan follows me in and takes the seat at the door, as he is not allowed at the main council table.

The rest of the council members are seated two on each side of Decipiér. Ryder, head of transport and Thiam, head-healer are to his right. Bethany, head of security and Bob, head of acquisitions to his left. Even though the table is circular, they are all scrunched up at the one end, with me on the other. I smile at Thiam and Ryder, who both nod back.

"So, now that we are all here, we can start." I've been to too many of these to really care what they talk about. So many words, yet so little use for them. 'How will we bring in more food?' I would say buy it, bring it in through the nearest breach. Boom. Done. But here, four meetings, five votes and three plan outlines later – still no food. This time, the meeting is about me though.

"Darby, we are concerned. Yes, you managed to apprehend the target, but the further management of its safety and our safety, it is just not good enough."

I took a deep breath, not breaking eye contact with Decipiér. "First of all, 'it' has a name, and he is a person. Grey is safe and if he had been briefed earlier and more extensively that whole incident in the forest could have been avoided." My mind is racing, and Decipiér looks ready to fire a counterattack, but I blurt out the rest. "Secondly, the whole reason for this mission was literally to save our worlds. Or should I use your own words 'extreme times calls for extreme measures'? Well, the mission is underway and the extreme times as you so nicely put it, are not getting any less extreme, especially if you won't allow me to do my job as I see fit." This produces a smile from most of the council, even a snort from Thiam. "Now, if you do not mind, I will get on with my 'management'." Illustrating the quote marks might be a tad too much, but to be honest, I'm furious. Where did he get off challenging my authority?

As I get up and stride out, Decipiér clears his voice and yells after me, "We will be watching you, Madam General!"

Callan gets up and claps my back as he trots after me. "You go, girl!" he says, whistling. Reaching the doorsteps outside the castle, I turn to him, grabbing him by his leather vest.

"Listen to me, Lieutenant. You better start remembering your rank, or I will write it down for you with my blade somewhere it will be very hard for you to miss when you stand admiring yourself in the mirror every morning. Is this understood?"

Nodding furiously, I let him go, noticing that by doing so he actually takes a second to hit the ground. The bustling square outside the castle, which is always filled with people, is suddenly very quiet, too quiet. And I suddenly get why. I look down at Callan, as he gets up, dusting himself off.

"Sorry about that, might've... Erm, no, I definitely overreacted there. I am sorry, Lieutenant." He looks almost scared. I change back, ignoring the stares from every angle of the square.

"No worries, General, I was out of line." His irritating, nonchalant manner is gone, so that is something. But it is replaced by that look I hate more than anything. The look that tells me that I am different. I am different, and people are not sure of what I am or what I can do. I do know. Well, not all of it. I am still learning, and I even scare myself sometimes.

"Let's get back to Grey, he needs to get his shit together as we have things we need to get done." The crowd has started moving again, but I can feel their eyes following me out of the square.

Chapter 10

Grey

I have seriously lost my shit. Staring at my ceiling I wish I was back in my own house. That is what I was good at. Being alone, doing my own thing, staying out of people's way. People are generally stupid. They play games, lie, take advantage and judge. I hate judgemental people. Closing my eyes, it is not hard to picture them. In the foster home. Always being the smallest, shortest, slowest. But that was all so superficial. It didn't bother me anymore. Much.

At school it was worse. I loved school, don't get me wrong. Especially when we got to read. It didn't really matter what it was. Maths, English, History. I devoured it all. And it all just made sense. It was naturally all connected, and it made me somehow feel connected to everything. I never found a connection to the other kids though. Maybe they didn't like how I knew the answer to every question in class. Or how my clothes were too big as they were hand-me-downs. It would've been fine if that was the case. Well, it wasn't. It happened on a Thursday. I remember it as if it happened every day. And it did, as I replayed it in my mind more or less constantly. It was quarter to twelve. At school, during my lunch period. I was twelve. Her name was Landon, and she was the closest thing I had to a friend in class. We sat together in English, and we bonded over Narnia. She liked Aslan, while I preferred Prince Caspian. It was so nice having someone who smiled to you occasionally, acknowledging you as more than wallpaper.

One day, Landon stopped coming to school. The teachers told us her dad had just died and that we should be considerate when she came back. After two weeks she returned to school, looking different. More guarded and sad. I tried to talk to her, but she avoided me. She avoided everyone. That day in class I slipped her a note, saying she was like the kids in Narnia. Missing her parents, or her dad in her case, and maybe the Wardrobe would take her away to Narnia. She smiled at me, taking my hand. That is when it happened. It started small, like a tinge of red when the Sun is coming up. Then it grew to a full blast of the sunrise. Though it wasn't warm at all, it was the opposite. Freezing. It rose up my arm, squeezing my heart and suddenly all I could think of was pain. I must have screamed, because when I opened my eyes, I had twenty-two pairs of eyes locked on me. Landon looked terrified.

"What did you do?" she asked me.

She looked better. Not so grey-skinned any more, and not so sad.

"What? I… I don't know."

She looked almost happy, but I could see she was scared. She didn't understand what had happened. I didn't either. After that, no occasional smile lit up my day. All I knew was the looks, the whispers of freak and weirdo following me through the hallways, and the only respite was reading. I eventually also discovered the sanctuary a pair of headphones gave, and then the movies. Escaping into other worlds became my hobby, and after a while, it became my life. It wasn't until high school when I discovered the world of fantasy and comic books. It shifted my focus to living in the world of fiction, and existing in the real world. The amazing feats of Superman, the extraordinarily happy and magical endings of Disney movies, but most of all it was the stories where the hero saved him or herself. Spiderman was especially a favourite, nerd turned hero. The more I read, the more I became convinced that I was living my own origin story. It was just very long, and I just needed to wait a little longer. Endure my foster dad's belt just one more time, followed by my foster mom's blatant ignorance.

After finishing high school, I disappeared. I was eighteen, and could decide for myself, so I decided to do what I did best – vanish.

Looking back, I wish I had known then. How much more there was. How I wasn't alone, that I belonged somewhere. As my thoughts keep unravelling, it only make me hate this place more. They knew what was going on and they didn't do anything, and it only got worse after that. Without anyone to turn to, I had no money, and I couldn't get a job, so I ended up on the streets. And life on the streets was no Narnia.

Moving from alley to alley to avoid the worst of the gangs, who were trying to recruit tweakers and lost souls to deal their poison. I mean, I wanted to belong, but not that bad. Instead, I starved half to death, finding food in dumpsters and trying to stay warm. One December night I was failing on both counts, laying in a corner of an alley, under some newspapers I had scavenged, listening to the inside of my stomach turning itself over. It hurt more than usual, and I think I was running a fever. Though the shivering was more habit than anything else. Rats were running along the wall behind me, and I was contemplating using them for insulation, or even food.

"Why aren't you from Narnia and here to save my ass, huh?" It was a definite low point, as talking to them didn't do much good, but it still helped me feel better. As for being invisible, it seemed like no matter where I went, people tried to approach me. Even they looked a bit confused about it and I stopped venturing to areas where I knew there were a lot of people. It made me feel even more lonely, so I made a few friends in the homeless community. But it didn't make me feel better. Every time I talked to one of the vets or tweakers who had ended on the streets I felt horrible. Sure, their stories were sad and depressing, but it was more than that. I always felt so drained. It seemed to make them feel better, because I became a popular guy to set up shelter next to for the evening. I didn't mind, as I started to like the company, but each night I would be just a bit more tired, a bit more exhausted. In the end, that same December night, there was an actual brawl over who got to set up his cardboard house next to my corner. The people involved didn't really know why, they just wanted to have a chat, they said. I guess they couldn't really explain it. I solved it by talking to all thirteen of them, listened to their struggles and worries, shaking their hands, and watching as they left, one by one, smiling. I sagged further and further down into my corner, finally closing my eyes, my stomach again hurting, and sweat running down my back. Being tired didn't cover it any more. I felt hollow and done, and sleeping felt like the only right thing to do, like I could sleep forever.

Had I known then what I know now I might've done differently. Darkness. It had to have something to do with all of this. Eader. Darby. All of it.

Anyway, little did I know it was one of the coldest nights that year, and being so exhausted I didn't wake up the next day to eat or move around to warm up a little.

I barely felt the nudging. The voices were more like a dream than anything else. The one thing that made me aware of

70

something happening outside the darkness I was drowning in was the warm feeling on my cheek. It stayed there and streamed through my neck, into my body like warm summer rain. After that, it is pretty much a blur.

I remember being lifted. Then nothing until waking up in a bed. It felt like lying on a marshmallow; soft and wobbly. Nothing like the steady pavement in the alleys. They told me I was in the hospital. I was dehydrated and suffered from extreme malnutrition, along with a fever caused by the hypothermia, all resulting in a severe case of anaemia. They didn't know who had brought me here, but they said they would take care of me. My stomach still hurt, but as this was no news to me, I didn't care. I was warm, safe, and food was offered freely, for the first time in three years. I took it.

The fever was not giving in though, and after a few days, it got worse, as did the stomach pain. Lizzie, one of the older nurses, had taken a liking to me, treating me as if I was one of her sons. Four days after I was admitted to the hospital, she came in, carrying my dinner, smiling with that same glint in her eyes.

"So, Grey, how are we feeling today? Ready to tell me some more stories?" Every day I had told her some made up tale of where I came from. I didn't want to share my real story, and I think she got it. She never asked questions, just kept me company while I ate and listened to the fantastic new story about me.

"Of course, Lizzie. Did you bring me my usual?" At this, she would always laugh, winking at me, and say something about how the cuisine here was five star. It wasn't, and she knew it, but I didn't mind. It was food after all. The stomach pain had increased to a sweet nine on a scale from one to ten, and I was sweating. I didn't want to complain though; after all, this sure as hell beat the alleyways of my every day. But that night I couldn't help it and as I reached for the green Jell-O (the red one was better), I groaned, squeezing my eyes tight as the pain intensified, throbbing in my gut. Lizzie had raised her eyebrows, eyeing my forehead.

"Still having that headache. And now your stomach hurts?"

I shook my head, telling her it was nothing. Touching my hand, she furrowed her eyebrows. The pain increased, but now from where she was touching me. Her worried look only intensified as a loud moan escaped me. She didn't believe me and proceeded to examine my belly, which at the slightest touch exploded in more pain.

"Oh, Grey. How long has it been like this?"

I shrugged, saying it is not that bad. My eyes told Lizzie a different story though, and she rushed off to find the doctor as my Jell-O slipped to the floor. In the few minutes she was gone, the nine became a ten. Lizzie's touch had made it worse. My pain riddled body couldn't process anything more though. Slipping in and out of consciousness, I saw the door flying up and Lizzie coming in, followed by one of the on-call doctors. He also touched my stomach, receiving the same result. I gave a short scream and slipped into darkness again.

When I woke up, I was in a different room. Monitors were beeping all around and Lizzie was sitting in the chair next to my bed, smiling when she saw me looking up at her. "Well, hello my superhero. Good to have you back!" I tried sitting up, but felt a sudden pain in my lower abdomen, and Lizzie pulled up my sheet, gently pushing me down at the same time. "No, you just lie down. Gonna rip them stitches moving around like that. Honey, your appendix burst. Must've been building for a while, but the inflammation got bad, and must've hurt something terrible at the end. Why didn't you say nothing?"

I just smiled. It had been a long time since anyone cared the way she did, though I still was very wary of her not touching me, and it made me feel horrible.

"Sorry, Lizzie."

She smiled again. "Don't you worry, Grey, we'll get you all better, and that is a promise. Now, ready for some red Jell-O?"

I stayed in the hospital for two more weeks and the day I was checked out, Lizzie came to see me off. No one had hassled me for paying for my care and I was so relieved. Knowing and again not knowing what would happen if I touched Lizzie, I gave her a big hug. I felt the cold feeling as my cheek touched hers. But it wasn't as bad as it had been, and after we let go, I could see a big smile on her face. Totally worth it. "Here, just to get you started honey, take care of yourself." She slipped me a small box, patted my shoulder, and hurried away, drying her eyes as she went. The box was small and red, with a lid and a blue ribbon tied around it. I walked out the sliding doors, holding the box and the new set of sweats I had gotten from the hospital. Sitting down on a bench outside, I opened the box. It contained three things – a letter, a roll of money and a medallion. I still know every word of that letter by heart, and remember how hard it was holding back the tears. That letter and that money ended up being my salvation. They got me off the streets, an education, and a place to live.

I touch my chest, feeling the medallion, cold against my skin. Lizzie had always been wearing it, and she had told me about how her husband had been a police officer and that the medallion of Peter of Alcantara had been her comfort as she waited for him to come home. I hadn't pegged her for a religious person, but it had meant a lot to her and had brought her husband home every night, at least as she told it. Holding it now, a small oval pendant, with the saint depicted on the front, I think back to the letter and the last sentence which made more sense now than ever, "Grey, you might not know where you are supposed to be yet, or what your purpose is, but this can help." Turning the medallion over, I re-read the inscription on the back, feeling that Lizzie might have been right. It reads, 'Patron Saint of Night Watchmen'.

Chapter 11

Grey

I wake up with a start, and it takes me a minute to realise where I am. Rolling my eyes I stretch out, looking up into the ceiling. It isn't like I wanted it to be a dream. I just don't know what I am going to do now, and it was so much easier when it was just me. Me, myself and no one else.

I liked it that way. Not that I had ever really had anyone, other than Lizzie. The closest thing I ever had to anyone caring for me. Relationships caused complications. Pain. I had enough with my own weirdness, and I have always had my escape into other worlds. They never judged me and there were always new places to discover, and characters left to meet. It suited me perfectly. Best of all was that I could feel whatever I wanted, and so did they, and we'd never bother each other with any of it. Sitting up, I realise the light has changed. How long have I been asleep? Not that I really know how time works here in terms of the day turning to night. Is there even such a thing?

No matter the time, I'm hungry. And I need a shower. My clothes are OK, but I haven't washed since I got here. Stepping into the bathroom, I strip down, leaving my medallion on and as I step into the shower, I spot a radio on the ledge under the mirror by the sink. Switching it on, I smile. The intro to *Hurricane* spreads out into the room, and suddenly it feels like home. Yes, it is one of my favourite bands, and yes, I know it by heart. But it is more than that. Whenever I left my house, I always brought my Bluetooth headphones. My music tuned out the world, made me feel like it was only me and gave me my own life soundtrack. Thirty Seconds to Mars is probably the most played band on my Favourites playlist, and Jared Leto's voice now takes me right into my own little world, as the water streams down my face, whisking me away to somewhere I feel like me again.

Getting out of the shower, now to the sound of *Irresistible*, I dry off and feel like a new man. How do people here know what my favourite music is? Not that I mind. I mumble along with Patrick Stump as I browse the selection in my closet. Finding a pair of ripped jeans, a black t-shirt and a pair of red converse almost seems kind of too good to be true, and I hope Lay won't be too disappointed for changing out her green robes. Next up – food. I grab a grey zip hoodie and a black leather jacket, marvelling over how everything is catered to my preferences. Almost like it is magic. Probably is. Getting out of my room is more mundane, as I actually need to open the door manually. Seems like the security isn't really bothered with people wanting to get out of my room. Opening the door, I freeze as I hear something. I shouldn't really be hearing anything, right?

"Hello?" I shout, feeling as nonchalant as I sound. This might seem silly, but on my way out I grab something that makes everything feel safe – an iPod shuffle, which magically just has all my favourite tunes on it too. So, with *Sugar, We're Going Down* on one ear, I jog down the stairs and run straight into Darby. Literally. Luckily, it isn't until I reach the bottom step, so the fall isn't that high.

"What the hell, Grey? Get *off* me!" She pushes me to one side and springs to her feet. The sheer force she has is more disorientating than the knock on my head from hitting the wall. I take a second to get my bearings, before clumsily getting up.

"Sorry. I just… didn't expect you, or anyone, to be here."

She blinks, and puts her hands on her hips. "And why is that?"

I thought she of all people would know. Not that I really know. Or don't I? "Callan said this was my house? Or at least… my room is upstairs," I finish lamely, shrugging.

"So is mine, stupid." Stupid indeed. I had just assumed… Well, she had said that I was the last… I realise I am not saying any of these things out loud and must look dumbstruck.

"Well I am!"

"You are what exactly?"

Damn, wrong words to say out loud!

"You told me I was the last one. The last Fior, or whatever. You mean, you are one too?"

She smiles sadly. "Yes, I did, and yes, I am. You were the last, but it doesn't mean there wasn't anyone else before you. There are always four of us. At least there should be. At the end of the last…" She stops suddenly, staring at the cellar door. "I need a drink for this. Want to join me?" She doesn't wait for an answer, just walks straight into the kitchen, the door slamming shut after her. Real inviting. I slowly take out the earbud still hanging in my ear and turn off my Shuffle, probably disappointing Ed Sheeran something terribly. And yes, I listen to Ed Sheeran, dude knows his shit.

Entering the kitchen, I find Darby on one of the barstools at the counter, holding a beer, with another waiting next to her. "I see you cleaned yourself up." Her eyes move her way from my Chucks to my wet hair before taking another swig of beer.

"Yeah." My brain seems to be malfunctioning and can't really come up with any words. Or put them into a sentence.

Darby is a freaking Fior.

"So we are the same?" I sit down two barstools down from Darby. There are of course four barstools, as there are four of everything in this place it seems.

"Yes, we are. But we are also different. I know, I know. More things to confuse you, I'm sorry, but seriously, it's true. All Fior are different. Different forms, different powers, different purpose. And I am sorry to say we do not come with an instruction manual." She puts down her beer and gets another one out of the fridge. "You want another?" I haven't even started on mine, but I nod absentmindedly, downing mine in one go. First now I notice it is a Stella Artois, one of my favourites. Having one in Eader just takes imported beer to a whole different level.

Grabbing the second beer Darby offers me, I look at her more closely. She had looked tired before, now she looks almost like a different person. Deadpan look, grey pallor, and no sass. I was starting to get used to her sass. "So that is what you meant when you told me to power up? To find out what I could do?"

She nods. "Yes, and I just wanted to see it for myself. It has been so long…"

"How long exactly has it been? Were you the one before me?"

This results in another long swig of beer, and it takes Darby a few seconds more to find the words it seems. "Yes. I was. There were two others before me and after the battle it was only me. Turns out though, I was wrong, because here you are." She struggles to get the last words out, and downs the rest of her beer. I wish I read minds. Instead, I take her hand. I know she is hurting, but nothing could prepare me for what I feel. Looking at Darby, her eyes are wide, and she grabs my other hand. It is like being punched in the gut by a freight train and I have never felt such angst in my life. The loneliness, the anger, the bitterness, the despair. I struggle to catch my breath and grip Darby's hands even tighter trying to steady myself. Closing my eyes, I see flashes of faces, I feel stranded and as if I am drowning, all at the same time. Sweat is running down my face and I can feel my strength draining.

"Darby, let go, please!" I gasp the words, not able to open my eyes. I feel her grip loosening and pull my hands back, falling to the floor. Still squeezing my eyes shut, I see the faces floating past. A man and a woman, smiling. I feel the remorse, the grief, and the longing, all mixed into one and it is too much to bare, my head splitting and chest pounding. As darkness is closing in around me all I can think is how I feel sorry for Darby, carrying that burden around.

I don't know how much time has passed by, but I open my eyes and see Darby sitting next to me. My head is still pounding. and I feel warm. Noticing me stirring, Darby moves to touch my arm, but I flinch, causing her to change her mind.

"Are you okay, Grey? What was that?" I groan, trying to sit up, but can't seem to find the strength. "Wait, let me get you some water."

She rushes away, and returns with a water bottle and a wet cloth, dabbing my face with the latter. After a few sips I manage a few words. "Food, please." I realise my initial goal after waking up has never been fulfilled, and that green stuff Lay fed me earlier has worn off a long time ago. After a few seconds, I have a piece of bread with cheese in my hand, eating as fast as my slow movements allow. "Thanks." The words come out in a whisper and Darby looks worriedly at me. She does however have the colour returned to her cheeks, and overall, she looks much better.

"I am so sorry; I don't know what I did. This has never

happened to me before!" The food is doing its work, and I pull myself up, putting my back up against the counter, next to the foot of my stool. Although my head still hurts and I feel the sweat trickling down my back, I feel better.

"It isn't your fault, Darby. I shouldn't have... I mean, I am the one who should be sorry."

Realisation dawns on Darby's face. "Your hand... Your power! Grey, that is amazing. Or... sorry, I mean, thank you!" Not that I have known her for that long, but Darby looks and sounds flustered. It isn't really a good look on her, but it makes me smile.

"You're welcome, I guess."

"No, you do not get it. I feel like, like I can breathe again. It is as if I have hope again that there is light..." She leaves the words hanging, as if she suddenly thought of something.

"...At the end of the tunnel?" I ask. It is the first time anyone has given me any idea of what it was I left them with.

"Have you any idea of what it is you can do, Grey? Or what you are? Or how dangerous it would be if he found out? Crap, he probably already knows." Darby gets to her feet and starts pacing around the kitchen. I continue working on my bread and cheese, noticing how little effect it's having.

"No, not really. Should'a would'a could'a really want to though." Sarcasm is my first responder, and he's stepping up now, 'cause I am pissed. "Why don't you share?"

"First of all, you look like shit." Again, sarcasm is bristling his muscles, getting ready, for that isn't really the information I'm looking for. "Sorry, but I am guessing you feel horrible, and I am so sorry about that. I have a lot of, uhm, baggage." Understatement was all I could think. "We need to get you to Thiam, because if I am right, with the hit you just took, you are

80

deteriorating faster than you can handle, especially with being low on food."

"You make me sound like a junkie. Can you just use small words?" Darby smiles at me; it even looks sincere. I must look like I'm dying or something. Again.

"I will explain later. Let's just say that your body is trying to fight off a large infection caused by a lot of negative energy, and it needs help." Still not helping, but I feel what she is saying. I do feel like crap. Helping me up, I lean on her, several groans escaping me, but I shake her off as to not activate this power again. I stagger out into the hallway, where Darby opens the door and leads the way out. "Again, Grey, thank you." The words are all but a whisper, and all I can do is nod, as I am focusing on putting my right foot in front of the left instead of my face. My heart is racing, and my legs are shaking, but I ball up my fists and force myself to walk. Down the stairs and past the large trees outside where Callan is waiting outside the barrier, jumping back as we walk through, popping out of nothing.

"Whoa, what happened? Did the house do that to you?" Wow, I must really be wearing this power. Not cool. Also not able to give a sensible response, so I just stare irritated at him.

Darby, however, has a more verbal answer. "No, you bloody idiot, he powered up, and it was too much for him. We need Thiam. Now!" She is walking behind me now, as if ready to catch me at any time, which is just pissing me off. Baggage indeed. This seems to be more than enough information for Callan, who nods once and takes off in the direction of the medical tent back at the small clearing. "Come on, Grey, it will all be all right, just keep walking." I want to answer and tell her to shut up. If it is the residual effects of what has just happened or because of the pain, I don't know, but I just need her to go away. We move up the slope after Callan, and I feel like my feet are glued to the ground. The shivers don't make it any better, and it becomes harder to hold my eyes open. I feel myself leaning over and suddenly I am leaning on Darby, until she can't hold me up any more. "No, Grey, that just isn't an option. Get up!" My body has other plans, however. I sag down to the ground, and can hear Darby sigh. "You better not be conscious enough to remember this, nerd." I'm probably not. Can't be. For through my half open eyes, it looks like Darby suddenly grows three feet. I feel myself being picked up and thrown over a shoulder. Callan must've come back. "Just breathe, Grey, we are almost there." Darby's voice echoes in the background. All I can think about is how I wish I had my headphones on, and could disappear to a safe place.

Chapter 12

Darby

I put Grey down on the first cot inside the med tent. He is unconscious and warm, clearly running a fever. "What happened? Was he attacked again?" Thiam comes out from his office, concern written all over his face.

"He..." I trust Thiam, but he is on the council and a very loyal servant of the city.

"Darby, I need to know what happened, and fast, if I don't, I can't help him!" He checks Grey's pulse and looks at me, a look of urgency now competing with the one of worry.

"He powered up. He is a Conduit, Thiam. Not a Healer, I mean, a Conduit, same as the First. He... he used it on me. But he can't control it, so he took it all at once. And you know just how much that is with me." If the news surprises Thiam, he doesn't show it, his only concern seems to be Grey. "His system is shutting down, he can't cope with the energy loss, and the darkness is drowning him. If he only had had the training..." Actually, he might have the training, but for some reason Grey can't remember. It bugs me, and I make a mental note to find out why.

"Darby, can you hear me?" Thiam is looking right at me, waving his hand. "I need your help!"

"What do you need?" I let my training take over, as naturally as breathing really, trying to forget what is at stake. "As I said,

Grey is fighting the Darkness, but he hasn't got the tools to do it. I am guessing he has done it before, but now his body, still recovering from the surgery, cannot handle it. We need to help him." I look at Grey, again lying on a cot, again in danger. He's definitely having a rough week. His hair is still moist from his shower, his chest moving rapidly up and down, sweat running down his forehead, and it almost looks like he is drowning in nightmares. "What do we do?"

"It will be similar to what you did last time, but this time it requires a more guided flow. We need to help push the Darkness out; it is not a simple refill. Take my hand and focus on the light, and remember to use your training. Do not let it in; it is a two-way street when we connect. Do you follow?" I nod firmly. Thiam takes my left hand and instructs me to take Grey's left on his command, and he grabs Grey's right hand, forming a circle. Thiam signals and I take Grey's hand.

At first nothing happens. Then, I can feel a pressure growing in my mind. It is powerful, and I can feel the Darkness. It wants in. I push back and gasp. Pushing back, I see Grey. No, I see into Grey. The Darkness is everywhere. It is killing him. "Oh no you don't!" I growl, starting to shove it out, mentally sending out Light, chasing the Darkness off. It is slow going, but I can feel Thiam doing the same. Little by little, we scrape it off, pull it out, extinguish it. I start to feel Grey's presence again. It is weak, but it is there. I also feel like I am invading. His feelings, his thoughts, they are all here and I do not want to intrude. One feeling is however so overpowering that I can't help but feel it. It is one of solitude. It is sharp, painful, and extremely convincing, like it is the only way to exist.

"That is enough, he can take care of the rest." Thiam's voice pulls me back, and I feel him letting go of my hand. I do the same, and I feel warm tears streaming down my cheeks.

"Is he…?"

"We did what we could, the rest is up to him. It is hard to say with attacks this extensive." He looks at me knowingly, and I drop my gaze. I do know, only all too well.

I sit down next to Grey, almost taking his hand, but I pull back. A Conduit. That's incredible! This might give us a chance! Small moans escape Grey, but at least the bad dream looks to have changed to mild discomfort, though he still looks feverish. How in the world has he managed this power? Like Thiam said, it has to have happened before! And without training or any idea what he was or how to control it. I feel sick. We just left him all alone. I should've…

"There is nothing you could've done. Not until now anyway." It's Lay, standing behind me. "Sorry, I couldn't help it, I was so worried."

"It is okay. I still think we should have done something sooner though."

Lay shrugs, looking uncomfortable. "I know, and I totally agree, General. But Decipiér…"

"Decipiér what? Tell me, Lay." Lay shrinks away. I power up, just a bit though, and look down at her, scowling.

"I do not know all the details, it is complicated. But several of the reports we got from the Watchers before you took over, they… At least I think we should've helped him. He was all alone, on the streets. I think he almost died at one point."

My incredulous look must be saying more than my raging thoughts because Lay takes another step back. Why in the world wouldn't Decipiér want to help Grey? I didn't admit that I had checked in on him once, that cold December night. It was after that I requested a closer follow-up on his case, then later the transfer. He was one of ours, a Fior, nonetheless. I got the whole protection thing, but you couldn't protect what was dead.

"I am so sorry," Lay whispered, looking devastated. "I was under orders, and couldn't tell you. I didn't realise…"

"It doesn't matter now, does it?" I don't want to hurt Lay, but I am angry and the words make me feel better. She shrinks back, but remains in the tent. It is all just so confusing. Another moan from Grey brings me back, and I feel horrible. The assignment, my nerdy annoying assignment. So alone. And that feeling I had gotten while fighting off the Darkness. It had been so intense, so all-consuming.

"How is he?" Lay moves up beside me, looking down at Grey.

"He is still fighting, but he is strong. He will be fine." I sound more convinced than I feel, but he needs to be fine. I need him to be okay. More than I realise. I can't lose another one. I have lost the others to the Darkness, but I can't lose Grey. Not like this. Not because of my personal demons. Lay puts her hand on my shoulder and squeezes lightly. If she read my mind or if it's just because she knows me, I do not care. It feels good having her there. Suddenly I remember. "Have you seen Callan? I sent him to get Thiam when we left Fior Mansion, but I never saw him after that."

Lay shakes her head.

"You both should go find him, Grey will be out for a long while and needs peace and quiet anyway." Thiam steps up to me, and starts to nudge me out of the tent. There aren't many people I would take this from, Thiam is one of a select few. "I will send word if there are any changes, now go."

I take one last look at Grey, looking more peaceful now, and step outside. A few of the Dust float around me, lighting up the now darkening surroundings. I need sleep, which I could've got waiting for Grey earlier, but I was so riled up after the council meeting, that I wasn't been able to. "Would you mind retracing our steps back to Fior Mansion, while I take a look around the camp?" Lay nods and flies off in the direction of Manawa. It really isn't like Callan to just disappear like this. He might be a complete idiot at times, but he is loyal and a fine Guardian. I search each tent and the forest surrounding the camp systematically, but after an hour I still have not found any trace of him. I hear the fluttering wings behind me, and spin around in time to see Lay fly in, holding Callan by the hands. His head lolling between his arms.

"Darby, help!" She lands awkwardly next to me by the main fire pit. Callan doesn't appear to be injured and he is breathing.

"What happened? Where did you find him?"

She tells me she had flown over the trail down to the edge of Manawa, covering the outskirts of the path, and suddenly Callan had just appeared. Out of nowhere, lying over a log. "I couldn't wake him, so I flew him back here." She looks tired, and I guess carrying a seven-foot grown-ass Guardian for over a mile will do that to you.

"Ladies, you mind helping me up?" Callan is lying there looking up at both of us, smiling his crooked smile. We help him up, though he struggles to find his balance and we help him back down on one of the logs next to the fire, which is now blazing in the dusk. He shakes his head, looking confused, a look I never associate with Callan. No matter how irritating his behaviour might be, he always looks to be in control, incredibly sure of himself and what he is doing.

"Lieutenant, what happened to you?" I use his rank, hoping to snap him out of it.

"Uh, yes, General, I... I don't know. I was running to get Thiam, and then... Oh no, how is Grey? Is he okay?" He tries to get up again, but it seems like his body isn't quite sure of how to get him vertical. I put my hand on his shoulder, pushing him gently back down.

"Grey is fine, I got him to Thiam in time. Now, tell me what happened."

Hearing the news of Grey seems to calm him down, and he takes a breath. "That is good, OK. Let's see. I ran to get Thiam, but halfway up the hill, I felt a tug. You know, like when we do a Shift. But I hadn't activated my Beacon, hell, I don't even have one on me! Then things got dark, and painful... and then I woke up to the gorgeous view of you two ladies." Yep, he is definitely okay. The news of him Shifting without tech, involuntarily like that, however, is not good. Not only is it incredibly dangerous as you could end up anywhere, or nowhere, but that means that the Eader was compromised. Crap, the situation is getting worse!

"General, you know what it was, don't you?"

I share my suspicions with my two most trusted Guardians, and both of them look horrified. "We have to alert everyone, and I will talk to Aron about increasing the sensors – we need to know how rapid the degradation is happening." Aron, the Boundary Mage, must have noticed something.

"I will do it," Callan says, getting up, playing around with the bullet on his chain. He looks to have shaken whatever dizzy spell he was under, and looks determined to make up for not doing his duty earlier. He must also know how close he was to really being gone, and maybe he needs some time.

"Thanks, Callan. And make sure Thiam checks you out, just to be sure." He nods and walks off at a brisk pace. Now more than ever the mission is crucial. I need Grey, and I need more time. But first, I need sleep. Not really thinking, I let my feet take the route past my tent in the camp, past the treeline, down the hill and towards Fior's Mansion. Before going in after Grey today, I hadn't been in there since... it happened. It felt like a ghost house. Haunting me with the memories of days past, which would never be coming back. Grey has ignited a small flame of hope however, and I feel it is time. And I really do miss those fuzzy slippers I left in my room. Walking down the slope towards Manawa, my thoughts float back to Grey. That feeling I had when being inside his consciousness. It hurt so much, on a deeper level than I thought possible. Coming from a boy, or a man always exuding his boyish nerdiness, I am amazed how he does it. I had known pain. I had inflicted it, and received it, but not on that level.

I finally reach the mansion, and after grabbing my bottle of vodka from the freezer, I jog upstairs, enter my room, second door on the right, and find my slippers. I also take a bath. It has all my soaps and a built-in speaker in the wall, rolling out my favourite tunes, led by Queen. How he had always loved the classics. Soaking in the water, I listen to the music, and empty half the bottle at the same time. After towelling off I revel in the privacy my room provides, feeling the buzz from the vodka, and eyeing the bed hungrily. I love this room. Sure, I have my own quarters back at the camp, and my Guardians know what happens if they interrupt me, but here, I know I am alone. I think that is part of the point with the mansion. The war with darkness is all consuming, especially for the Fiors. But coming here, you know it is only you, your personal space, and it gives you all you want, within reason. For example, I know that the first thing Grey would have wanted was his wall of nerd – TV and PC, though that doesn't fly here. I don't know why, maybe because we are actually expected to exit the room at some point. My room has a panoramic view of Manawa, and it only goes one way, so I don't really worry about anyone watching me. I throw my towel on my bed, put on moisturiser, and go through my closet, locating my favourite nightie – my oversized Bon Jovi 'Slippery When Wet' – tee. It still smells of him.

Just like old times. I turn up my tunes from the bathroom, now playing 'You Oughta Know', to drown out the sound of my thoughts. It's like Alanis is trying to tell me something. But I ignore it. There is probably much for me to figure out still, but right now I don't know of any mess I need to fix. I need to catch some Zs. Throwing myself down on my bed, I stare up into the ceiling, trying not to think. Not about the Darkness, the mission, my lost friends, or about Grey. Which is pretty darn hard as that is pretty much my life right now. Damn it! Things used to be so much easier before I went to Earth. Before Grey. No fuss. No confusion. Definitely no nerds. I think back to the council meeting, the night before I left Eader, almost five years ago. We had just had an attack in the western quadrant, which wasn't really unusual. The reason for the meeting was the seriousness of the attack. We had been overrun, and barely been able to shut it down. The attacks had been increasing in strength over the last fifty years, but slowly, and it was normal to have fluctuations, so we thought nothing of it. This had however been an extreme peak, and we needed to figure out what to do.

After much deliberating by the Manawa Elders, we still did not know the reason behind the attack or how they had broken through our defences. There had been suggestions though, one more crazy than the next – global warming was to blame, it was because of the internet, it was because David Beckham missed the penalty kick for England in the Euro 2004, or because of the

Kardashians. Needless to say, we got nowhere. Ryder, the most respected of the council members then got up, silencing the hall.

"There has been a development in the integrity of the Eader. I was unsure, but after conferring with Aron about recent activity combined with today's events confirms it. Our defences will not be enough; the Eader is weakening."

This might not have been a very calming message, but Ryder was a straight shooter and did not like politics. The crowd in the hall on the other hand, did not appreciate his candour, and exploded in shouts of anger and panic. Decipiér stepped in, raising his hands, calling for silence. "Not to worry, what Ryder meant to say is that we know what the problem is, and have a plan in motion to fix it." He sent Ryder a look, challenging him to say otherwise. Ryder on the other hand only shrugged, staring back deadpan.

With that, the meeting was over, and everyone but the council was cleared from the hall. The door had barely clicked shut, before Decipiér exploded in Ryder's face. "Could you have been less subtle?" he shouted sarcastically, waving his arms to emphasise his point.

"Yes, but people need to know. They need to be prepared."

I agreed with him – being caught unaware was not really a good defence strategy.

"Of course they don't need to know, not until we know what we should tell them." Yeah, Decipiér wasn't really a likeable guy back then either. Still a pompous douche, but I also knew where he was coming from – he was scared. I think we all were. "First we need a plan, and for that we need to know why this is happening and why it has gotten worse now." Turned out that was easier said than done and none of us could figure out why. So what do you do when you can't stop the water from rising? You build a stronger dam.

Ryder cleared his throat, fixed his eyes to mine, and said six words I will never forget, "We need Grey, the last Fior." I had just stared back. What did he mean? I was the last Fior, and we all knew it. Decipiér had started on another rant about risks and that it was too soon. Thiam had nodded, mumbling something about that it was about time, while the two others just sat there, looking grave.

"What the hell are you on about? What last Fior?" Surprise registered in every one of their faces.

"Ah, you do not know. Well, you wouldn't, would you? It was a 'need to know' I guess." I wanted to punch that smirk off his wrinkled little face. Decipiér sat back, knitted his fingers together in front of his face and sighed dramatically. "The youngest Fior was targeted by the Darkness, and we were forced to take extraordinary measures to ensure his safety, as he was only nine and had remarkable abilities. Grey was therefore relocated to Earth during the battle though he was lost during the Shift due to the instabilities in the Eader. He was however located by one of our Guardians who followed him to Earth, unauthorised I might add, and has been monitored ever since. And I would like to keep it that way."

"That would be a mistake. And you know that Guardian had no time to gain authorisation, Decipiér," Ryder again spoke up. As head of transportation between Eader and Earth he was the authority on the Eader, along with Aron, and everyone knew to listen when he had something to say. "As the Eader is weakening—"

"Rules are rules, and we don't know that," Decipiér whined.

"—We cannot ensure Grey's safety anymore, seeing as the Darkness is allowed to roam more freely, along with the increase in Dark activity on Earth."

Decipiér could not argue with Ryder, one rarely could. I couldn't find the words. I barely remembered the last Fior. He had just been a kid. And I thought he had been killed along with my friends.

"I see your confusion, and I am sorry, Darby. When we saw what was happening, we mounted an evacuation for the young one, and there was no time to include you, seeing as you were fighting with the others." Ryder tried a smile, but it fell short, and I could see his regret. I knew this story. The Darkness had come, in full force. Seeking, smelling out the Fiors of Eader, the youngest one not standing a chance as we had been betrayed from within, the rest taken out in the ensuing battle. All except me. "So we left him all alone?" My voice was but a whisper in the big hall. Ryder hesitated, but met my eyes firmly. "We kept a watchful eye and set up protections in his house when we found him. Thank the Eader he is such a recluse and almost never left. And a silver lining from us not being near him for all those years, the Darkness was unable to track him." At the last part I jumped up. "He lost his home and any connection to his people for years, and you talk about silver linings. He is staying here, we are keeping him safe, and that is final." There were no objections, which I didn't hear anyway as I left the hall. That was the December night I ventured to Earth, with Grey's location passed to me by Ryder, and the rest is history.

Back in my room, I feel warm tears running down my cheeks. So much for not thinking about any of it. Instead I shut my eyes, drifting off into nothingness.

Soft knocking wakes me up, fresh new tears dampening my cheeks, revealing a not so peaceful sleep. I brush them away, pushing the dreams down. I do however feel rejuvenated, with a slight headache, which I can thank the vodka for, but I must've gotten a few hours of rest. Looking at my watch set for Earth-time, I see that I got more than I bargained for. Diving into my closet again after washing my face and tying up my now dry hair, I pull on a pair of Levi's jeans and grey NASA t-shirt, with the hooded denim jacket, and Dr Martens boots. It feels amazing. I walk over to the door and reaching for the handle I suddenly realise with a jolt who the source of the knock has to be. Ripping open the door, there he stands, leaning up against the door across the hall, looking no worse for wear.

Chapter 13

Grey

"Took you long enough." It really didn't, as I had no idea which room hers was. I have gone around in circles, knocking on the three doors that weren't mine. I have just heard a door slam and leant back to wait for her.

"You too, how was your nap?" I must say, Darby almost looks normal in her new attire, but her attempt on sounding brazen fails, as she looks half grief-stricken and half guilty.

"I am so sorry; it was all my fault. If I had known, I would have never…"

"Never what? Told me about yourself? Opened up?" I try to sound reassuring, but I am all kinds of angry. It's the first time I feel like I actually helped someone with this cursed ability of mine, and she is taking it away.

Darby looks hurt, but I can't find the words to make it better. I don't want to make it better. "I… I'm sorry."

"Well, at least I got to know something more about you." I brush past her and go down the stairs, into the kitchen.

"Grey! Grey, wait!" Darby comes running after me. I turn around, just in time for her to put her arms around me, and squeeze me tight. I don't know what to say, or do. So I just stand there, lamely patting her back. "What you did… You have no idea. Thank you."

She quickly takes a step back as if scared to repeat the deed, drops her eyes and stares at the ground. I shrug.

"Not to worry, I don't know how, but I am not always 'powered up' as you call it. And don't mention it. Glad I could help. It is the first time it felt good." She gives me a questioning look, but I turn away, heading for the fridge. Thiam had tried feeding me with that green stuff back at the med tent, but I said I would eat when I got back here, and now I really need it. Grabbing a ham sandwich that has been magically prepared, I lean up against the counter, looking at Darby.

"You know, you really should've gotten a therapist or something, that was a shitload of, well, shit to carry around with you." Darby looks up at me, with that annoyed crinkle back above her nose.

"Thanks for that. It isn't something I like talking about with anyone."

That I can understand. It had been a lot. The pain of losing her friends, the bitterness of being left alone, the loneliness of being the last of her kind, the anger of getting to know he was still alive, but no one told her.

"Did Thiam tell you about your power?" I shake my head, and Darby sits down on one of the stools next to me. "I did promise I would explain later, and this is later." I turn towards Darby, eyebrows raised. Being so close to finding out what this… thing is, which has haunted me and distanced me from everyone for so long. It is daunting to be honest. Putting on my best casual look, I smile. "Sure, lay it on me."

Darby clears her throat, and shrugs. "So, you are a Conduit. You can sense Darkness, absorb it, transfer it, use it as a weapon. You are a child of both worlds, dark and light. Or, let me put it like this, have you ever felt colder or warmer around certain people, or felt like you could easily read people around you?"

I nod; feeling like what she says is very obvious. Isn't that normal?

"That isn't just a normal thing." So, that's a no to normal. "You can say that you are an empath of sorts, who can read, feel, and take away people's emotional burdens. If they are scared, hurting or otherwise in pain. You can make it better. What you did for me was just that, you absorbed it. Alleviated my pain. Our healers can do it too, transfer light, but in very limited amounts." She takes a break, waiting for me to take it all in.

"Go on," I say impatiently. Taking it in is apparently what I do, and I have been waiting for forever for this, no breaks necessary.

"Okay then. The consequence of this is, like you might've gathered, that all the negativity, pain and hurt is transferred to you, and you need to find your limit. This is something we can help you with, finding your limit and transferring it out again. But in short terms – too much of it, you get sick, and you die, as the Darkness will overwhelm you."

I realise I am still holding my sandwich and take a big bite out of it, not really hungry anymore. Holy chimichangas. I am a freaking sponge for Darkness and Light. Not really the cool hero title I was looking for. Captain America! Iron Man! Superman and… The Sponge. Nope.

"Grey, you need to realise that the power you hold is the greatest one a Fior can have. You are giving us a fighting chance against…" Darby stops talking, almost like she is catching herself just in time.

"Against what, Darby? Come on, I need to know what the hell is going on, and I need to know it right now!" I can see her fighting with herself, struggling to figure out what to do.

"Grey, first of all, as you might have realised, I am not just a

97

Fior, I am also the General of the Eader Army. I have certain responsibilities."

"You're a what now? A general? You? But you're so…"

I stop dead when I see the look on her face. I don't even know what I was about to say. Young? Female? Short? None of the above are safe to say out loud that's for sure. "Eh… busy? How old are you anyway?" The raised eyebrows and steely gaze speak volumes and I swallow hard. Nailed it!

"My age is actually none of your business, dude! But sure, busy. And because of my duties as a general, I answer to the people of Eader, and my job is to keep both Earth and Eader safe. As you already know, Earth is constantly in a battle for balance between light and dark, but the scales are being tipped more than we can adjust it, and the darkness has been gaining a larger foothold on Earth the last twenty-five years or so. Especially since the Fiors were killed and you had to leave." Darby holds up her hands, stopping the flood of questions I have, which I ignore.

"You say battle, and talk about fighting against it. How do you fight darkness? I feel like punching shadows isn't really effective?"

"Actually, that is a good question," she acknowledges.

"Yeah, surprising, isn't it," I say dryly.

"Anyway. The Darkness has its own guardians called the Majin, who attack us to weaken Eader's defences and their goal is to take us out, leaving an open highway for the Darkness. These Majins need to be fought in hand-to-hand combat – guns will not work here in Eader, due to the magic protection spells put up. There are combatants with powers on their side as well; they are called the Eilne, the Polluted Ones. They need to be fought with Light, using our powers. And lately it seems like they have increased in strength and numbers, as our defences are weakening. The other two Fior were killed in the biggest battle we have ever had, and we think we were betrayed from the inside. Someone was after the Fiors but ended up killing them instead. It was a massacre. After that, no new Fiors have been born." She is struggling to hold back her tears and anger, I can feel it rolling off her, and it's seeping into my skin, making me ball up my fists. "We got you out—"

"—And then promptly left me to fend for myself, thanks for that."

Darby looks hurt but goes on. "—And after that it has been more or less quiet. Only the small intrusion here and there, but the constant is that the Eader has been thinning down. We have not found the source of it yet, but with the attack on you in the forest and Callan disappearing today…"

"Callan is gone? What happened?"

"He is back, and he is recovering. He fell through a breach in the Eader without the proper preparations, which can be lethal. But yes, both incidents indicate that things are escalating again. Cox himself was here, which shouldn't be possible, not since we put up those defences all those years ago."

When she speaks the name, I feel like someone has punched me in the gut with a block of ice. I drop my sandwich, feeling as if I might throw up. "That name. It is him, isn't it? The man in the forest? With the voice?"

Darby nods gravely. "He is the Darkness's right-hand man. We do not know much about his powers, only that he has not been able to pass through the Eader in a very long time, until now, and that he, together with the Darkness, wants to destroy all light in this world and on Earth."

All that's missing right now is a fitting dark score to go with the ominous vibe set by Darby's words. Maybe Hans Zimmer could dish up something.

"So Darth Cox has infiltrated the Resistance, disturbing the Force and wants to bring everyone to the dark side?"

Darby looks confused for a second, but then tilts her head. "Yeah, that pretty much sums it up. You up for it?"

Let's see – fighting some scary ass Darkness, with freaky new powers in a place between places? It isn't like my calendar is full or anything, and I did just finish up all my job assignments and my last degree. And it will probably get me back home.

I give her a crooked smile, pick up my sandwich, dust it off, take a large bite and wink at her. "No worries, the Force is strong with this one!"

Chapter 14

Grey

I wish the Force was stronger. The next few weeks are hell on steroids, and then some. After Darby's dark pep talk about the end of the world, she sets up a training schedule: for my powers, for physical fitness, and weapons training. She even sets up different mentors – Thiam for my powers, Callan for weapons and fitness, and in addition, Ryder, for transportation and knowledge on Eader. And I thought I was done with school.

I start with fitness, both with and without weapons. I hack away on dead trees with an axe, my puny hands blistering against the hilt, do ten rounds running around Manawa and up the hill behind my house towards the camp carrying a sword and a pack filled with an increasing amount of rocks – all before breakfast each morning. Though the rounds around Manawa are slow, and often with Callan literally kicking my ass to get me moving, my lungs and legs on fire. After eating, I have a session with Thiam on channelling Light and Dark, only in small doses. We work with small animals, and actual shadows and light – with the goal of sensing emotion from the animals, making them feel more comfortable if they're scared and not absorbing their fear, but instead filtering it out and dispersing it harmlessly. It takes me a long time to just be able to trigger my powers, even longer to begin to push back the flood of Darkness. I need long breaks after each of these sessions, which only pisses Ryder off, as I meet him after. The first meetings with this guy are gruelling. He barely speaks, only stares broodingly at me, while handing me books on Eader history.

"Hey, these aren't even in English, man!"

Walking slowly over from his chair in the corner of his house, he smacks me on the head. "I am not to be disrespected, Grey. I am Ryder, Master of Transportation, Keeper of Knowledge. You will address me as such."

I feel like he is more of a glorified bus driver with a big ass library. "It is quite a mouthful, sensei. But question still stands. Ouch! Sorry, Ryder. Jeez!"

Needless to say, I have a headache after these sessions as well. As it turns out, I can read the weird languages after a while and could comprehend them easily enough, if I just don't try too hard. It just sort of comes to me – which makes me prefer Ryder's sessions in the end, because you know, books. So I read up on the details of everyday life in Eader, from the different cultures gathered here, to the mystical powers of the Eader itself. Sometimes I get an itch in the back of my head, telling me I already know this, making me feel as if I'm wasting my time. But each time I grab for the thought, it vanishes.

"What about how Eader came to be, Ryder? Anything on that?" I ask Ryder one afternoon, as I'm looking through a book on the merchant routes from Earth to Eader. Ryder sends one of his usual glowering looks.

"Read what you are told, boy."

"Actually, it is Grey, Fior of Eader, Conduit of…" I leave with a headache that day, too.

After Ryder's sessions I can barely think straight, and pass out in my room, not even bothering to undress.

This goes on for weeks, each day the same, feeling like I'm

getting nowhere and both brain and body feeling like it has been trampled. Then, Callan thinks I have mastered the basics and can handle more on the other hand, so he adds combat training.

"You should now have built enough stamina and strength to be able to keep up with a combat situation. If it had been a normal training education, you would have gone through basic training, studying strategy and different fighting styles, along with fitness. But you ain't got that kind of time, dude. Look at it as cramming last minute for a test. So, sword-up, you're gonna need it!"

Yup, he isn't kidding. It isn't like I have never done any fighting before – it is just that it was more virtual than anything else. I could kick your ass in Tekken and I am one of the most feared elves in Azeroth, but when Callan comes at me, I have no clue how to defend myself. Which several bruises all over my body can now attest to. Callan shows no mercy, and after every attack, and me losing, he helps me up and shows what I did wrong, and how to improve. In his mind it's better to learn by actually doing it than going through motions without an opponent. Learning by bruising, as he calls it. To help my progress he sets a schedule for several of the other Guardians to fight me, which is not much of a fight as they are all superior to me in strength, speed, and skill. Callan has told them to not hold back, and I'm grateful we're only using blunted weapons. By weapons I mean weapons plural, as in fists, swords, spears, axes, clubs, quarterstaffs, knives, and even boomerangs. I am surprised my nerdy arms can even hold them, and my shoulders and hands burn as I attempt to block Callan's and the other Guardians' attacks. The fairies who prefer the use of quarterstaffs come at me from every angle. I think at least Lay will go easy on me, but she's the fiercest one of all. Combat fairy indeed!

"Stop, please, mercy! Seriously, gimme a freaking second!"

I yell, which only makes her go harder.

I'm three weeks into weapons training, and this, alongside all my other 'courses', is beginning to have its effects on my body and my general mood. One highlight is that Ryder has started to explain about transportation between Eader and Earth, about the tools they use to measure safe breaches – meaning stables zones of light which can be exploited by the tech they call a Beacon. I haven't been allowed to try one yet, but I'm really looking forward to going home for a spell. At least I am until Ryder tells me that the first Shifts would be from and to safe locations in Eader only. I really do want to go home, but I am also starting to like it in Eader, despite the harsh schedule. I want to get some of my stuff from home, however. From all my training, at least I understand much more of Eader now, its people and its purpose. My level of fitness has increased, and I have now doubled the amount of stones in my backpack, hack through the dead trees faster with hardened palms gripping the axe hilt, and do twenty rounds around Eader each morning, Callan having to at least work a little to kick my ass. It is the power and weapons-training that are the worst. I have started to grasp how to automatically absorb and disperse negative energy. But it is not giving too much away that gets me. In addition, absorbing actual light or dark is proving to be impossible. The goal is to extinguish the candle in Thiam's office and then reignite it, but I'm having little luck. Emotion is easier to grasp, but the physical aspects are a lot harder. Even so, Thiam persists, and I don't want to let the big man down. Callan, on the other hand, I want not only to let down, I want to pummel him. I never come close enough however, though I'm getting better at evading attacks from my assailants. Problem is, if I evade one attack, I receive three more as a prize.

"No, no, NO! You need to duck and move towards her,

cutting off her attack and pulling her off balance." I can't see how I can pull Lay off balance as she has wings to keep her pretty darn steady. So now I'm on the ground, begging for a time out.

"Fine, take five. And you might want to plug up your nose, it's like a bloody waterfall." He walks off, laughing to himself. One day. One day I will beat the living crap out of that guy.

"If you are to achieve that, you need to keep your guard up, and also work on your counter attacks. Here." Lay hands me some paper towels and I stuff pieces of it up my nose.

"Thanks," I mumble, nodding to her.

"He is our best fighter, you know. Besides me, of course." She winks at me. "You are lucky to have him train you."

At this, I'm not the least surprised. Callan might be an irritating asshole, but he does know his stuff. Lay walks off, leaving me to feel sorry for myself. Which I am extremely good at. Always the victim. I'm so tired of it, and I suddenly feel something building. Somewhere deep. The hollowness filling with fire. I get up from the ground, pull out the paper from my nose and stretch out my hands. It is like they are firing on all cylinders. I hear someone walking up behind me. Without thinking I take a step back, kick out and hit the person in the stomach, surprising myself with how accurate and quick the response is. Spinning around I see it is Callan. I grab his arms as he flies back, but he has got one leg underneath himself and is already on the counterattack.

"Bro, what the hell?" he yells as he throws his first punch. I catch his left in my right side, but at the same time pull out his front leg, disrupting his balance, and as he falls towards me, I catch him in a headlock. I squeeze his windpipe and I know I have him. He thrashes in my grip, trying to loosen it, but there is no doubt – I am in control, I am holding his life in my hands and as I tighten my grip, I let the anger seep from me into him. I feel him lessen his efforts, giving into the Darkness, into me.

"Grey, let him go!"

As if from far away, I hear Lay screaming. She has her quarterstaff pushed up against my back and I know that a flick of her wrist could unleash a world of pain. Suddenly I see Callan's face, it is drab, his eyes are closed, and his hands are slowly releasing their grip on my arms holding his neck. Backing away I drop him and Lay runs to his side.

"What did you do? How…?"

Callan looks awful. His skin is totally grey, and he is shivering.

"Grey, I need you to go get Thiam, now!"

I snap out of it and does what she tells me. Thiam is at his desk in his tent and comes running as soon as I call him, and we return to the training field by the fire pit. Lay is by Callan's side, holding his hand.

"Thiam, you have to help him. Grey, he…" She doesn't finish the sentence, but it looks like Thiam gets the message. He rips open Callan's shirt, and puts both hands on his chest. I can't help but notice all the scars criss-crossing his otherwise very ripped chest. What has happened to him? With closed eyes, Thiam is chanting.

"Grey, I need your help. You need to take it back." I back away, but Lay grabs me by the neck, pushing me down towards the two on the ground.

"You will undo this, now." Her usually buoyant voice is now dead serious and sounds almost menacing.

"I'm sorry. It just… just happened." My stuttering seems to fall on deaf ears.

"Take his hand, and do as we practised. Right now!"

I do as he says. I just want to fix it. Taking Callan's hand, I immediately feel the Darkness, helped by all the practice. Focusing on his pain, I start attracting it, pulling it in. Immediately it is clear that it is more there than what I infused during our fight, but I do not care. As I did this to him, the least I can do is fix it for him. The flow of Darkness is immense, almost as powerful as the one I received from Darby. The flashing of moments of pain, confusion, anger, and loss overwhelm me, and I can feel the Darkness overwhelming my own defences.

"Grey, that is enough, let go!"

Thiam's voice comes from far way. Ignoring it, I continue the transference and at the same time make sure to return Light to Callan. The effect is immediate, as less Darkness is pulled from him, and I can sense him coming around. Someone grabs my shoulders and yanks me backwards, making me lose contact with Callan. Falling backwards as in slow motion, I see Callan roll over, coughing, and Lay helping him up. As I hit the ground, I try not to think of the fact that this might be like the fifth time I pass out in this hellhole. I lie there, trying to stay conscious, but I hear that voice, that British-pig-in-purgatory screech, and he is laughing.

"Ah knew ye wid unlock it, Grey, soon we wull be th'gither again." As I black out, I see Thiam, Lay, and Callan staring at me, none of them moving to help.

Chapter 15

Darby

I hear the screaming before I see them. I run around one of the lieutenant's tents, and see Callan struggling to get up, Lay and Thiam helping him up. Grey is on his back a few yards away, motionless, head to the side and sweat shining on his arms and face. "What is going on? What happened to Grey?" The words come rushing out faster than I can control them, and my mind is racing.

The three on their feet just stare at me, then glance at Grey.

"Talk to me now!"

Grey looks like he did after the incident at Fior Mansion. That boy is seriously more often knocked out than not, I suddenly realise.

"Thiam, talk, now!" My voice is no longer that of a friend. Thiam straightens up, regarding a General, with a dark look in his eyes.

"Madam, Grey used the Forbidden on Callan. I do not think he meant to. He... he... attempted to take it back, and more." Callan looks scared and really out of balance as he leans heavily on Lay.

"There was so much darkness. I could feel him taking it. All of it... If he hadn't..." Callan swallows hard, trying to straighten up. "He took it back, and then some." The look in his eyes mirrors the feeling I had down at the Fior mansion. I glance down at Grey, who is still lying there. Sweat is pouring down his face and a low groan escapes him. Taking back what he did must have taken a lot, and after performing the Forbidden exchange to start with, Grey is in bad shape. Again.

"Thiam, help me with Grey." Thiam does not move. He looks straight at me, with an unwavering gaze.

"Madam. He broke the law."

I take a step towards him, willing myself to grow to look down upon him.

"And then he tried to set things straight. He did not know what he was doing. Do your duty and tell me how he is!" My voice is level and firm and, reluctantly, Thiam moves over to Grey, and checks him out.

"He has a pulse, but I can feel the Darkness overwhelming him. He is stronger this time and might make it out on his own." Seeing how pale Grey's face is, his body twitching as if the nightmare in his mind is coming to life, I can't help but feel scared. Thiam is of course right. It is against the law to help anyone who has done the Forbidden as it is a force of Darkness. With Grey being a Conduit being able to channel the Darkness, it just makes it worse. The judgement for this crime is the Darkness itself, and it will decide if you live or you die. I can't change the law, no matter how important Grey is for Eader and the future of Earth. My shoulders sink and I shrink down to normal size, sighing heavily as I go.

"You are right. It is up to him now." I convince Lay and Thiam to help me carry Grey to my tent, putting him on my cot so I can keep an eye on him. The others can't seem to get out of there fast enough, which is understandable. After they leave, I sit down next to Grey's cot, covering him with a blanket, and put a damp cloth on his forehead, which is the most I can do without breaking the law. I sit back against the back of the chair and close my eyes. It is my fault. I should've helped Grey with his abilities. I am the only one who knows how they can get out of hand. Especially when it comes to the Forbidden. It is never easy to talk about, and I wonder if that is why Grey didn't know about it, as Thiam is one of the people who has felt first-hand how a life can be ripped away by the foul act.

The Forbidden is when dark powers are used to harm another person. Stealing someone else's life force. This is what we are fighting every day, and to have it done by one of our own, no matter how innocent the intent had been, is just horrible. The law is short and concise and unyielding – if you have performed the Forbidden, you will not receive any relief or aid in possible consequences put upon you. That meaning, if you are injured in self-defence, or have Darkness inflicted upon you in return. It does not matter; you're on your own. Should you however survive the ordeal, you will be exonerated. There have been occurrences where the perpetrator has gotten away scot-free. When this happens, the person would be at the mercy of the council. Maybe Grey is in better hands now to be honest. Decipiér, with his whole family being killed by the Darkness, would not be merciful. Then again, we all have history with the Forbidden.

During the last Great Battle, Lay lost her parents to an Eilne of the Darkness as he stole their life force, infusing them with Darkness. She was only a little girl, and he left her to witness the whole thing. They were consumed in front of her eyes and then crumbled to ashes. I know it still haunts her. That feeling of helplessness is what has spurred her on to become one of the fiercest warriors Eader has ever known, bested only by one other. Thiam lost his wife, also a healer, as she tried to help injured Guardians during the same battle. One of them was so panicked that in desperation, he stole more light than she had to give, resulting in the Darkness taking her from him. It was hard for

Thiam to blame the Guardian, of course, as he himself is a healer, but he has not been able to put it behind him. He spent several years on Earth after that, in Gaza, helping people there. He blamed everyone and everything, and it took seeing all the darkness humans survive on a daily basis to make him return, wanting to stop the Darkness spreading. Which was not something he could do from the Earth side.

As for Callan, all I know is the scars he carries and the fierceness with which he fights. He never talks about it, all I know is that his family was of Earth. There was an element of family abuse in there, but all I have gotten out of him since he came to Eader is that he is 'never going to forgive him'. Which I assume means his father. No matter the reason, the Forbidden is ugly and is a tool of the Darkness. How the hell did Grey know how to perform it? It is something that requires training, lots of training, and it isn't exactly any kind of training we offer here in Eader.

Looking down at him on the cot, I can't help but feel a bit disgusted as well. He has stolen life. Perverted the purity of his own kind.

Then again, I feel sorry for him too. He never asked for this. Being here just six weeks, asked to accept a world with magic and evil, and agreeing to battle against a Darkness he has never known. He has done everything they have asked of him, and then some. Looking at him now, tossing and turning under the sheets I covered him with, eyes squeezed shut in pain, chest tensed, and teeth clenched. I can see the muscles in his arms and neck contracting as if he is tensing to fight – which I guess he is, for his life.

Chapter 16

Grey

It is like running in water while being dragged in every direction. I can't breathe, everything hurts and at the same time I feel like I want this. Like the pain feels good, but at the same time it burns every cell in my body. Looking around, there is nothing but mist. It isn't black, which is weird, as I assumed the Darkness would be, like, black. But there is dark green and blue mist and I try to move through it while feeling like I am being spread thin across a piece of toast. It feels excruciatingly amazing. At the same time, I know it is wrong. That I shouldn't be here. Trying to free myself only drains my strength; it would be so much easier to just stop. Just float and feel the pain, enjoy the pain. Wow, and I thought I used to be emo. Shaking my head, I realise this is the Darkness working its mojo on me. I need to fight it. If I only knew how, though.

"Ah, mah laddie, there is na fightin' this. Yer mine now, shouldn't hae tried tae be the hero… givin' that light back tae the Guardian boy." Cox is in my head. Goddamn Bogeyman. Well, he can talk all he wants, I am not staying here!

I do the only thing I can think of – I start to absorb the dark and disperse it around me, which isn't easy, as I am all but drained already. My movements become easier, and the pain lessens. I absorb more, and feel a new pain starting to build in my stomach. It feels more honest and familiar, like that time in the alley. Clenching my teeth, I grab on to it and increase the flow of my power.

"What are ye doin'? Na! Impossible... it cannae be!" Cox almost sounds scared. "Ah will stop ye, laddie, yer wee tantrum is nothing but noise, just ye wait!" His voice fades away, but at the same time, something else sparks. Floating lights in a clearing, a fire pit, a winged boy, a battle. It all comes in rapid flashes, overwhelming me. The training sessions, the companionship, the feeling of belonging and family. Why family? Who were they? The power. The city of Manawa. A group of children, but me being different. More feelings and faces flood in, putting some pieces of the puzzle back in place. My time in Eader had been a time of peace. Of friendship. And then it came to an end. Flashes of fire, fighting and flight. All blurred together in a torrent of images and pain. As the images stop, I feel I can move again. The pain in my chest and stomach is still there, but the mist has subsided, and I am laying in a field of fluff. Clouds and cotton. No, wait. More like a hard cot and pillow.

I force my eyes open, and when they finally find their focus, I see Darby sitting over me. I have so many questions I don't know where to start. How is Callan? What did I do? Who were the people I had seen while I was out? But as I open my mouth only quiet moans escape me, and to my surprise Darby smiles at this.

"Thiam! Get in here! He made it out!" I see Thiam come into focus a few seconds later and he grabs my hand to check my pulse. I try to smile, but float away again on my cotton clouds. This time I do not dream, but rather I wake up in the med tent in the same cot as the last time, feeling like a truck ran over me.

"We have a lot to talk about, Grey, but first, eat this." Darby is sitting next to my cot again, but this time she comes bearing gifts. It is a Big Mac. Ah, bless her heart. I devour the offering, and then chug the bottle of water next to my cot. Feeling just a bit better, I inch myself up into a sitting position, trying not to aggravate my angry ribs which must have taken the brunt of the force as I escaped the Darkness. "Yeah, you have six broken ribs, which Thiam is refusing to heal for the time being, says it is fit punishment. You must've put up a hell of a fight to get such a severe physical injury from the Darkness." I feel like I know only half the story here, but I do not argue. Even though I do not understand fully what I did, I know it must be bad. And the physical injury, sure, tell me something I do not know, but I deserve it. Darby looks worried, like she can read my mind.

"Grey, I need to know. Do you remember what happened?" Darby almost looks terrified as she asks.

"Yes, and no," I croak. "I remember being annoyed with Callan, and being tired of being beat up. Then I felt almost... electrified, and it was like instinct took over. I knew what I was doing, but at the same time I did something I shouldn't have been able to, like my body remembered something it shouldn't have. At the end of it I just did the only thing I could, I reversed what I was doing. It was wrong, it felt right... but I knew it was wicked. So I tried to reverse it. Please tell me I reversed it!" I plead.

Darby smiles sadly and I start freaking out. Even though I can't really get up, I try, which must look pitiful. "Grey, relax. You stopped yourself and Callan is fine, you took back what you gave and then some. You almost killed yourself. We... I... After what you did, the law says we aren't allowed to help, so you had to help yourself. Which you did. You might have some apologies to make, but everyone is fine." She still looks a bit apprehensive, and I do not blame her, as I do not really trust myself at this point.

114

"I remembered something when I was out. Only flashes. But the feeling of family, pictures of Eader... it all came flooding back. I think I even remember you, even though you looked a bit younger."

Smiling, she gets up. "I am glad you are starting to remember. Get some rest, I will try to convince Thiam to heal your ribs, though it might take some time." With that she exits the tent, leaving me to my thoughts, and the pain. Wow. It has been a few weeks since my last bout landed me in here, but I am getting really tired of lying on my back. At least without a book or a gaming console to keep me entertained. The pain, however, is more or less becoming a latent companion, dropping in unannounced. Well, I'm not just gonna take it, and I have a fresh batch of questions which need to be directed at the right people. In this case, it is the last person I wanted to talk to, but to hell with it, it has to be done.

I inch my way up, my ribs screaming obscenities at me, which I ignore. Staggering my way to the entrance of the tent, clenching my teeth, I peek out, making sure no one sees me. When it is clear, I take the quickest route to the Lieutenant's barracks. It is clearly getting late by Eader standard time, as there are few people around and I don't attract any attention as I more or less stumble and fall into Callan's office. I remember the route from my fresh archive of memories, same as how I know that Callan will be pissed at me. He is after all my best friend.

Face planting is not my intended start of this conversation, but it makes an impression at least. Smashing my cracked ribs into the floor also makes an impression, and I almost pass out from the pain. Rolling over, I see Callan lounging on his cot in the corner, holding a vodka bottle. "Smashing entrance there, buddy," he mutters.

"I remember you as more of a scotch person," I croak from my pitiful position on the floor. Callan laughs, throwing the bottle in my general direction. It is more or less full, and the content spills all over his desk where it hits. "So you remember now, do you?"

I sit up as best I can, leaning against the desk. "Yeah, at least that bottle we stole from Ryder while he was sleeping. I have never felt so sick in my entire life, this moment excluded perhaps." Readjusting myself, I cough, covering my mouth with the inside of my elbow, which comes away bloody. A rib must have pierced something when I fell. Crap.

"Callan, I am so sorry. I don't know what happened and I wish I could take it all back." Callan shrugs nonchalantly, but won't meet my eyes. He looks OK, but at the same time he doesn't have that bravado I have gotten so used to.

"I know you didn't mean it. I felt it when you took back what you gave. You took away so much of the shit I have been... Anyway, I know you are a good guy, Grey. If you weren't, I wouldn't be here. And I am glad you made it." The words bring up such a feeling of relief I could cry. Ever since I woke up, I have been doubting my sense of right and wrong. That feeling of enjoying that pain, it has messed me up. So hearing Callan spell out how I instinctively acted right, well, it helps. Smiling at him tiredly, I feel grateful.

"Thanks man, and why didn't you tell me before? That we know each other?" At this he laughs. I remember that laugh and it makes me smile even more.

"When you didn't remember me at the fire pit, I didn't want to force it. Darby had told me you might not remember, so I was prepared. It did suck though. I missed you, bro." Looking at the vodka drying on the carpet around me, I raise an eyebrow.

116

"Really, I remember less bottles being broken and more being emptied the right way when we stole the captain's stash, the last time we hung out, man." I cough again, and I feel blood running down the side of my mouth. Something definitely got poked the wrong way somewhere.

"Well, last time you were more of a fighter, less of a nerd. You could also take a hit, and it looks like you are falling to pieces over there." It is my time to laugh, and it hurts as much as the coughing does.

Clutching my ribs and clenching my teeth, I croak, "Well, Stinky, last time I could beat you with my hands tied behind my back." I end this with a coughing fit and sag sideways to the floor.

"Of all the things you could remember, you have to remember that stupid name." Callan picks me up from the floor and throws me over his shoulder, something my already crunched ribs do not appreciate, which I underline with a muffled scream. It is harder to stay conscious this time, and as I jostle around on his shoulder I fall in and out, snapping back to consciousness in the med tent. Maybe I should just move my stuff here.

Thiam is back, and by the looks of it, and feel of it, he is still refusing to heal my ribs.

"He gets it, and he made it through the trials by himself. Look at him, man, something has been punctured. He is freaking spitting blood." Callan and Thiam notice me looking at them, and as if on cue, I have another coughing fit, struggling to catch my breath, which is a lovely mix of blood and low moans.

"It is fit punishment, either he heals, or he doesn't." Callan looks ready to pummel Thiam.

"You bloody well know what will happen. He is bleeding internally, and he cannot heal that himself. I forgave him, now fix him, you large oaf." Being a worshipper of solitude, I have never got the whole bromance thing. Like Riggs and Murtaugh, Steve and Tony. Sam and Dean. It must be the pain, it is so cheesy, but it feels awesome, like I have a brother. A brother who has my back. Another coughing fit is building and my body tenses in preparation. It's as if Thiam senses it. He shoves Callan back, puts both hands on my chest and presses down. As a reflex my hands try to push him off, as this is the same lovely pain as in the dream, only this feels like it is the right kind of pain. I feel my hands hit the cot, and hear Callan's voice. "Stinky and Shady, ride again."

Chapter 17

Darby

I get the news about the whole thing the day after. It is Callan who shares. I feel like he is keeping certain details out – but the important thing is that Grey is healed. Meaning I have to remember to thank Thiam. It must've taken a lot for him to see past his own reasons for not wanting to help.

Grey has resumed his training sessions, though Thiam refuses to train him anymore, maybe his way of putting his foot down. I walk down to the training field to check out Grey's progress. Turns out I don't even need to see it to find out. Sounds of heated fighting reach me as I exit my tent. Of wood hitting wood and taunts being exchanged. As I round the med tent I see them, or at least I think I do, because it is more like a blur. They are moving around the training field, unnaturally fast. Which makes no sense, as Grey shouldn't be able to match Callan, on any level. But he is now. On several occasions I can hear Callan swearing as Grey gets him, though there are several in return as well.

"Excuse me, are you done with your little dance already?" They stop abruptly, only two metres from me, both with intense glares in their eyes.

"Dance, huh?" Grey says, breathing heavily.

"You heard me. Would you mind taking a break, so I can have a word with you guys?"

I'm not really asking, and turn around as I finish the sentence, walking over to sit by the fireplace. The two men follow me, rather reluctantly, but no petulant reply comes my way. The guys stay standing as I sit down, with my back to the pit.

"Now, would you please tell me what changed in the mere day since I last saw you boys?" The two exchange looks, smiling. Callan shrugs, cocking his head.

"Well, I just got my bro back after he went all soul sucker on me, and now we are celebrating."

I raise my eyebrow. "Soul sucker? Okay. So, Grey, what do you remember? Clearly your combat training has come back?"

Grey is being uncharacteristically quiet, looking towards the forest. As I say his name, he shrugs. "Not much really," he says, shrugging again, still looking away. "I remember Callan, training, and a few bits and pieces of growing up here. But that is about it." Bollocks. I was hoping there would be more, but at least he can fight. Which means it's time.

"Well, Callan, you know what that means?" Callan winks at me, which I let slide for the time being, and he bangs Grey on the back.

"Yeah, bro, it is time for you to go to the Academy!" Grey only blinks at this, looking more than confused.

"Academy? More school? Seriously?"

I roll my eyes. "Yes, you need to hone your skills as a Fior."

"Isn't that what I've been doing these past weeks already?"

"Stop your whining," I chide. "Keyword there being 'weeks', you moron. You think you can come up to the required level of skill with a mere six weeks under your belt? Please. Even with your memories boosting your fighting skills a bit." I am saying this while picking out something stuck under the nail on

120

my little finger.

"And you couldn't have informed me of this earlier? What, busy with your manicure or something?" Grey's getting mad now. What else is new?

"It was need-to-know, and now, well, you need to know. Additionally, it isn't like you take new information that well anyway." At this Grey is making a sour face, mockingly whispering 'additionally' under his breath. I start on the nails on my other hand.

Callan laughs. "Yeah, you needed to come up to a certain level of competency before joining the Academy, bro. Let's just say you needed to pass the entry requirements. Which you now do. Sweet as, man."

Grey doesn't look very happy about this, but shrugs, this time with a smirk on his face. "On the plus side, maybe there will be someone there with some real fighting skill?"

"Oh yeah, you are looking for some more ass whooping, are you? I'll show you…" And they're back at it. Which is good, as I was almost afraid Grey lost his sarcastic humour for a moment there, and I've been kind of getting used to it.

For a second, I consider joining the fun, but then I remember my awesome responsibilities, and turn away to start my walk down to the castle. As I pass the med tent, Thiam pops out and joins me.

"How are the guys?" he asks, avoiding my gaze.

"They both seem fine, back to training. Grey even started to remember…"

"That's good." The abruptness of Thiam cutting me off catches me off guard. He is usually the mellowest person you could meet. But something about Grey has pushed the wrong buttons. I decide not to prod him with any more questions, so we walk down to Manawa in silence.

As we come up to the castle, I can feel the apprehension. What in the world am I going to say? Lost in thought, I walk through the creepy entry hall with Thiam towards the main chambers, where the rest of the three council members are already waiting.

"Ah, General and Thiam, so glad you decided to grace us with your presence. Not been up to more forbidden activities now, have we?" Decipiér's play on words puts my nerves on edge, but I simply smile and find my usual seat.

"Now that we are all here, I think it is time we decide what our next step should be." Ryder has gotten up, and as per usual, he has the council's full attention. "I have been conferring with Aron, and the General, and there are clear signs of degradation in the Eader's integrity. After an incident just a few weeks ago, involving a lieutenant falling through a breach without any tech, in addition to having an increasing number of visits from Cox himself, we need to find out what is causing this, and how to stop it."

It's like the room is holding its breath. Ryder sits back down, a look of gloom on his face. We all knew it was bad, but having it spelled out like that makes it all the more real. Glad that Callan has conveyed the incident to Ryder so quickly, it makes me appreciate the annoying brat a bit more, but before I can dwell on that further, Thiam gets up.

"We all know that we had planned to use Grey to help us fight this evil, but after what has happened, I am not sure we should…" He takes a deep breath. "I do not think we can trust him. After being in contact with his mind and soul on several occasions, I have sensed a presence of Darkness in him that scares me, and after what happened yesterday with the Forbidden act, I am against using him for our aid."

Even though I know Thiam had deep apprehensions against healing Grey after yesterday, I didn't know he felt like this. All I can do is stare at him. He, on the other hand, stares into the tabletop.

"We appreciate your thoughts on the matter, and will take it into consideration. As I have gathered, Grey is now to undergo training at the Academy, and we can keep an eye on his progress there for the time being. The more pressing matter should be how we protect the Eader, should it not?" Bethany, Head of Security, speaks up, which I am grateful for, as I myself am not sure of what to say.

"Right you are, Bethany," Bob, Head of Acquisitions, says. "If we cannot trust the Eader's natural defences, we are soon to be overrun, and yes, this will also affect our supplies. It is an issue we cannot afford to postpone."

After this, the room becomes quiet. Too quiet. Decipiér just sits there, brooding.

Enough of this. "What we need is a strategy, enabling us to protect ourselves, and at the same time investigate the source of the problem. I suggest we stop all Shifts for the time being, keeping all forces here. We set up a grid patrol, making sure to cover as much of Eader as we can. At the same time, no one should be wandering off alone, so have double watches set up. In addition, Ryder, you and Aron must have some sort of way to find out where the breaches are more prominent and there is a higher likelihood for an attack?" A nod from Ryder confirms this. "Good. Work on identifying the worst ones, and then I will assemble a team to go investigate the matter, but not until we have secured Eader." I take a deep breath and brace myself for any counterarguments, but having a plan seems to have invigorated the council, as they are now nodding and sitting up straighter.

"Well, well, look who decided to put on their General-hat today." Decipiér seems to finally have decided to join the meeting. "Not a bad strategy, General, but why should we trust you to take this quest to find out what is causing all this? I seem to recall that your latest responsibilities have not been exactly successful to say the least. Our new guest even went and broke the law by performing the Forbidden. And he is your responsibility, might I add."

Wow, way to contribute to finding a solution. If he wants a pissing contest, fine. "Decipiér, I do not remember you ever having any combat training, strategy skills or even having picked up a sword. Your duty is to the people and to keeping the peace in Eader, and mine is to keep Eader and Earth safe. You are nobody's ruler, as this is a democracy, and we all have our areas of responsibilities. Remember your place, and I will remember mine." Not able to control myself, I have grown about five feet and am now towering over the rest of the council, both hands on the table, staring needles into Decipiér, who cleverly enough has seated himself again. "Then we are all in agreement?" The council nods, including Decipiér. "Excellent. Ryder, let me know of your findings, and work with Bob to stop all Shifts for now. I will start assigning the new patrol duty. In the meantime, Bethany, Thiam and Decipiér, do what you can to assure people that they are safe, and implement a buddy system, making sure no one is wandering off alone. And as for Grey—" I look straight at Thiam. "He is my responsibility, and as he is a Conduit, he is burdened to always battle the darkness within him, which we should all grant him clemency for, and try to help as best we can." I nod once, meeting each of their gazes to make sure they get the message. As I leave the hall, I make sure to change back, but still have to bend down to avoid hitting my head on the door header.

That went well, right? At least we have a plan, though we do not have a fix. For the time being, I hope fixing the symptoms will be enough. At least until I can figure out what the cause of the Eader's weakening is.

Thiam catches up to me as I exit the castle, and we walk out of Manawa together, again in silence. As we reach the campsite, Thiam stops. "General, I am sorry for my directness earlier. I had to speak my mind, and I will stand by it. But I do also acknowledge your point," he says, sounding resigned.

"Thiam, I do understand where you are coming from, and right now I agree. There are too many variables with Grey we cannot be certain of, and until we have clarified these, he will not be a tool to be used for any defence work. You have my word on that. But he will be allowed to prove himself, as we all deserve a second chance." Thiam sets his shoulders and nods, and takes off in the direction of his tent. As I turn around to leave, I see the back of Grey, turning around the corner of a tent, along with Callan. Great, how much of that did he hear?

Chapter 18

Grey

So that is what I am, huh? A tool. That is just awesome. Callan and I didn't mean to overhear Thiam and Darby's conversation. Just bad luck, really. But now I know, I guess, and it is not like I asked for any of this darkness and light bullshit. It was them who left me all to myself and then to just pull me back here to do their bidding.

"Crap, did you hear that? Sounds like you've been benched!" Leave it to Callan to just downplay the whole thing. Maybe he's right. I just want to never use my so-called gifts again. "Now, ready for that beer?"

"Absolutely!" If he's being gracious, oblivious, or just doesn't care, I don't know, but I appreciate the distraction Callan provides. The epiphany I had when recalling my first memories was nothing short of mind blowing. I felt like a small part of me could rely on someone else for the first time in my life. It was kind of terrifying, but it also made me feel more like a whole person than ever before. We head into Manawa, passing my house and entering the busy lower-level streets. I haven't had the time to go sightseeing yet with my busy schedule, so this is my first time in here. There are street vendors, selling all sorts of mystical objects, from potions to some weird looking pizza. As I am about to stop to ask about it, Callan pulls me along.

"Better not dawdle at these booths, you never know what

kind of weirdness they have put into it." I swallow hard, and nod once. We continue past pottery vendors, bakers, blacksmiths, and swordsmiths; and they even have a candy store which just looks awesome. I notice all the Guardians patrolling the streets and people whispering to each other with worried looks, but there are so many other things to look at that I push the thought aside. We pass by Manawa elementary school, and I stop and stare. It is built as a spiral, crawling three times around a huge tree. There are ladders and ropes connecting it to the ground and as I watch I see kids fighting with swords on a balcony and others having a food fight further up.

"That can't possibly be safe, man? They are just kids!"

"Ah, the good old days! Don't worry. Here kids grow up fast." We move on through the streets, and I try to get my bearings, but I soon realise I am lost.

"How big is this place?" I ask confusedly, turning around in a small square. Callan shrugs.

"Manawa grows as is needed. Stores, storages, stables, and stoves. Added or removed whenever needed. Magic, remember."

He walks out of the square, heading down a narrow alleyway and I stare dumbfounded after him. Magic? Stoves? "Hey, wait up!" We continue exploring, and I start listening to the different people in the streets. A satyr arguing with a nymph over prices on bark bread, the nymph bristling in her green dress as the furry hooved satyr tries to get a two-for-one deal.

Later, we pass a group of people watching a football game on the big screen at the pub, between what looks to be Norwegian teams Rosenborg and Molde, according to the commentator, who announces the imminent defeat of Molde. One of the spectators is a troll, who is showing his utmost displeasure in a tirade of curses not fit for any audience.

"Hey, Callan, how is it everyone speaks English here?" Callan pats my back and scoffs.

"Dude, we ain't." I stop abruptly in front of what looks like some kind of potion seller's store window. Filled with bottles and vials of different coloured liquids and blue smoke leaking out through the doorway.

"What do you mean, 'we ain't'? English is the only language I know!" I say, clearly thinking Callan is pulling my leg.

"We speak all languages and no languages here. Ever heard of Babylon? Where there was only one language? Or wonder why it is so easy for you to read and understand different languages? It's just..."

I cut him off with a wave of my hand. "Let me guess. Magic?"

"You got it mate! Now, ready for more sightseeing?"

I sigh. "Sure thing."

Callan pushes me along, stifling a cough, as the blue smoke is getting annoyingly thick. "Good, because I have someone I would like you to meet. Grey, meet Shawna, the town mother hen. Or isn't that right, ma?" We are in a small dry cleaner, complete with a coin wash and a small coffee stand. Shawna is a dwarf woman with red, rustled up hair and a red apron to go with her red cheeks and kind green eyes.

"Oh, Callan, you rascal. Always with your charming words." I shake Shawna's hand, bending down to take the cup of coffee she is offering, and she waves us out of the store.

"Now that is a woman, let me tell you. If I..." Callan stops short, dropping his coffee. "Oh crap, there she is." I follow his gaze and spot a tall, blonde woman, with lean arms, grimy face, and long legs. She is wearing a red bandana in her hair, form-fitting jeans and a white, dirty T-shirt, giving her that tomboy look about her, with the 'don't mess with me' attitude to go with it. Adding the three sheathed swords she has slung across her shoulders, she looks pretty badass. When she spots Callan and me, she nods smilingly, brushing her blonde braid of her shoulder as she walks by. Callan waves lamely in response, turning after her.

"Wow man, strong game you got there. Friend of yours, I assume?"

Callan turns slowly back towards me, with a faraway look in his eyes. "Huh? What? Oh. That was Morgan. Kinda got a crush on her. Best swordsmith in town." With that he starts walking again, face so red I wonder how there isn't steam coming off it. I laugh and trot after him. As if to forget what just happened, Callan starts pointing out different town characters we pass, such as the town drunk, Henderson. He is a yeti and works as a barber. Needless to say there have been certain incidents, but according to Callan, he is good in a fight. Which are usually situated in a bar. Then we follow the smell to the best baker in town, Dagan. As we buy a Manawa-pretzel each, we listen to him whistling, 'Can you feel the love tonight,' and Callan whispers that Disney-tunes is Dagan's thing and I should never comment on it, as it will result in getting smacked into tomorrow. We pass the town seamstress as well, Addison, who sings to her fabrics and materials to make the best suits of armour, black suits, and fiercest Halloween-costumes. Once, I think I spot someone resembling a certain Mr Potter, but he is too far away to get a good look at his forehead.

We turn a corner, and head even further into this maze of trees, houses, and tree huts. With ladders hanging down and signs attached of who lives there or what they are selling up there. There are so many colours, from the signs to the clothing people are wearing and the colour of the houses. It feels like walking in a rainbow-land, if it weren't for the earthier tones, that is. We pass through the bustling foot traffic of men and fairies – I guess they like walking too – a unicorn – not kidding. I even see what must be a centaur, but walking next to this I spot something else that puts them all to shame – the movie theatre.

"Thought you might like this," Callan says as we walk up to the front of it. I have no words. Only a few unintelligible sounds escape my mouth, which is now hanging open.

"What…? How…?"

Callan starts laughing. "Bro, you are just so articulate. Yeah, like I said a couple of months ago, we are pretty set up. So, of course, we also have a movie theatre." I nod slowly, and look up at the beautiful monstrosity. It looks to be three stories tall, with stone walls in gothic architecture, even with the cool gargoyles on each corner of the roof. It has columns in front and posters plastered all over the front wall.

"There are movies here, from all over the world? In every language? But how? The scheduling alone must be a nightmare."

"That is a great question, let me show you, dear sir." Clearly, Callan is enjoying this immensely. "Like, I know it has been a while since we've hung out and all, but you used to like movies way back then too; doesn't seem like you lost that, nerd." He smirks and walks on in front of me into the cinema. I don't even have any sass to come up with a proper comeback at the moment, so I just follow him in, staring at everything. The posters show movies in every genre, every language it seems, and it looks like it must contain every movie ever made, stapled on top of each other, making it a beautiful mosaic of wonderful, cinematic magic. Inside I find a large lobby with velvet ropes, columns disappearing into the domed ceiling overhead, but just one big

130

door, along with the candy shop of course. The red carpet – yes, a red carpet on top of the marble floors – leads up to a screen in front of the huge double doors, where Callan is waiting, leaning nonchalantly up next to a column. "So, what do you think? Impressed?" Of course I am. But I don't get it. All those posters, such a big place. And only one door. No place to buy tickets. Reading my face can't be very hard, as Callan chuckles. "Come over here, smarty-pants, and check this out." He points at the screen, which I now am looking down upon. There is a huge button and a handprint. Remembering what happened last time, I am reluctant to be pulled into a screen. But Callan beats me to it. He pulls my hand down and puts it on the screen. The screen immediately lights up and starts talking.

"Hi, Grey, welcome to Manawa Cinema Magic. What will you be watching today?"

"Uhm..." I stutter, not knowing what to say.

"Oh, I am so sorry, we don't seem to have that title in. We do however have more or less every other movie in the world. Would you like to try again?"

This time I was ready. "Do you have a database I can check out?"

"Of course we do, press menu on the screen and it will take you through them. Just speak up when you have decided."

Wow! This is great. I press menu and start looking through the categories. I feel like I am at home, sorting through Netflix, never deciding on anything. So many options! Even TV-shows! Having a small nerdgasm. Apologies.

"Seriously, this is amazing! But, what now? So I pick a movie and go in and see it?"

"Yep, that is more or less it. The basics are that the door reads the entrants, and as you can see, there is one screen here. If they were to walk in anyone else, another one would be available. And yeah, pick a movie, go over to the doors, and use your handprint – which is more or less you logging in. And voila! The theatre has an infinite amount of rooms, so it doesn't matter how many people pick different movies. And there is of course awesome seating, great candy, and you can pause to go to the bathroom." I feel like I have found my happy place, and could more or less just move in. No such luck, however.

"Ready for that beer now?" Not really. Kinda wanted to start the world's greatest movie marathon, but we leave the movie theatre, with me vying to return as soon as possible.

"Magic? What do you mean by that really? I get the whole light and dark thing, but magic?" We are passing through a tight alley between two huge tree trunks, and come out in what must be the dining district. There are restaurants and pubs on each side of the street, with more or less anything you could want. Italian, Irish, Scottish, Indian, and Lebanese. Flags are hanging everywhere, and the Irish pub is blaring its folk music. Awesome! "Well, it is all in how you use it. Technology in its own right is only magic humans have figured out. Your manipulation of light and dark energy is also magic. How Addison sings to her clothing is magic." Not quite convinced, but I nod.

"Crap! I haven't got any money."

Again Callan smirks. "No worries, compadre, I got you covered." He pulls out his hand and shows me his right wrist, where a small Celtic circle is tattooed, with a fox in the middle. "Every person in Eader gets one of these, you will too, and this is our form of payment. All your wages get stored in this, sort of like a personal QR code. Let's just say next round is on you!"

We sit down at the Scottish pub, Grasshopper's Feast, ordering a round of St Mungo's, making sure to steer clear of the local Eader beer, and Henderson the Yeti sitting in the corner, snoring. The pub is half full, but according to Callan it will fill up, as the day shift is going off duty soon, and the shops are closing up as well. Just like Callan predicted, no less than five minutes later, the street is full of people, along with the pub.

"So man, what do you think?"

I look at him over the rim of my glass, as I chug down my beer. "About what? Considering all that has happened, it doesn't hurt to be a bit more specific." At this he laughs, copying my move with the glass, and ordering two more as a waiter passes by.

"I guess you are right, Shady. Well, let's start with Manawa then." He winks at me, already knowing the answer no doubt. I blurt out with how weird it all is, and especially how great the cinema is, and after that, we just talk about everything. How mean Darby can be, which movie we are going to see at the cinema, who is the better fighter – which is me, of course – and finally, we talk about when we were younger. How Callan used to steal my training sword, and getting into trouble with the Swordmaster, the tall, always angry, but nonetheless best swordsman in Eader. How we used to go exploring in the forest after dark and how it was there where we discovered I could control shadows. It is only the memories of Callan that have returned, everything else is more or less still a blur. It's when we are having our fourth beer the question pops into my head.

"There are so many different species and people, and I know the Eader is the source of them all. But there are so many, and there are kids? Do they... erm."

"You mean, do they wham bam to make more?" Callan interjects ever so eloquently.

"Sure, let's call it that," I say.

133

"Well, you have to understand that Eader has been around for forever, and yes, there is some sexual interaction going on, even cross species – though no hybrids are ever produced. It is like the recessive and dominant genes when deciding eye colour – one wins." I blink. Seriously, I do not think I have heard Callan use such big words before.

"Ah, I see," I mumble, trying to imagine a dwarf and a yeti hooking up, but shake my head to get that image out of my mind.

Meanwhile, Callan goes on. "The people living here are either descendants of Fior or from Earth, with different cultures, possibly religions, and most often looks. That does not matter here, as we do not judge. There is no value more important than the work you put in and the sort of person you choose to be." He takes a gulp of his beer. "You can call it a purer sense of worth that no Instagram account or flashy wardrobe can ever measure." Nodding, I empty my beer, squelching a burp.

"Sounds pretty awesome, man," I admit. "Callan, who is this Cox guy anyway? Nobody seems to really know what or who this guy is, other than the fact that he is a really not a good dude." At the mention of the name, Callan's eyes darken and his grip on his now empty glass tightens.

"He is the Betrayer. The Scottish asshole who turned his back on all of us."

"How did he betray us? The asshole part I get, from first-hand experience!"

"That is just it, Grey. You know who he is." Callan looks really uncomfortable now, not really making eye contact but looks ready to throttle his glass. I ease it out of his grip as it looks near well ready to shatter.

"What do you mean? How should I know? My memories aren't the most reliable at the moment, so spill."

"Fine already. Darby probably filled you in on there always being four Fiors at all times, right?" I nod, apprehension building. A Callan so serious is not something I'm used to and quite frankly it's unsettling. His eyes are dark, his hand now fiddling with the bullet on his chain. "Well, the Darkness has its Gatekeepers too, called Eilne. Cox is one of the last Eilne. He is a Dark Warrior, who disguised himself as a Guardian. He was the best fighter in Eader, and he can transform Darkness into physical weapons, destroying the Light. He revealed himself during the Great Battle and let the Darkness in before the battle started, also revealing he could wield the weapons of darkness. He personally killed Jared, the fourth Fior, with a Darkness-battle axe, and vanished in the middle of the fray. After this, no other Fior was delivered by the Eader. Grey, Cox is the one who taught us how to fight – he was our Swordmaster." Something clicks into place in the back of my mind, and I see a face. Dark, hard, shadowed eyes, hair combed back into a black ponytail and a black, bushy beard. Emotions of respect and fondness crash with anger and hate. I hear a 'crack' and look down at my now shattered glass and cut hand.

"Oh crap."

Callan smiles sadly. "Crap indeed."

I feel an anger building inside, which is weird as I hardly remember this person, but my mind is definitely remembering something. Betrayal. Hurt. Bitterness. What Cox did, uprooted my whole life. Darby's life. Thiam's. And so many more. "What kind of a monster would do such a thing?" I am seething, and by the look on Callan's face, he is too.

"We don't know, and don't call him a monster. He must have had his reasons." I'm wrong, Callan is mad at me. But why? "It is not something that can be forgiven. But he was our friend, our mentor. A leader. He wouldn't just do something like that without having a plan, or some kind of motivation."

"Yeah, I see how you can defend him. Really. He only killed

all those people and betrayed your friends!" The anger and confusion just make everything worse, and I am shouting now. People in the pub are starting to notice, too. Callan laughs sardonically.

"Easy for you to say, isn't it? Being a Fior and all. Entitled from birth, basically royalty. People fawning over you. Some of us don't have that luxury and have to fight for what we want in life. Along with having to fight for your friends and family. You haven't had to fight for anything in your life!"

This makes me take a step back, and I bump into a dwarf behind me, almost tipping me over. I mutter an apology and turn back to Callan, who is smiling at me. It doesn't reach his eyes. I sigh heavily, and smile sadly back at him. "Shows what you know, Stinky." I turn around and walk slowly out of the pub, feeling everyone's eyes on me as I leave. With my hands in my pockets I follow the winding pathways through the city towards the city limits, on the opposite side from my house. I kick the dead leaves, trying to avoid people I meet. As I leave the city, I hear the faint whistle of 'Hakuna Matata' in the distance. Pulling my hood up, I turn right as I reach the forest, taking the pathway skirting the city back to my house. Alone again, just the way I like it. Stupid people. I reach my house and walk up to my room, relishing in the emptiness. A feeling I have sought refuge in for my entire life and now it seems it's the only place that I feel comfortable in any more. The sweet pain of loneliness. Wow. Could I be any more emo? I kick my sad ass back up the stairs and in anger I punch the wall, hitting the entry panel, and as if in revenge, the door sucks me in with violent intent, almost catapulting me onto the bed. "Yeah, you are right. I am an asshole. Sorry about that." And now I am talking to walls.

Chapter 19

Grey

I lie in bed, wishing I could remember more of my past here in Eader. Then again, why should I want to? Even with all the struggles I went through back on Earth, I survived. Me. Grey. Without anyone to lean on. Except Lizzie, that is. Staying away from everyone was both a necessity and a tactic to avoid pain. Having Callan back in my memories is messing up my mantra – people only cause pain, so I stay away from them. Callan has reminded me of this by being a douchebag, getting me back on track. But it didn't help that my fucked-up powers intervened as well. The bad feeling was seeping into my soul, settling nicely in that familiar hollow in the middle of my chest. I did have one loophole though – if I ever met anyone with superpowers, I would make an exception to my policy of staying away from people. Now it turns out I have superpowers. Maybe not so super. People here are close to being superheroes, though. Sort of. Living in an inverted globe fighting darkness to protect the stupid people of Earth. And oh yeah, my old mentor was spearheading the whole operation to take down everything good in the world. My head is spinning. Never been on a rollercoaster, but this must be what it feels like. So excited and blown away by, well, everything. Magic is freaking real, I belong somewhere, I have people who know me, I think – it's bloody terrifying. Wow, I am emo-ing out more than usual, such a loser.

I must dose off, as suddenly a loud ring sounds through the house which springs me out of bed. Doorbell perhaps? Turns out I'm right. After running downstairs, I peek out the door, and see a dwarf at the end of the pathway to the house. Right. Only Fiors allowed at the house. I walk up to him, which startles him as I must just be popping out of thin air.

"Erm, hi? Can I help you?" I must sound pathetic because the dwarf does not look impressed. He eyes me up and down, before reaching up to me with his hand.

"Hi! I am Ragnar, and I am here to bring you to the enrolment ceremony, Grey, sir."

"Enrol—what now?" I shake his hand, feeling like there is something I should be saying or doing. Bow maybe? No, I am a 'sir'? What? But before I can do anything however, I feel a tug behind my bellybutton and my confused frown turns in to a full-blown freak-out-face. And then there is nothing. I feel my feet hit the ground hard and I gracefully fall face first into the dirt. As I roll over, I open my eyes, and stare up at the sky. Yes. Sky. Or wait. It's Dust! Thousands, no, must be millions of little Dusties flying above me – lighting up everything. This everything is a field, with lots of people standing around looking down at me. Behind these rude staring people, I see a large building. Or it is more like a fortress. In the middle, there is a large spire with a navy-blue flag, and on each corner a round guard tower. Baileys stretch between them, and I can see guards patrolling on the battlements and area surrounding the castle. They even have a draw bridge, and I can see larger structures behind the tall walls. Please, let there be dragons somewhere, I think to myself, imagining myself slaying the largest one.

"Yep, there are dragons, but they are very rare, and they do not need to be slain as they are some of our best aerial fighters, aside from myself, of course."

I awkwardly get to my feet and start looking around, where I come face to face with Lay, who is sporting her best combat gear it seems, all shiny and silver today. Intruding as always. I brush myself off and look annoyed up at her. A notion she immediately picks up on. "Sorry, Grey. Bad habit, I know." She shrugs apologetically and flies off towards the fortress. Great, my charm strikes again. And I haven't even had my morning coffee yet.

Like everywhere else in Eader, we are surrounded by the impossibly tall trees. The air seems a bit chillier, and I pull my jacket around me. Where is this anyway? I don't recognise any of it, except for the same murky, mushy moss, evenly spaced trees around the large clearing with the occasional rock or dead tree breaking up the pattern. The light is almost magical as it flows in waves of the ocean of Dust above, making the usual dank and depressing dusk feel like it is the dark giving you a shimmering hug instead. Darby did say something about the lack of Sun, but at least there are the Dusties.

Everyone is standing haphazardly around. A few dwarves, some elves it seems judging by their pointy ears, but lack of wings, several fairies, mostly in uniforms, and a few humans. They are standing talking to each other, looking impatient almost.

"Everyone, if you would quiet down!" A booming voice is coming from the front of the fortress, and I recognise it as Ryder's. The crowd starts shuffling towards the sound, and I skulk after them, not really in a mood to interact with anyone. I look around for Darby, but can't see her anywhere.

"I realise that you are all here to support your friends and family, or you are just bloody curious about our new recruits. Well, too bad," he growls. "If you are not enrolling today, would you please sod off!" I snort, smiling to myself. Gotta love that guy. Seems like he was right too, as more or less three quarters of the people here leave, some disappearing in pairs into the woods, others fly off or just disappear mid-air, a lot of them accompanied by a dwarf.

"It is because dwarves are our best excavators, so they are the best to find their way through layers. They work for the transport department." Lay is back, but I try to smile and nod. After everyone has left, we are only six people left. Lay, Ryder, a fairy girl, a tall man dressed in full combat gear, a round, older woman, and myself.

"So, you two are our new trainees, are you?" The fairy girl nods, and I just stare. No need to confirm, they all know who I am, and I am in no mood for small talk. Ryder stares at me, sighing.

"You have both been training for today, you, Sawyer, due to special circumstance, and yeah, Grey." I frown at his condescending tone, but just shrug. Whatever.

"This is the Academy, where you will receive the necessary training to fulfil your new roles. These roles will be assigned to you as we find out what you are made of, along with your strengths, and more importantly, your weaknesses, of which I am sure there are many." He stares at me as he finishes his sentence. I just stare back. "As you both know, I am Ryder, and the leader of this teaching establishment. This is Roberta, and she is the quartermaster. She will provide you with all the necessary equipment and clothing for your training, and if you have any questions, she is the woman to ask."

He gestures to the round lady to his right, who nods sharply. Seems cosy.

"This is Ren. He will be overseeing your overall progress,

reporting back to me." This time it is the tall Guardian man who nods, and he even adds a smile. Though, somewhat cocky, with his hands on his side making him look like a combat-ready Superman. "Lay here hardly needs an introduction, but she is your combat instructor."

Lay waves and smiles, winking at me. I smile half-heartedly back, and the fairy girl swallows hard as Lay is introduced.

"Now, your magic instructor is busy teaching this morning, but you will meet him later." Magic class? Unreal! I must look like a gleeful idiot because Ryder clears his throat meaningfully before continuing. "If you would both come with me, we will commence the enrolment procedure," he announces. At this, the fairy girl draws a quick breath, eyes widening, and follows the four others over the drawbridge, and into the fortress. The drawbridge is hanging over a gorge, which as I stare down, doesn't seem to have a bottom. Inside the fortress there is a large courtyard, with stone arcades encircling it, and several hallways beyond them. There are stables off to the right, what seems to be the main building in the centre, and what could be the barracks off to the left. We walk across the courtyard, where Roberta and Lay leave us, and head off in the direction of the barracks. Lay winks at me and I stare glumly after her, wishing I could go with her instead. Way to leave a teammate behind.

I follow Ren, Ryder, and the fairy girl into the centre building, the one holding the spire. It is built with dark stones and has no windows, and gives off a menacing vibe as we pass through the large black stone doors. I feel like the sentries' gazes on the wall are following us in, which might in fact be their job, though it makes my hair stand on end. As we get inside, I am about to relax a bit, but then I see what room it is we have entered. In the centre, there is a pedestal. An obsidian pedestal holding a blue flame. Holding is a strong word, as it is more like it is floating above it. Around the room different corridors lead off, either up or down staircases, probably to training areas or classrooms I assume, but in this room, there is only the blue, or maybe more turquoise fire in the centre dancing and throwing its eerie glow onto the jet-black, stone walls. The light is strange and cold, especially when the doors slam shut behind us, and it flickers in the reflection across the glossy walls. Looks like no Dusties allowed.

"Now, we will make this as painless as possible." The way Ryder always starts his sentences with a calm and deep 'now', is starting to annoy me. "You will both be tried by the Flames of Eader, known as the Dán. Dán is a kindling of the Eader itself. Which is of course to say that the flames will not burn you, but nevertheless, it will be a trial by fire. The results will be given in the colour of the flame. The warmer the tone of the flame, the more powerful you are. In addition, you will be given an insignia, which will be tattooed on your wrist. Your mark of Eader." Ah, so this is what Callan meant. My way into the magic world at the cinema. Bring it on! "As we know the roles you will take on, there will not be any assigning of these; you, Sawyer, a combat fairy; and you, Grey. Well, still a Fior."

I grunt.

"Sawyer, dear, would you come here, please?" Ryder's voice is now softer, and looking at him slightly bent forward with his arms outreached in front of him reminds me of a cosy grandfather. The young fairy girl swallows hard yet again, making big eyes at me after she hears Ryder mentioning me being a Fior. She inches her way up to Ryder, fiddling with the hem of her leather vest as she goes. She reminds me of Lay, with her lithe, athletic body and pointed ears, but she has long, braided blonde hair and a dark green dress under her brown leather stitched vest. "You are training to become a combat Guardian, are you not?" Ryder smiles down at her.

She nods nervously; now clenching her fists on either side of her hips. She looks very apprehensive to this whole thing – does she know something I don't? Probably. "Not to worry, just step right up to the Dán and follow the instructions," Ryder coaxes in a soothing tone. As if bracing for impact, Sawyer steps up to the blue flames and seems to freeze. Her eyes glaze over, and she appears to be saying something, then she smiles, and steps up and into the flames on the pedestal. I almost scream out as the little girl is consumed by the flames, but no one else moves. We just stand there. The blue flames still flickering. Then suddenly Sawyer gently appears again, smiling, and steps down towards Ryder again. She turns around, and then waits. The flame seems to consider her for a while and then it starts to change, and it changes into a dark purple otter. Seemingly swimming in the air above the pedestal. "Ah, very good, Sawyer! Dark purple is a very strong colour for a fairy combat guardian. And the otter, grand! Feisty little fighters they are." Sawyer blushes and nods slightly. She is instructed to show her right wrist, and sure enough, the same knotted Celtic circle as Callan had, though this with an otter tattooed in the middle. "Ren will now show you where you can find your class, and let you get settled in."

Ren nods once and escorts Sawyer up one of the staircases to the left.

"Now, let's get this over with." An annoyed chill runs down my spine. Ryder frowns as he beckons me forward. "Same goes for you, step forward and follow the instruction of the Dán. No messing around, shadow boy, or you'll burn." Ah, so he has heard. Well, of course he has, he's on the council. And the grandfather impression is totally gone. I can't tell if he is kidding about the burning thing, but I glance over at the flame which is now back to a normal, blazing blue. As I step closer, I can feel waves of cold air rolling off it, and I stop right in front. Glancing back at Ryder is no help, as he is just staring at me with a dark look. Okay then. As I look back into the flame however, I freeze. I hear an eerie voice coming from the flames, pulling me in:

"Step right up, step right in,
then we will see where to begin.
Reveal we will, and it won't take long.
Uncover secrets and powers, feeble or strong."

Before I know it, I relax. My shoulders slump down, hands falling limp at the sides. "That is it. Do not try to resist. Come join me, Grey."

"Actually, I am fine right out here." I do not want these flames to search my brain for whatever they are looking for, but as I try to resist, the urge to do as it says just grows stronger and I feel myself getting pulled into the flames. They are cold, but not uncomfortable. At first, I can see Ryder standing outside in the round room, then he is gone, and the flames are everywhere.

"So, Grey, why are you here?" I go to open my mouth, but find that I can't. "Oh, not to worry, no need to articulate any answers. We will find all we need." We? Who are we? Suddenly I feel the flames getting hotter. "Hm, this is not... Wait." The little man's voice sounds strained. "It can't be. No!" I frantically look around me and then feel myself get pushed off the pedestal. I land on my hard back, getting the air knocked out of me. Ryder stands over me, looking worried.

"Boy, what happened?"

Coughing, I am about to answer, when I see the light reflected on the wall start to change. I turn to see the flames, which are now anything other than blue. They are growing in size, and intense heat is rolling off of them. The colour is growing from turquoise to navy, passing through different stages of purple, then pink then red, then blood red, before they seem to be turning black. As they grow, it changes form and each side elongates, into what looks like wings. Finally, the wingtips each touch the opposite walls, and a phoenix is floating in the air above the pedestal, the bottom half with tailfeathers, the top with head, pitch black. I look down at my wrist and see an ordinary Celtic knot there, but no phoenix. There is nothing inside it. Ryder's face is pale, and he stares wide-eyed at the phoenix. At the same time, I feel a searing pain on my back and jump up from the floor, tearing at my shirt, screaming. The pain is sharp and hot, and seems to be covering my entire back. Ryder steps over and rips off my jacket and shirt, which I think is quite rude, but he holds me by the shoulders, my back towards him.

"What is it, Ryder? What do you see?" My voice is half-panicked, half-indignant. The pain is subsiding quickly now, but I can still feel the burn. Ryder still isn't answering, but his grip on my shoulders is tightening painfully. "It can't be," he mutters. "I knew you... but the colours... Not the phoenix. Not since..."

"Wow man, that is fascinating and all, but could you be any less helpful?" Yep, Mister Sarcastic stepping up, right on cue.

"Oh, sorry, Grey." He releases me and I spin around to face him. I note that he used my name, which isn't a good sign.

"Ryder, what just happened to me? What was that phoenix all about, and what colours?" My heart is racing, and it is pissing me off. Ryder sighs deeply. He grabs my wrist to check the tattoo and then drops it again, shaking his head as if confirming something.

"Now, listen to me." I roll my eyes, which ordinarily would

earn me a slap in the back of the head from this guy. This time however, he is just observing me curiously. "As I mentioned earlier, the colour of the fire will pinpoint the strength of a Guardian's power, or in your case, the strength of a Fior. A Fior is more or less always stronger than any regular Guardian, which really goes without saying." I nod impatiently, crossing my hands over my chest, now feeling annoyed and naked. "Well, usually a Fior will reach a hot pink or a light red, which is looked at as very powerful."

"So, what is Darby's colour then?"

Ryder smiles. "You would have to ask her. These things are considered to be very personal, you see."

"But I saw Sawyer's flame?"

"Yes, you did. I had asked her beforehand, and she was not very fussy about it."

He was being so patient with me, I almost wanted him to yell at me, slap me in the head or order me to read his entire library. Something. "Your flames were blood red, and not only that, it had two colours. Which happens sometimes. But never with black. Black is a sign of..." I could more or less guess where he was going with this. Having more or less made movies and comic books my life, it didn't take a master's degree to realise black was a bad thing.

"Let me guess, Darkness, right?"

Ryder nods. "Indeed it does. It might be due to your power, mind you, which is clearly much stronger than any of us originally guessed."

"Then again, it might not be," I add cheerfully. "Anyway, moving on. What is up with the tattoo on my arm, and can you please tell me what is happening with my back. I thought we were supposed to get the symbol on our arm."

"Yes, right you are. To be honest, I have never seen this happen. And it has not been documented either as far as I know.

So I am not quite sure what it means. I can tell you that you did get your phoenix however." I swallow hard. It isn't like I hadn't concluded as much, but I just didn't want to admit it. Walking over to the wall, I brace myself, and in the shimmering light from the now once again blue flames I see it – on my back is a black phoenix with red details on the tail and wings. Wings stretching from shoulder to shoulder, tail feathers hanging down my spine and a fierce face in the middle of my shoulder blades. It is actually quite stunning, and it isn't like I'm a stranger to tattoos, but somehow this feels like something more. "I would keep this to yourself, Grey. Your wrist tattoo should work like any other however." I study the one on my wrist closer, and it is just like Callan's was: Celtic knots in a circle, but nothing inside it. Ryder hands me my now torn shirt, which I take and put on like a short-sleeved jacket. "Now, you will be starting your courses tomorrow, and will be joining the advanced class for combat training, beginner's class for travel and magic, and you do not need to take language and culture adapting courses, as Fiors pick up these things much faster than other Eadorians." That last part is news for me, but I shrug, and nod. "Eloquent as always, young sir," Ryder remarks dryly and ushers me out of the room and into the courtyard. There, Ragnar the dwarf is waiting for me.

"Sir, are you ready? Oh, I see it is casual day at school today. Nice shirt, sir." I can't tell if he is messing with me, but I am too weary to care.

"Let's just go."

Ragnar nods, grabs my arm and it goes dark for a second, and then we pop out back outside my house.

"Thanks, man," I say to my ride.

"No worries, sir. See you tomorrow at eight a.m.!" With that he is gone, and I make a beeline for the door, in dire need of a beer and a proper mirror.

Chapter 20

Grey

Ragnar is not kidding about the a.m. call. I had set my alarm clock. I hadn't known what time it was anyway, as it's never really clear what's night or day here. So I had just set it to quarter to eight. Plenty of time to spray some water in my face, put some deodorant on and pull on my favourite black jeans and a Batman shirt. Because today I have a feeling I'll wish I was Batman. Grabbing a cheese sandwich on my way out, I step outside, and can feel it has gotten a bit chillier. The gloomy light is however growing on me. I close my leather jacket and spot Ragnar, who is standing outside the boundary waiting, right on time. He greets me cheerfully, which I feel is blasphemy so early in the morning, but I dutifully take his hand as he reaches for mine, and we are off. I'm getting much better on the landings now and manage to stay on my feet this time as we arrive outside the Academy. During the Shift I had kept my eyes open, and could see this wasn't just an act teleportation, moving instantly from one place to another. It's more of a vertical movement, navigating some kind of extra layer, a shortcut of sorts maybe? Could it be that there is even more to this place?

Before I can think more about it, I hear shouts, and see Lay floating down towards me. "Right on time, trainee." Trainee, wow. I feel like an apprentice Avenger. And not in a good way. She lands next to me. "Well, don't just stand there, join your class." I look over towards where she is pointing. Left of the drawbridge I can see people are gathered. As I draw nearer, they seem to be about five women and six men, all dressed in combat gear. Meaning boxing bandages and protective gear for legs and head. I feel so out of place I wish I could master the Shift right here. "Extra gear is inside, trainee," Lay says and leads everyone inside to the Training Hall, which is downstairs from the onyx walled room housing the Flames of Eader. When I walk by, it is still hovering above its pedestal. "Grab boxing bandages and please lose the jacket, Grey." Lay's voice is commandeering, but I can hear her smile through it and roll my eyes. Always the bossy one. "You might think so now, Grey, or should I say Batman," she says, eyeing my shirt. "But just give it a day, I will make you wish you hadn't rolled those sparkling purple and blues at me."

We are down in the Training Hall. The room is filled with mirrors, punching bags, floor mats and all sorts of weapons, and below an arched ceiling with beams stretched across about five metres above. I walk over to where the protective gear is stashed and grab black boxing bandages. As I have never tied any sort of bandages on myself, I get help from a fellow trainee, a lithe, sandy haired guy named Haines. Three times around the wrist, three times around the middle of the hand, then in a cross motion covering the knuckles, the thumb, and then again around the middle of the hand before finishing around the wrist. I never knew how complicated preparing for a fight could be. Hell, my fighters in my games were just always combat ready. To be honest – they never really needed protection, as I was always winning. Just kidding. Or not. I on the other hand, am not always winning. And I have been fighting Lay, so I know what I'm getting into, or so I think. Haines knocks his fist against mine as he finishes, nods at me, and goes to stand with the rest of the class.

"So, finally we are all ready," Lay shouts. "We will pick up on where we left off yesterday – which is basic defensive moves in hand-to-hand combat. As mentioned, knowing these moves will intuitively help you move and counterattack without a second thought in a fight, with or without a weapon." I am inching over to the rest of the class as I feel a hand on my shoulder. "Grey, would you help me demonstrate?" Knowing it isn't really a question, I swallow hard and nod, turning to face her. "Grey, we are just going to have a light sparring match, with moves we practiced with Callan, OK?" I nod, and she turns to the class. "Now, as you all know, I can read minds, which to be honest is an unfair advantage. But in this case…" She doesn't get any further, as I try to swipe her left leg with my right, while driving my elbow into her stomach. I must be getting lucky, as my elbow connects, though only briefly as she manages to step back with her right leg in time to follow the movement of my attack. "Yes, surprising your enemy is definitely a strong strategy to use when you are outmatched by your opponent." Really? Outmatched? I can feel my anger surging. I'll show you, little fairy. I feint right, and drive an uppercut against her chest, which she dodges almost too easily. "You see, where your enemy tries to outsmart you, you need to be the smarter one, and use his attacks against him." After my hit and miss, I drive my right leg in a back kick, which she seems to see coming a mile away, and twirls away to the right, only to send a lazy kick to my hindquarters. The rest of the class laughs. "Again, overconfidence will be your enemy."

I feel my cheeks flush and head over to stand at the back of the class.

"Now, pair up. Grey, you are with Daryuen. He will show

you what moves we are focusing on today." She winks at me, which can't be a good sign. Turns out I am right. A tall, broad-shouldered man with his long, black hair in a ponytail steps up to me and nods.

"Daryuen," which is all he says. I feel like saying 'Hodor' but realise it might not be the right time for jokes. He looks intimidating enough, with his large bulging muscles in his bare arms and legs, and intense brown eyes. I nod back, and get into my fighting stance, Daryuen doing the same. He demonstrates carefully the simple jabs and cross-combos with feints and kicks, along with the defensive counter to follow each attack. It looks like a slow-motion mime fight scene. But all in all, it is pretty basic stuff. Taking a deep breath, I start circling him, sending small jabs in his direction, making sure I am never in half-distance to him. This seems to be annoying the big brute, and he meets me halfway with a right cross in my chest, making me stagger backwards. How is a man of his size so fast? Shaking it off, I close in again, a bit more careful this time. Daryuen nods at me again, as if to make sure I am good to go. In reply, I kick him with a side kick in the gut, which he takes without as much as a wince, grabbing my foot and sending me flying again. Okay, so superfast *and* strong. I need to up my game. This time I wait for him to approach me. He comes at me with a one-two punch combo, which I dodge followed by an uppercut into his solar plexus. This time I get a reaction at least. When I step out from his reach I send a kick behind his knee, knocking him out off balance and follow up with a right cross. When it connects, I feel like my hand is breaking and immediately step back, clutching it. Daryuen laughs as he regains his balance, holding his jaw. He nods once again, and steps away.

"Good job, Grey. Not many are able to land a solid hit on

that guy." Lay comes up to me, and slaps me on the back.

"Which is why you paired me up with him, I am guessing," I grumble.

"Well, yeah. Rolling your eyes will get you that much at least. Daryuen is a giant, and packs quite a punch. He can also take most punches. How is your hand?"

I notice I am still cradling it, but try to flex it and it feels okay. "It is fine, just took me by surprise is all."

She nods. "Be glad I told him to go easy on you," she mocks and turns around. "Okay class, good work. Now, I want three rounds on the Ranger before we move on."

"The Ranger?" I ask curiously.

"Just follow Haines, and try to keep up." I run after the class, and see Haines hanging back to wait for me.

"Okay, I won't wait for you, mate, but I'll show you where to start. Savvy?"

"Sure thing," I mutter. Haines' British accent makes him sound like a posh street rat, so dude seems cool enough. We run up to one of the towers where a zipline is anchored, disappearing in between the trees at the edge of the clearing. People are throwing themselves off of the top, vanishing into the distance. "Just use your hands, the bandages are designed to withstand the heat." Which are all the instructions I get before Haines is off after the rest. I am last. I climb the wall at the edge, and gasp as I watch Haines zoom through the air no less than twenty metres above ground into the tree crowns across the estate. I grab the wire with my wrapped hands, take a deep breath, then launch myself into the air.

The speed is incredible, and I feel my hands getting warmer, but nothing too bad. As I get closer to the trees, I see a net just inside the treeline and the others crawling up. I brace myself and let go just in time to reach it. I won't say slamming into a net at high speed is advisable, but I manage. Getting my bearings, I start climbing after the rest. After a while I see a platform where the net ends, and after getting up onto this, I inhale sharply. There is a whole obstacle course set up here, at least ten metres above ground. Ropes and ladders made out to create a pathway through the trees along the edge of the treeline it seems. The architecture of the elementary school in Manawa is starting to make sense. My next obstacle are the monkey bars across nothing but air, almost holding my breath, before doing the Tarzan swing over to a new platform, refraining from doing a jungle cry. Then comes a balance bar with a punching bag swinging out of nowhere trying to knock me down, several ropes I need to swing between to reach another net, then another set of monkey bars after climbing down the net before reaching a last platform. It just ends. Should I go back? But then I hear Haines's voice from down below.

"You gotta jump, mate!" Jump? Sure thing. Just jump into nothing. Below me I see tree brush and more greenery. Worst trust exercise ever. Whatever. So I just step off. I fall the five metres that are left to the ground and drop into a small lake. Of course, there is a lake here. Resurfacing, I see the Academy in front of me, realising I am now at the back of the estate. I start swimming after Haines, who I see is getting out on the other side. I am dead last, and it is getting more tiring by the second. At least the lake isn't all that big, and I reach the edge quickly. I run after Haines who is just entering a side door into the walls surrounding the Academy. As I get there, I see a staircase and as I step through, I feel a humming go through me and my wrist tattoo getting a bit warmer. Security perhaps? I pump my arms as I run up the stairs, and suddenly I am at the top again, just in time to see the back of

Haines as he zips down into the woods all over again. What had Lay said. Three rounds? At least the name makes sense now. I also realise that Darby was right. My previous training was just the entry requirement. With burning lungs, I jump off the tower for the second time.

After what seems like an eternity, I finish the last two rounds, and barely manage to keep up with the rest. If keeping up is finishing. Wow, my training with Callan has really paid off, compared to my couch potato starting point at least. As I think that I should thank him for that, I remember the last time I saw him and decide against it.

"Awesome job, mate!" Haines slaps me on the back and smiles. "Thought we lost you on that last round!" Referring to when I forgot about the punching bag in the haze of exhaustion and almost got knocked down.

"Yeah, me too. Why the hell is it so far above ground?"

"To keep everyone on their toes and focused. Don't worry, only a few have died falling down," Lay says lightly as she enters the room. "Good job, everyone. Now, as you have all warmed up, we will start weapons training. Everyone, arm up. Grey, get over here." Warmed up? Is she for real? I stagger over, sweat dripping and stare darkly at Lay. "Don't give me that tone, Grey. We aren't playing around anymore; you need to take this seriously." I am not even surprised when she answers my unspoken resentment, and grab the water bottle she hands me. "As you do not have a chosen weapon yet, I will train with you today to help you figure out which weapon will fit the skills imbued upon you by the Blue Flame. Everyone here is adequate with all weapons as fighting requires flexibility, but we do also have specialised training for the weapon we are born to fight with. There are tests to go through to find the right one, and we will do this today."

I nod once, emptying the water bottle and dry off on one of the fresh towels in the corner of the room. As I turn around, I see the others with their weapons. Three with quarterstaffs, four with swords, two with battle axes and two with two knives each. "As you can see, there is a preference for the sword and quarterstaff, but as I said, your weapon of choice depends on what lies within."

She turns to the class.

"Okay, we will all be helping Grey today to find his weapon, and go through the tests. This will mean that you will have to perform at the top of your game with your weapon as well, so don't think this means going easy on you." Her eyes narrow and everyone nods. Turning back to me she says carefully, "I know you are tired, but it is in this state you are able to pull out what is truly needed to succeed in battle, which will mean your ultimate weapon will be the one which helps you succeed." Not really getting what she means, I just shrug. We start with the axes, where I fail immediately. The balance is completely off, and after Rin, a dwarf with orange hair, short beard, and one of the axe wielders, manages to cut my shoulder, Lay calls us off. "Next!" she yells and Narila, an Asian looking girl with green hair, golden eye shadow, and pointy ears, making me guess she is an elf, approaches, holding her two daggers. I get two as well and they feel better in my hands. I have been trained in all the different weapons, both with Callan and with Cox. I shudder, blocking it out.

What will be different now, I don't know. Even though I last longer with the daggers, something feels off. Lay stops us again and gives everyone a break, as everyone is doing simultaneous drills as I am fighting my opponents. After the break, the quarterstaff is up, and I am paired with Raimy, a tall, blonde

Amazon looking woman. She has long hair in two braids, shimmering green eyes and holds herself tall, almost like royalty. She does not hold back, but neither do I and we go round after round, both holding our own. In the end however, it is as if I get unsure of my attack and in that split second, Raimy knocks me to the floor.

"What was that, Grey?" Lay demands, walking over and dragging me to my feet.

"I don't know. It just felt like…"

"Like you didn't know if the attack was right?" Lay finishes for me.

"Yeah, something like that," I murmur.

"Okay, we are getting somewhere," she says, and walks off. I have no idea what that means, but follow Lay over to the sword rack. "We are left with the swords now. There are, as you know, three types that are used here, the double-edged longsword, the scimitar and the short-sword. You will try each one." And I do. The sword is by far my favourite weapon, and I do quite well. But in the end of each match I'm still left the loser. First, Daryuen knocks me down using the pommel of his longsword, then Kazuki, an Indonesian fellow with a Mohawk and a wicked grin, wins by slicing my calf open with his scimitar before Katie, a blue haired girl with a gnarly offensive manoeuvre, knocks my short-sword straight out of my hand. Each time, that feeling of not being able to trust my weapon overwhelms me in the end. Lay explains that I don't have to win, but that I will know when I find it, and we're running out of weapons. Lay looks to be thinking hard. She gives us another break and runs off up the stairs.

"Don't worry, mate, Lay will figure it out, she always does. I remember when Kazuki here was looking for his weapon, it took him like a thousand tries." He chuckles and glances over to Kazuki who turns around at the mention of his name.

"What was that, Haines?"

"Oh, nothing, old boy." Because of Haines's English accent and his laidback attitude, he is growing on me, and I smile.

"Something funny, new guy?" Kazuki walks over, throwing his scimitar across his back.

"No man, all good."

Narrowing his eyes, he stops right in front of me. "No, you know what is good? The rumour I heard about your enrolment ceremony." He sneers at me, grabbing my wrist. "Ah, looks like the rumours are true, nothing there." He sniggers. I tear my hand from his grip, feeling my heart pounding in my chest. No one says anything, but I can feel everyone staring. Haines cocks an eyebrow.

"Nothing? Well, at least he has something between his ears, eh, Kazuki? I know you weren't as lucky." Stopping short, Kazuki glares at Haines, but he doesn't seem to come up with any witty response and stalks off.

"Thanks, you didn't have to do that," I say.

"No worries, he makes it so easy, and he is an asshole to boot. Good fighter, though." I nod and grin.

"Okay, here we are!" Lay is back and carrying a black wooden box, about the size of a lunch box, with silver threads delicately decorating it. "We will just try this, Grey, and if it doesn't work, we have other alternatives, sound good?" Shrugging, I step up and she hands me the box. She eyes me interestingly, but says nothing. "I will be fighting you this time." As I have been fighting her on several occasions, I think nothing of it and shrug. The class on the other hand starts whispering and some gives the standard, mocking 'ooh' sound. I open the box and my eyes widen at the sight of its content. Two silver knuckles gleam in the box, each with inscriptions in a language I cannot read, for once. I look surprised up at Lay, but she just smiles, standing on the mats with her own quarterstaff. "You ready?" As we are inside, she is limited to using her legs, and not her wings, though this hasn't really stopped her from winning before. I put down the box and grab the silver knuckles. How is this fair? Hand-to-quarterstaff combat? But I put them on and join her on the mats. I get into position and feel a calmness rolling over me. Locking eyes with Lay, I raise an eyebrow, daring her to attack. Knowing her moves a bit, I anticipate her attack, but she waits for me. I feint a left jab, which I know she will see coming a mile away, but I want her to. As she moves to take advantage of my obvious feint with the staff, I step in and thrust an uppercut into her unprotected side, she grunts, and I roll out of the way as she lashes after me with her quarterstaff. "Not bad, trainee." This time, she comes at me, thrusting the tip of the staff towards my stomach, but I knock it aside with my knuckle, doing half a pirouette and hitting her jaw with a left jab. She rolls with the punch and hits me behind my knees with her staff. As I am about to fall over, I do something I have never done before. In mid-air, I put one hand on the ground, doing a sideway flip and come up with my hand squeezing Lay's throat. There is nothing but silence and my heart pounding in my ears.

"Wow, that was... What was that?" I release my grip and look around.

The class is staring at me, some whispering, "Did you see how fast he was?"

Another replies, "I barely saw him at all!"

Lay is smiling, rubbing her neck. "That, Grey, was you finding your weapon. You are the first silver knuckle user in a very long time. With your speed and reaction time, and in time, strength, you will be a force to be reckoned with. It is a very special weapon, keep them safe." She pats my arm. "Okay everyone, that is it for today. Hit the showers!" I look down at my hands. The knuckles gleam in the light from the fire in each corner of the room. Cool. I walk after the others, looking forward to a shower, as Batman is completely soaked, then remember I do not have a change of clothes here. "Not to worry, just go to the showers," Lay says. Nothing is private around that woman, I think, and jog after the rest, stuffing the knuckles in my back pocket.

The showers are weird. It's more or less just a small room with nozzles angled towards the centre and it cleans you, clothes and all, by spraying this green mist at you. It smells like pine trees and pumpkins and takes less than a minute. It's awesome.

"It is for efficiency's sake," Haines explains as we head to lunch. I nod. Wicked. My muscles are sore, but I feel good. People in class are cool enough, besides Kazuki, and I feel like I can hold my own. As we grab a quick lunch in the mess hall, Haines tells me about how the courses at the Academy are limited to skill and speciality, such as for healers, which requires strong light magic and knowledge of anatomy, and combat fairies with aerial training and Dust manipulation. He also divulges how people have been going missing and they have stopped Shifting people out to Earth. "I even heard rumours that a vampire was spotted in the eastern ravine, there is supposed to be a large breach there in the Eader. Though we aren't supposed to know about the breaches at all. They are keeping a tight lid on it all." A chill runs through me as I realise what ravine he must be talking about. And then I start wondering how anything really has a direction here. Do they have poles here too? I am left with a sour taste in my mouth about the whole thing, scary and confusing. But before I can ask Haines about any of it, a bell rings. Hopefully next class will help take my mind off it, which just happens to be Magic class.

I have been looking forward to this since I was told about the Academy. My sessions with Thiam haven't exactly been rainbows and unicorns, and now I think maybe there will be more than just making rabbits feel good about themselves. Maybe I will finally get my wand. Turns out, I am not that lucky. The room is nothing like an ordinary classroom. It, like every other room it seems like, has no windows, but is lit with Dust flying around, there are pillows everywhere and small glass orbs filled with different coloured glowing light floating in the ceiling. In each corner there is a yellow brazier, heating the room.

"If you would, please find your seats."

A tall, older man steps out from the flames in the corner, or more, the light in the corner, as I realise that he must have Shifted here. He does not seem to be bothered by the heat from the flames he just walked through. We plop down on the pillows spread out on the floor, which makes me feel like I am three years old and in kindergarten. Which, when I think about it, I never really had tried. I notice there are more people here than just people from my previous class.

"Ah, welcome Grey. My name is McFadden, and I am your professor in magic. I have been in contact with Thiam, and I know you have been working on the essentials," he says, looking intently at me. "But that was just the basics, you must know. We have been working on force magic the last month, and your partner will help you as we get started. First, we will repeat the rules. No direct contact, no indirect maiming, no supplementing power from *any* other sources." He says this last part staring intently at me. Ah, I see. He knows too, Thiam has definitely told him. "So, we will start by repeating the exercise from yesterday, working with levitation. As you should all remember, besides you that is, Grey, light is all the colours in the spectrum – like a rainbow when fractured through a prism, meaning it has many layers and characteristics.

"It moves like water and can work over different frequencies. Using the physical characteristics for light and dark, where it fills the air around us, we can manipulate the air by exploiting the same physics – but with magical properties. We can, by manipulating the light, move objects, or even ourselves and our opponents in battle. Now, everyone, get on your feet." McFadden says all this in one breath, and it makes my head spin trying to follow it. It seems like the rest of the class is used to it, as they immediately leap up and stand next their pillows and are instructed to try to levitate it off the ground. I slowly get up and recap what he said. When he started in on the science explanation, it all suddenly made more sense. I close my eyes and try sensing the light around me, but I feel more of the dark and decide to use that instead. I focus on the dark around the pillow and push up. The familiar tug in my stomach tells me it is working and as I open my eyes, sure enough, my pillow is floating. So is every pillow in the room. Everyone is staring at me. I swallow hard and release the energy. The pillows fall softly to the ground, and I shrug apologetically.

"What? Did I do it wrong?" I cross my arms. Seriously, it is getting old, me being the centre of attention all the time.

Professor McFadden steps over. "Eh, well. No, I guess you didn't. You actually did it quite well. I see the rumours are right, and you can use dark energy as well, my boy." I just stare at him. "Yes, well, let's try focusing on using the light energy for now, shall we?" In response, I gather the little light energy I can sense in the room and lift the pillows again, the light flickering.

"That okay, Professor?"

He swallows hard. "Yes, quite so."

I let the pillows drop again and he walks away. For the rest of the class I am tasked with lifting other, heavier objects, while the rest of the class struggle with the pillows. No one is talking to me, even Haines is focusing only on his own pillow, which is barely wiggling on the floor. I remember being told that Guardians can also do magic, though it is much weaker than a Fior's ability. It's weird how easy it is to reform the energy into a concrete force. And with each try it gets easier.

At the end of the class, Haines comes over. "So, how are you doing over here?"

I shrug. "I'm good. You?"

"Ah you know," he says, cocking his head to one side, "Us mere mortals need some more training." I laugh, and he smiles.

"Mortals, really?"

"Aye, you know, you are like the Special Forces, or the Avengers, while we are more like the ground support. Good to have you on the team, mate." He winks and walks off.

Me, an Avenger? That would be cool. I do have powers, and a definite fatal weakness is too much Darkness. What had Darby called me? A Conduit. What are my real powers anyway? Before I can ponder more on it, the Professor calls for attention.

"Good job, everyone. Find your seats again, please. Tomorrow we will start working with each other, knocking over an opponent. I want to remind you that our power will come from who we are. Remember that what you have inside is what you can draw strength from. Use it to your advantage. Creativity is key." Well, that could explain it! Survival of the nerdiest, or the one best to find shelter in fictitious worlds. Finally, it would pay off.

At least, it can't hurt.

"I will leave you with a quote by the great Albert Einstein, who said 'the monotony and solitude of a quiet life stimulates the creative mind,' meaning, I want you all to remember your meditating exercises each night. And Patrick?" A young man, with black hair and freckles I hadn't noticed before stumbles to his feet, knocking over one of the lights by the wall.

"Yes, sir?" He mumbles, fidgeting with his blue shirt.

"Be a good lad and gather up the pillows." With that he walked into the light and disappears again. Patrick nods frantically and starts pulling on the pillow Haines is sitting on. Not the sharpest knife that one. Meditating? Sure thing.

"So, see you tomorrow, man," Haines says as we exit the room, leaving Patrick with his pillows. I nod, and he waves as he walks off, towards the barracks.

As I hitch a ride with Ragnar home, I think every day cannot be like this, right? I am wrong. The next few days are exactly the same. Training, magic class and history, which I absolutely love, because books. I am not an outsider, except for freaking people out with my magic skills, even though I am trying to downplay it. On the fourth day, at the end of the day, I am about to go look for Ragnar, as I remember I have left my jacket down in the Training Hall. I trot down the stairs and find my jacket next to the protective gear.

"So, new guy uses Darkness, does he?" Kazuki is walking towards me from the doorway as I turn around, a menacing look on his face. "How the hell did they let you in here, you freak?" He stops in the middle of the room and slowly draws his scimitar.

"Nothing gets by you." I am sick of this. Kazuki has been

glowering at me since the first day in class. And I have met enough bullies to last me a lifetime.

"No, it doesn't, and neither will you, you freak."

"Freak again. Well of words only goes so deep with you, huh?" I wink at him. Wasn't the smartest thing to say or do, but he made it so easy. After all, weird and sarcastic is my default setting.

Kazuki sneers and takes a step towards me. Knowing it isn't a good idea, I take out the silver knuckles from my back pocket and put them on, tossing my jacket back on the ground.

"You think those things can stop me, do you?" he growls.

"What, no freak this time? Running out of ideas, are we?" I mock and Kazuki cries out as he charges at me.

As Kazuki attacks it is as if times slows down, I see his attack coming and I dodge it easily, sidestepping as he attacks again. I feel a bead of sweat trickling down my neck, the strain of today's exercises and magic training having taken its toll. Pushing it aside, I focus on keeping Kazuki at arm's length, only using defensive tactics, which is no problem as my hands and arms are deftly holding my aggressive opponent.

"You are really taking this way too seriously, man," I say as he comes at me with a flurry of attacks, which I brush off easily, only feinting a couple of jabs at him in return. He takes a few steps back, breathing hard.

"What are you?" he demands. Then it dawns on me. He doesn't know I am a Fior. Maybe no one in my class does. I just took for granted they all knew. In my moment of realisation, I take my focus off Kazuki, and he takes advantage of this. He leaps towards me and slashes down at me. His sword tip rips open my shirt and makes a thin cut diagonally across my chest, separating bat from man. I stagger back and see a drop of blood running down. Footsteps echo in the staircase, and Daryuen and Haines come jogging in.

"Hi guys, we heard a bloody ruckus, what is…" But before Haines can finish his question, I charge Kazuki. Who the hell does this guy think he is? He barely has time to realise what is happening as I hit him hard in the gut, followed by a knee to his nose as he doubles over. As I spin away, I feel his sword against my back and realise he must've lashed out after me. My shirt is barely hanging on any more, so I tear it off, feeling sweat and blood running down my chest.

"Guys, why don't you put your weapons down, eh?" Ignoring Haines, I close my eyes and search for sources of light around me, then opening them again, I start channelling the light around my hands and silver knuckles, and at the same time behind Kazuki. I walk slowly towards him, grinning wickedly. Kazuki screams and charges, and as he sets his foot down, merely a metre away from me, I push up with the light energy, making him do a backflip and land hard on his back. His sword flies away and as he tries to get up, I set my right foot up under his chin and lean over him.

"What am I? I am the Fior who is sick and freaking tired of your insecurities. Do you yield?"

Kazuki's eyes widen in shock, and he nods frantically. "I… I am so sorry, sir," he croaks. As I step back, he springs up and bolts for the door. Haines and Daryuen are still standing there, frozen, gawking at me. I pick up the remnants of my shirt off the ground and put the knuckles back in my pocket. Turning around, I walk back to get my jacket, ignoring the other two.

"Wow, your back! Is that a phoenix? Wait… is that your insignia? That is bloody cool, mate!" Haines's excitement doesn't penetrate my bad mood, and I feel my manly resting bitch face settling. Might be the reason why people have branded me a troublemaker, I don't know. I walk back towards the exit, and Haines is waiting, Daryuen having disappeared. "Oh, come on, give a lad a break, now would ya?"

I just walk past him, not interested in any sharing. I feel my hands trembling. What was that I did with the knuckles and the light? All I want is to go home. And not to the Fior Mansion, I want to go home to Earth. As if I didn't stand out enough, now everyone will know what happened. As I step outside the main castle, I take a deep breath. The fresh air feels like it is giving me new life, though I do wish it would rain. Actually, when I think about it, there isn't much weather here at all, just cold and dark. I make a beeline for the drawbridge and run Darby over, literally, who was standing talking with Lay next to the barracks. She pushes me off her and jumps to her feet. I awkwardly follow suit.

"What the hell, Grey?"

As I get up, with my back to her, she gets quiet. Crap, my tattoo! I hastily put on my jacket, wincing as I stretch my cuts from Kazuki's blade. As I turn around her shocked expression turns into worry as she notices my bloody chest. Then that crinkle between her eyes makes an appearance.

"What did you do now?" she grumbles, crossing her hands in front of her chest. Is she serious right now? I just stare at her, letting my deadpan look do the talking. When that doesn't seem to do the trick, I say my thoughts out loud.

"Are you serious right now? It is just a scratch. Why do you assume I did something wrong?"

"Because almost every time I see you, you are either unconscious or injured, and it is always because of something you did. Need I say more? You really need to get your shit together." I roll my eyes, and Lay stifles a laugh.

"That is just great. Well, you are wrong. And maybe I like having my shit lost, huh?"

Darby purses her lips. I fight the feeling to scream. What an awesome first week at school. At that moment Ragnar makes an appearance, and I couldn't be more grateful. Without a second glance at Darby, I grab his arm and he takes the hint, taking us out of there.

As I enter my room, I groan. Looking in the mirror I hardly recognise myself. The person staring back has a hard, grim look on his face. Where did the guy from this morning go? I take a shower, washing away the blood and bad memories, and head down to grab a beer, not caring that it's a school night. I am not the guy to start moping or getting depressed. It just isn't my thing. Now, the getting angry thing, with a hint of fuck off, that is more my speed. I bring my beer into the sitting room and turn on the TV, where randomly switching through the channels does nothing for my mood. It looks like they have more or less every channel in the world on this thing. How long have I been at the Academy? Seems like forever, at least it feels like it, though it's only the first week. I know days are longer, but I have started to get used to it, getting the energy I need. Though not today, my eyelids are getting heavy, and I don't even hear the empty beer bottle fall to the floor as I fall asleep.

The rest of the week goes by pretty much the same, but with a different kind of attention. Everyone has heard about the fight with Kazuki, the show of powers and the tattoo. It results in me being ostracised, like a freak on display. But it's the same drill I was used to in high school, with stares, whispers, people making room for me as I walk down the hallways. I had thought they would be different here. But as I'm only one of two Fiors and after what I have done, I don't blame them. So I decide to keep my head down and do the work. My time improves drastically on the Ranger, my body getting stronger and leaner. And my fighting skills too. Haines is more or less the only one who talks to me.

One day on the Ranger, Haines shouts, "So, Fior huh? I promise I won't hold it against you!"

I know he was trying to be casual about it, but I can tell he's treating me a bit differently. Almost reverently. We do however grab a beer at the end of the second week, which I manage to pay for with my tattoo. I need to get the lowdown on how much money I have on this thing.

In Magic class I stay in the back of the class, trying not to overdo it, as I have decided I would rather focus on my combat skills. I haven't talked to anyone about what happened in my fight with Kazuki, but I don't want to either. All I know is that I have way more power inside me than anyone knew, and I'm not sure I want to find out what that means. To sum it up, I'm mad, more or less fuming all the time, which seems to be affecting people around me as well, as Lay one day corners me and orders me to snap out of it, pointing to my hands, where small wisps of dark energy curl around my fingers. Circumstances do however improve a bit when it's finally time for me to have practical Shifting lessons. Minor downside? Darby is the teacher.

Chapter 21

Darby

It's not my choice to teach Grey Shifting, but with all the rumours in town and whining from the council… Let's just say, I'm the natural choice. After all that has happened the last two months, he's like a live grenade getting tossed around and I'm the one holding it when it blows. Shifting is however a skill he needs before we can move forward with the mission. Which is becoming increasingly more time sensitive. There has been an increase in attacks and disappearances, and the Guardians have their hands full with keeping everyone safe. Decipiér will only give the okay to a mission when Grey is ready, which means he needs to be able to Shift. Especially since dwarf transfer is only local. With his Conduit powers we may be able to sense a pattern, just something to point us in the right direction. Currently I am standing next to the fire pit, waiting for Grey to get here. He has already been at the academy now for four weeks, and I have heard he has made progress, not that I have been able to check in, with all the council meetings, strategy sessions, and checking of defences. I actually haven't seen him since he ran me down a little more than three weeks ago, half naked and bloody. I remember the look he had in his eyes, almost wild, most definitely angry. I shake my head and start pacing around the fire, which is casting shadows in every direction in the creeping darkness. I can't remember the last time it has got this dark here in Eader and it's getting under my skin, like the Eader has already fallen.

Suddenly, somebody comes walking towards me out of the shadows, making me jump, though it takes me awhile to realise that it is him. He looks older somehow, with the beginnings of a beard and broader shoulders. But what really takes it home is his eyes. Like he is somewhere far away, but still with this piercing look. Grey nods as he approaches and gives me one of his crooked smiles – and I see the old Grey in there, glinting in the purple of his eyes.

"You're late," I grumble, tearing my eyes from this half-stranger in front of me and continuing to pace as he sits down on one of the logs around the fire.

"Sorry, General, didn't know what clothes to wear for a Shifting session." I frown and he winks and smiles at me again and I relax. Grey is definitely still Grey. Nevertheless, I wonder what happened between now and the last time I saw him. Speaking of which.

"Well, at least it is more than you wore last time I saw you, which is an improvement."

He shrugs.

"Okay, let's just get started. I will explain the basics of Shifting to you—"

"Ryder already did that during my first few weeks here though, so—"

Ignoring him, I press on. "—Which are important to know because the basics are your only safety net, as Shifting is perilous and you can only rely on yourself when doing it. Yourself and your Beacon that is." I tap my own Beacon, the bronze buckle attached around my waist, stamped with my insignia, the dragon.

"A dragon? Wait, is that like your mark?" Before I can

answer he pops up and grabs my wrist to see.

"Yes, it is," I growl, yanking back my hand. Grey slides back down onto the log, smiling mischievously. "As I was saying, each Beacon is custom made for each user. But you already knew this, right?" Grey sticks his tongue out and I go on, and I try not to smack him on the head. "We will use this fire as our source of light and our goal is to travel to the inside of my tent." I point in the direction of my tent, two tents over from the med tent. "I trust you know its location well enough?"

"Yes, ma'am. Are you inviting me to your room, General? Do you take all your trainees there on the first date, or am I just special?"

I crinkle my nose in annoyance, taking a deep breath. "You better be taking this seriously, as this is extremely important, and you can easily get lost while Shifting. End up in places you really don't want to be."

Grey stands up, straightening out the collar of his leather jacket. "Don't you mean the mission is important and you don't want me screwing it up for you, me being just your tool and all." The abrupt change from his playful tone to bitter resentment startles me. Ah, so he had overheard Thiam and me that day.

"I did not mean it like that, I—"

"Whatever," Grey cuts me off, giving me his best deadpan look. "Let's get this show on the road, shall we?" He walks to the other side of the fire, stopping and stuffs his hands in his pockets, expectantly.

"Right." Suppressing the urge to pummel him, I lift up a Beacon buckle, brandishing a Phoenix. "This is your Beacon. I will show you how to activate it in a bit. The most important function it has is to pull in as much light energy, or also dark energy in your case, as is needed to fuel the Shift, and it has to be enough to, first of all, take all of you, and second of all, go all the way to where you want to go. If the source isn't big enough you can risk losing part of yourself in the journey, either physically or mentally, or end up between layers or only halfway to your destination. Are you with me so far?" Grey gives me a double thumbs-up, nodding enthusiastically from across the fire, the light dancing across his face. "Well, good," I say, trying to keep the snark out of my voice. I fail. "The Beacon will connect with your mind, and automatically absorb energy, while you focus on the destination. When it is ready, it will connect to your wrist tattoo." I glance up at Grey again, and he is looking at the empty circle under the cuff of his jacket.

"So, my back then?"

Shrugging, I admit, "I am not sure to be honest. But we will find out. The tattoo will let you know with a warm tingling, which you might have sensed when activating through using it for payments or opening security doors earlier."

Grey is nodding. "Been meaning to ask you, how much money is on this thing anyway? Haven't really been briefed on my contract or whatever."

This time it is my time to smile. "There isn't really a contract for Fiors. Let's just say you have the black American Express, so don't worry about that."

Grey stares blankly at me. "Not quite sure what that means, to be honest."

"Oh." And I had been really proud of the Earth reference myself. "Hm, you have unlimited funds. Does that help? You can't put a price on a Fior's contribution to Eader." More blank staring. "Anyway, are you ready to try this thing?"

"One more question." Grey comes back around the fire. "How does that translate to Earth currency exactly? Do you have a bank account or something?"

Raising an eyebrow, I smirk. "What, urging to go shopping or something?" Then I catch myself, remembering Grey's life on Earth. It is too late however, as his expression darkens.

"No, not really, just wanted to know."

"Well, let's just say you have a travel budget, and it is well within reason."

More shrugging. This is going great! Just great, I think, mentally face-palming myself.

"Now then, the basics are?"

When I get no answer, I smack him beside the head, getting it out of my system, and he grudgingly repeats the steps, "Enough light or dark energy, focus on destination, wait for signal from Beacon."

"Great!" I beam at him. "Then you push the Beacon, and the rest will take care of itself. Before you try, let's do a dry run. And as you can use both light and dark, we will practice both with you." He nods.

"So now, okay, close your eyes and focus on the light of the fire, the heat, and imagine yourself absorbing it, much like you have practiced before. Then, imagine the insides of my tent from when you were there last. Getting the details right isn't that important, it is more the feel of the place." As I am talking, I have closed my own eyes out of habit. As I open them, I see that I am talking to air. "Grey? Where did you go?" No answer. "Grey?" I shout louder.

"Present," I hear from behind me, and there he is, striding out of my tent. Looking down, I see the Beacon with Grey's Phoenix stamped on the side still in my hand. "How did you...?" I stutter.

Grey stops in front of me, looking a bit shocked, but no

worse for wear. "You tell me, you're the expert!" he says accusingly, crossing his hands in front of his chest.

It takes me a minute to compute what has happened. Somehow Grey managed to Shift manually – without a Beacon. Which is… unheard of, really.

"Let's try that again, this time use dark energy. Focusing on the darkness and the cold around you."

"Alrighty!" He promptly shuts his eyes, before opening them momentarily. "Same destination, General?"

"Oh, stop calling me that," I chide. "No, this time try for outside the Fior mansion. We need to check your range. If it works, I'll meet you there." He shuts his eyes, and within a minute, he disappears. Damn! I promptly activate my Beacon and a minute later I pop out at the Fior mansion. There, Grey sits on a rock waiting for me nonchalantly.

"Funny meeting you here," he quips. I start pacing again.

"It must be because of you being a Conduit. No other explanation. It is just instinct. Incredible. No one ever gets it that quickly, and you doing without a beacon…" I realise I am muttering to myself, and stop, straightening up. "Good job, seems like this is unnecessary, but you can keep it as a souvenir, I guess," I say. I throw him his Beacon buckle.

"Cool! Every hero has his tool belt."

I don't know if the play on words is intentional, but it makes me feel bad, nevertheless. "Anyway, we will spend a few more days practicing your targeting skills, and testing out the effect shifting has on you, then we will go. How are you feeling by the way?"

Grey stops playing with his tool belt and looks up. "I feel fine, a bit tired maybe, that is all. Go where, exactly?" I can see a gleam of hope in his eyes, and I know what he is thinking.

"Yes, Grey, go to Earth. We have been given approval for a mission to Earth, to investigate the… whatever is happening."

A big smile breaks out across Grey's face. "That is the best news I have heard in a long time! When?"

"Two more days, we need to plan and prepare, then we go. Sound good?"

"Sounds awesome!" He looks like his regular old self again, with a happy gleam in his eyes.

"There is however a small catch."

Grey stops his small happy dance and turns back to me. "What? Nothing you can say can ruin this for me right now."

I beg to differ, I think, not really wanting to ruin his mood, but there's no getting around it. "Callan is coming too."

And there it is. The smile fades and a hint of this newfound darkness seeps into his eyes again. "Yeah, that ruins it."

Irritation is building now. "You know what, this is far bigger than some bromance quarrel between you two imbeciles. Get over it. Callan is our strongest fighter and I need someone with me who I can trust."

"Yeah, get that – wouldn't want you to just have someone like me along."

I swallow hard, not wanting to take the bait, but realizing that I need to talk things out with the guy. "Meet me at the fire pit tomorrow, at ten, and be on time this time. I have talked to Ryder about your lessons at the Academy, and due to the circumstances…"

"What circumstances? You haven't told me squat, which is really not that surprising considering your track record of sharing information." I feel myself growing with frustration and anger, and Grey takes a step back. "Whoa! What the…"

With a sharp intake of breath, I realise the growth of

frustration was more literal than I wanted it to be. Closing my eyes, I shrink back. "You will know when you need to know, which is tomorrow. Now, get out of my sight!" When he doesn't move, probably in shock, I turn around and move up the hill back to the camp.

The next day, Grey is already waiting for me at the fire pit when I get there and he jumps up, ready to fire questions at me. Before he can, however, I hold up my hands. "Just wait, okay. I have some things I want to say to you, and all questions, which you clearly have, will be answered after. Deal?"

"We have an accord," he states poshly. I sit down, shaking my head, and he follows suit, minus the head shake. I start with filling him in on the situation, with the Eader thinning, increase in attacks and patrols. And what the goal of our mission is.

"You really think I could be of any help? I have been what, a month at the Academy, and most of it has been..." He stops himself.

"Yes? How has school been, Grey?" I prompt. A shadow passes over Grey's face.

"It is just like being back at school on Earth. The good old days," he says dryly, and I get the feeling I've stepped onto a touchy subject. I let it lie, and move on with the briefing instead.

"Moving on," I say, my tone awkward, trying not to look at Grey. "We do hope that your powers are the key, that is true. And the conversation you heard a few weeks ago... It was wrong of me to call you a tool. You are more than that. You are... a Fior. Like me. Which you got a brief demonstration of yesterday. Meaning, I think you should know my powers, as it is important trusting that I will have your back in the field, and you mine."

"Well, this is about freaking time. Power up!" I feel like he has been waiting for a good long time to say that to me, but I oblige. I grow a good ten feet, towering over him like a giantess. At the same time I summon Lika, my familiar.

"This is Lika, who I have already told you about." The white Samoyed dog leaps across the fire to Grey and slams him to the ground, making sure his face is all clean.

"It's—" Lick, lick. "Nice to—" Drool. "Meet you, Grey." Lick, Lick. Lika barks, jumping off of him again and runs to my side. "Hi boss," she says, poking my leg with her snout.

"Whoa!" Grey gets to his feet and stands across the fire, staring at the two of us. "That is some major power there, Gen... I mean, Darby. Tre-freaking-mendous! What else can you do?"

"What, this isn't good enough for you?" I say sardonically, shrinking back to normal size, but keeping Lika around, more or less to keep me sane around Grey.

"Oh sure, it was grand, really imposing, a giant show of..." I send an annoyed pulse in Grey's direction, which knocks him off his feet, but not before he absorbs it and sends it like a boomerang back at me. It slams into my head like a wave of static energy, and I stagger backward.

"So, that is the famous pulse. Not a massive fan of your own medicine, are you?" Grey croaks.

"Stop with the size puns, would you? I get it."

"I kinda like them, boss," Lika says, wagging her tale. I send her a treacherous look and she whines, sitting down, lowering her ears. "Sorry."

"Don't blame the dog. Who is, by the way, amazing. What is she?" At this Lika perks up a bit. "You would be amazed of how glorious you look. Ever thought about auditioning for Godzilla?"

That is it! "Would you please stop being sarcastic and just shut the hell up?" I am shouting now, having had about enough of this glib twat.

"Wow. Okay, sure." Grey shrugs non-committedly, holding his hands up.

"Great," I growl.

"Yeah, great," he mutters sarcastically. I can't believe it has only been like fifteen minutes of this session and I want to kill him already. "Lika is my familiar, along with Riley, my lynx, they are part of my Fior powers. I can call them using said powers, and they are as real as you or me."

I start pacing again, avoiding looking at Grey.

"Okay. Any other questions?" Grey shakes his head glumly. "Brilliant. Today we will start work on Shifting to Earth, only in theory though. It is more complicated than Shifting locally. This time, the factor of perspective will be important." My student is eerily quiet, and when I look up, he is no longer there. What the…? "If you are not back here in ten seconds, I swear…"

"Calm down, I am right here." He is behind me, petting Lika, who is enjoying a belly rub, tongue lolling out of her mouth.

"You shouldn't misuse your powers like that."

"Misuse? I walked over here. Not my fault you aren't paying attention."

I curse inwardly. "Oh, sorry. Did you hear what I said?"

"Perspective. Important. Got it," Grey sums up, scratching Lika behind the ear. Traitor.

"Yes. Perspective is to a problem, what a mirror is to a conceited man – feedback can get very one sided. Change the mirror into another person, however, and you will get a whole range of feedback, depending on which person you ask. You get what I am telling you?"

"That my outfit needs a second opinion?"

"No," I sigh, rolling my eyes. "But you could use a total makeover, to be honest," I remark, eyeing his choice of navy-blue sweatpants, white t-shirt, and his red Chucks in the chilly morning air. "What I am saying is that you need to change your perspective, let other possibilities enter your mind, to bend the light or dark energy, so it can travel to another plane, to Earth. Change the perspective, and the problem is no longer a problem."

"You know you are talking to me, right? It is not like I have trouble imagining extraordinary possibilities or anything." Grey gets up, and puts his hands on his sides. "You mean that I need to think four dimensionally in regard to our plane of existence? Moving not only through space, meaning in x, y, and z directions, but also in time? Sure I can do that. At least I get the general idea of it."

I frown. Sometimes he can be such a nerd. Which is kind of comforting to be reminded of. "Yes, and no. You are forgetting one important detail. We are not only removed from Earth in time, but also in terms of frequency. Meaning it is more of a matter of fazing through to the right frequency. Not in terms of light or sound, but in energy. We use polar coordinates for this, as the orbital alignment of the planes puts them in the same system, with the same centre, so we only differentiate on their radius to find the right depth to travel to. We need to faze inwards towards the centre so to speak."

"Stop for a second," Grey interrupts.

"No need, I was more or less done," I say sourly.

"Whatever. I just need to get my head around this." He starts pacing around the fire. "Earth and Eader are situated around the same origin, meaning they each have a set distance to the surface?" I nod, almost chuckling from his serious nerd face. "Okay, so navigation would be done from using the zenith and azimuth angle only? But what is the reference point?"

I cock my head questioningly. This time it is Grey's time to sigh.

"Do you use the same reference points as on Earth? You know, north, south, east and west?"

"Ah, yes. We do, the movement of Eader follow the movements of Earth, so these are closely associated with each other, same with the calendar being the same, only with a slight delay."

"If by slight delay you mean like an extra year per year, sure. Slight delay." Grey lightly scoffs, smiling crookedly at me.

"At any rate, don't know what you meant about those angles, but I think you have the right idea at least."

Again, the nerdy face is back on. "Ah, you can compare the zenith angle with the direction you get when standing in the centre of a sphere faced in the direction of x, then swinging your head to the left or right. The angle your head then makes with the original direction you were looking, is the zenith angle. And, if you stare straight up from the origin, then lower your gaze, that is the azimuth angle." He looks very pleased with himself when he finishes, and I smile.

"Yes, that sounds about right, at least, I recognise what you mean. We use other words for it here, like latitude or longitude, but sure, you stick with those. No matter, as long as you get the gist of it." I am actually very impressed, but I am not about to tell him that. "We have different tools to determine the angles and such, as it is rather hard to stand in the centre of anything here or on Earth. It will be in your Shifting-kit, along with other necessities."

"Oh, cool."

The silence stretches, and it doesn't take long before it gets painstakingly awkward.

"So," I start, walking over to Grey. "Ryder talked to me

180

about you, or not you, but about Conduits."

"Oh, did he? What did he say? Other than how rare they were, and that a crazy Scottish dude wanted my services, that is. Would be awesome to know what the hype is all about." Grey looks sincere and we sit down on one of the logs.

"As you know, the libraries burnt down and many of our Scholars were assassinated in the Great Battle, so most of our knowledge was lost, but he did tell me that Conduits were people who brought together, melded, led, a channel for conveying energy, power, both good and bad, and could often tip the balance, they were also protectors, so yeah… you get the point. There is more to you than meets the eye." I hope I get my point across, even though I am ever so ineloquent about it. As I hate to think that we are using him just as another tool. That is not what we do here in Eader. People matter.

"Was that a compliment?" Grey says, arching one eyebrow.

I roll my eyes. Typical him. "More like a hopeful statement, Guardian. Now, let's start training."

The day passes slowly, testing out Grey's abilities, which seem to be without limit, though it gets taxing in the end. At one point, I send Grey to the top of the Academy, by giving him a set of coordinates, and also allowing him to figure out the elevation difference, to not end up inside a wall, and while I wait for him, I start to consider my surroundings. Each day seems to present a new colour of grey. Filtering just a bit less light, casting longer shadows, making Eader seem like it's sinking into a sombre slumber. Worse is the cold. It's like it's seeping in through the ground, pulling colour out of everything. Not that Eader had been that cheerful and warm to begin with. It is however colder than before, and it doesn't seem to get as light any more, even with the Dust looming around. As I am lost in thought, Grey pops back into view, grinning.

"So, how did you do?"

He saunters towards me, then stumbles and ends up taking a knee in front of me. He grumbles as he gets up. "Got there fine, though I overshot it a bit and ended up two metres over the tower." He strokes his hindquarters and I start to get an image of what happened.

"Well, at least you are not stuck inside the sediment." I look around and sigh.

"What is it?" Grey asks, attempting to sit on one of the logs by the fire pit, but quickly getting up again, muttering about stupid towers.

"Oh, no nothing. Just that the darkness seems to be thicker today, is all."

"Ah, I am so getting used to the gloomy light and light being set to lightly Dusted, that I am hardly noticing it any more. But I guess you are right. Thought of it more as a change in season. Isn't it usually like this?" he asks. I shrug, not really wanting to get into it.

"You know what this light reminds me of?"

He shakes his head, while trying again to gently sit himself down. This time, he succeeds.

"It reminds me of you. As your name is kind of an ironic name – Grey, between light and dark. You do know, your Eader name is Liath, meaning grey?" I do not wait for an answer, as my mind is racing. "Yeah, grey, light and dark, twilight, manipulator of each force of energy." Not thinking about my audience, my thoughts wander. Grey, so free to go wherever, whenever he wants. An unpredictable warrior. Not that I think he needs to be leashed. Or should he be?

"So, Liath, really? What does that make your last name

182

then?"

"My last name?" It feels like I am listening through a thick wall of cotton, and I have to will myself to listen to what Grey is saying. "Teine? It means fire."

"So, a fire spouting dragon then? Neat. Totally makes sense, to be honest."

"What is that supposed to mean?" I growl. But realise I have just proven his point.

He raises an eyebrow, and smiles his crooked smile at me.

I clear my throat.

"Have you heard the stories around town then?" I ask. I don't really want to bring it up, but feel like knocking this guy down a few notches.

"What stories?" he asks apprehensively.

"Ah, no, nothing special, really. Just about the people who have gone missing or been injured in recent attacks. The whispers about the new Fior being here to save everyone." I stare at him, daring him to come with a witty comment. He doesn't. There is just silence. As it stretches on, I study his expression and it looks like he is far away, the dark morning casting shadows across his pale face.

When I think he will not say anything, I catch myself. Wait for it.

"I have been wondering about something." And there it is. "How can Eader pay for everything anyway? I haven't seen any banks or anything around town." Ah, we are not talking more about it, but hopefully the flippant attitude about the mission took a hike.

"Oh, famous people of Eader patented ideas through the ages – telephone phone, light bulb, Tamagotchi, steam engine, Walkman and so on. We cannot take credit for everything – such as the internet – brilliant idea! And the rubber duck! Anyway, the royalties are more than enough to keep Eader running." Grey seems to be considering what I have just said, before firing the next question at me.

"What about when Lay and other non-human people go to Earth? Do they not, I don't know, stand out?"

"That one is more scientific, than anything else. You see, when inhuman Guardians go to Earth, light and dark bends to conceal their features, which make humans see something they can understand."

"You mean, like diffraction?"

"Eh, sure? Point is that the humans on Earth cannot perceive the wings on a fairy for example."

My patience is running out, but it feels good talking about these things. After my stay on Earth, I feel more distracted and reminding myself of how Eader works and what it means to be a Guardian, well, it helps. I will not forget again why I am doing what I am doing.

"So, is the interrogation over?"

"Nope, last one. I know I knew Callan from way back when. Did I also know you? Were we like, friends or whatever?" Ah. Been waiting for this one.

"First of all, yes, I knew who you were, but we didn't know each other. Let's just say we didn't belong to the same crowd. And second of all, I fought in the Great Battle when I was only twelve, you…" I take a deep breath. "You were sent away to Earth due to your powers. End of story."

"But…"

"No, topic closed," I snap.

"Wow, touchy."

"Aren't you the master of the obvious?" I say dryly, seating

184

myself opposite him across the fire.

"Yep, goes well with the lady of understatements." He smirks.

"Don't you make quite the couple then," says a voice coming from off in the darkness. Callan steps out of the dark and I can feel the tension. It's palpable and I can sense an increase in the energy surrounding the clearing.

When neither of the two men say anything, I break in. "You are just in time. Have you been briefed on the mission?"

Callan nods once, standing just at the edge of the light of the fire, casting a flickering light across his face. Grey sits rigid on his log, eyeing the log intensely.

"Good. We will be ready to leave at daybreak tomorrow, as Grey has mastered Shifting."

I hope this will evoke a positive reaction from Grey, but nothing happens. I remember these two, back in the day and just a few weeks ago being like two peas in a pod. And now...

"Guys. We have important business to attend to. It would be prudent of you to put your differences aside..." I let my words die out.

Both men are avoiding each other's gaze.

"You look like crap," Grey suddenly says.

Callan straightens up. "Oh you know, mileage can be rough."

"Clearly."

The silence is agonizing. "Well, now that that is settled." It isn't, by a long shot. But it doesn't matter. "We will be travelling tomorrow at eight a.m. Be here, packing only the essentials."

Callan nods again, glancing in Grey's direction. "Not me you need to worry about. Shadow boy on the other hand..."

Before I can react, Grey has scrambled to his feet and tackled

Callan at lightning speed. Pummelling each other and yelling curses, they roll around kicking up dust.

I sigh, growing about ten feet before picking them both up by the waist.

"So, as I said," I whisper, my enlarged vocal chords more than enough to make myself heard. "We will meet here tomorrow, packed and ready to go. No more bullshit from you two. Am I making myself clear?"

The men look more like boys now, startled and shameful looks on their faces. They both nod in silent compliance and I set them down on opposite sides of the fire.

"Very well then!"

I stomp off into the dusky afternoon, smiling darkly to myself. Nothing like showing who's boss.

The next morning, Decipiér heads me off as I am walking to the clearing from my tent.

"You are prepared for the mission?" he asks, flying down from the thick of the trees. He has probably been waiting for me. Creepy.

"Yes, I am. We are leaving within the hour, so if that was all?" Of course it isn't.

"Callan is going with you and Grey, as ordered?"

I frown. "Yes, you were very insistent. Anything else?" He looks flushed and won't really look me in the eyes.

"Oh, no. Just wanted to see you off." And without further ado, he flies off again.

I shake my head and steer towards the fire pit, where the boys are already waiting for me. Callan dressed from head to toe in combat gear, finishing the look with a pair of sunglasses. Always so understated that guy. Grey is wearing his regular red converse, with dark blue slim jeans, a black t-shirt, and a suit jacket with leather details. Both of them are wearing a dark expression and giving each other the silent treatment. It feels like travelling with two toddlers arguing.

"Morning," I try, smiling. When I receive no answer, I send them both a pulse, forgetting about the boomerang effect I had experienced with Grey earlier. Sure enough, I get half the pulse back in return. This mission is really off to a great start. "Shall we?" I ask sarcastically, firing up my Beacon.

Chapter 22

Grey

Okay, so this is freaking awe-and-then-some! Even though it is basically the crack of dawn and I have had more than just a few crappy weeks. I am officially going home. Which makes it all worth it.

"Before we go," Darby says, turning to face us. "I need you to be on your best behaviour."

"Why are you just looking at me?" She rolls her eyes. "Because you are the only one that I am talking to. Callan I can trust as my lieutenant. You…"

"I am a rogue agent. No, Ronin. No, wait, a masterless vagabond…"

"How can you be so mind-bendingly annoying and damn smart at the same time?"

I smirk. "It is one of my magic powers."

The disapproving cute frown is back. "Oh shut up."

"Shutting up."

She scowls at me. "Are you ready?" Callan stands to the side, being uncharacteristically quiet. When Darby asks the question, all I can think is, you do whatever you want, I am out of here. I start envisioning my destination, which is remarkably easy, as all I need to do is clear my cluttered mind and think of home. Earth is so different from here. With its people, the weather, the seasons, and the different smells. All that talk about dimensions put it into perspective. But to me there are more dimensions than just these. It will sound weird, but there is an emotional dimension. A feeling, as sense of where I am going, and pinpointing where I feel like being right now is not hard. Home. Home in this sense being Earth. I shoulder my leather duffel bag, which contains only the essentials, like my music, silver knuckles, and house key.

I nod to Darby who is standing there waiting impatiently, and before she can argue, I say, "See you at home," and quickly Shift away. The feeling of not just moving from place to place on Eader but actually Shifting planes is incredible. I keep my eyes open as I have become accustomed to doing and I am glad I do. I can see the layers I usually see when moving laterally on Eader, moving like an almost frozen ocean of light and dark, with all the other colours of the spectrum mixed in, but as my destination is set for Earth, I see another, similar ocean floating just over this. It is like having two translucent pictures put over each other and you have to focus your eyes to set them apart. I feel myself drift over to the new ocean, which seems to be brighter than the first one and navigate to a portal near my house. Which is hard to explain, but it is like finding the right nuance that feels right to where I want to go. Which is home. I step out under a large oak tree three houses down from my place. The street is quiet, and everything is frosted. The moment I step out I hear a faint ringing in my ears. Probably a side-effect of the Shift between planes. I had been wondering if my powers would work on Earth, but turns out as I stretch out my hand, just for fun really, and suck out the light of the nearest lamppost in the grey morning light. Turns out they do. I feel like bloody Dumbledore! Seriously, I need a catchphrase! Or a street name – like the fearsome Light Sucker! No, that is terrible. I will work on it.

My house is dark, newspapers thrown haphazardly around the entrance. I wanted a head start. Get here first, just be home. Alone. The plan is to go to a larger city, but I have a few plans of my own. I trot up the stairs and by force of habit put my hand on the door. Right. Earth. I pull out my key and enter.

It is pitch black inside as I return from the longest walk ever. I switch on the lights, using the light switch this time and run upstairs to get my hoodie, as it is way colder than I thought it would be. Which isn't weird, as it's like ten a.m. at the end of November. Which means... Crap. Well, perfect timing to be honest. Other than the date, everything is as I left it. Wishing I could take a shower, jump into more Teen Wolf episodes, or spend some time on my computer, which would be well deserved after that hellish detour. No such luck however, as when I come back down, Darby is standing in the hall.

"What the – hello! Eh. Welcome?"

"Nice save. Welcome, my ass! This is what I mean by trust. What confused you? The word which is clearly not in your vocabulary, or my warning before we left Eader?" Okay, that is hurtful, but I do not care.

"I have a few errands to run, and to be honest, I needed a trip home. Which frankly, I deserve, after you kidnapped me the last time I was here."

"We didn't..."

"Whatever you choose to call it, I have stuff to do here too. Which can easily coincide with the mission."

Darby sighs and squeezes the ridge of her nose between her thumb and index finger. "Fine. Mind telling us what this 'stuff' is?"

"Actually, I do. But let's not fret about that now. I am just picking up a few things here, then we can be on our way."

Without further ado, I turn and walk into the kitchen. I spot the letter from Lizzie and grab it, along with the necessary paperwork and stuff it in my leather jacket pocket. My laptop is on the counter, and I quickly switch it on to check on the world and what it has been up to. Which looks like to be the regular nonsense and mayhem. I feel the negativity seeping in, as if it is in the air. All these stupid acts of violence and malice, no wonder the world is going to hell. The ringing in my ears is back, and I feel a faint cold creeping up my spine. Weird. As I stand there brooding in the corner of my kitchen over stupid people on Facebook, Darby walks in.

"So, nice house," she says, jumping up and seating herself at the edge of the counter. The room is dimly lit, and the horseshoe counter swings around the kitchen table and backdoor into the garden.

I slam the computer shut. "Weird being in here after only stalking from the outside in, I guess," I state matter-of-factly, grabbing an apple as I pass her.

"Hey!" she yells and storms after me. "You know I was only… Wait. What is wrong with you?" She pulls me by the elbow, as I am about to go back into the hallway. She quickly releases it. "Damn, you are cold!"

"Gee, thanks," I mutter.

"No, really. You are actually cold. What is wrong?"

I look at her and sees she looks concerned. I shrug. "I don't know, guessed the ringing and the chill was just a side-effect of the Shift or whatever."

"Nah, that doesn't happen, not even for Fiors." She starts pacing like she always does, which makes her look like a crazy person, trying to walk back and forth in this cramped kitchen. "It must be that you are sensing the dark and the light with your powers!" She starts smiling.

"Wait, what? No, I have been living on Earth like for forever. It isn't like I have been walking around like an icicle with tinnitus all these years."

She waves me off. "No, I get that. But after you have been to Eader, your powers must have been amplified and as a *Conduit* you are more prone to noticing the forces of power."

I must look utterly dumbfounded because she laughs while rolling her eyes.

"Okay, listen. Darkness breeds darkness, same with light, and it has been multiplying on Earth, making it easier for attacks on both sides for Eader. Here the light is intensified, and with the changes, there is a lot more darkness as well, which makes it a wild power environment. It is bound to affect you. I am sorry I didn't think of it earlier."

"So you are saying I am like an antenna for black and white mojo?"

"Sure. But you should be able control it, using your training. Remember how you have to open your senses to feel the energy around you?"

Nodding, I get what she is getting to and immediately try to shut down what I guess is my energy valves or something. It works and I smile.

"Did it work?"

"Yep!" I walk into the living room and sit down in my huge reading chair. Darby follows me in and sits on the armrest of my couch, while admiring my home theatre setup.

"Sweet! This we can use to our advantage. If you can track the energy flow, we can try and get a handle on what is really going on." She claps me on the back and heads for the hallway.

"Hey, what do you mean 'track'? And where is Callan?" I

192

picture him going through my stuff upstairs and run after Darby.

"I sent Callan on a perimeter check. I am tired of being your babysitter. And the tracking, we will see what we can find out, but there is magic in everything we do – we have simply forgotten about it. Magic is everywhere. In a touch. In a feeling. In a discovery. In a dream. Which may seem like capturing lightning in a bottle. But every action stores life, energy, light or darkness, in every nuance."

"So, it's like making a Horcrux."

Darby stares blankly.

"A Harry Potter thing. Never mind."

"But yes, all things can serve as a vessel, it just depends on what energy surrounds it, and it will adopt certain characteristics. Hopefully, through sensing these vessels, you might be able to deduce some sort of pattern?"

With her framing it like a question doesn't really inspire confidence, but sure thing.

When I don't reply, she jumps in. "So, yeah. Nice house. Quaint and all with the, eh, retro interior decorating. But give it up, Grey. How can you…" She stops herself, biting her lip.

"How can I afford it?"

She suddenly looks ashamed, but it is my turn to jump in.

"I have a good friend who helped me out a lot when I was… alone." The last word comes out more darkly than I intended, and Darby looks at me with pain in her eyes.

"Grey, I…"

"Anyway, the house came with the furniture and the upkeep is not too bad, so, I like it," I ramble on, trying to avoid Darby's eyes. Truth is I got the house from Lizzie after she inherited it from her father, furniture and all. "She helped me get started after… anyway, after I graduated, I came up with this idea, and it helps pay the bills, I guess."

This time it is Darby's time to stare blankly at me. "You graduated? From where?" But then it seems to dawn on her. "Ah, the reason for all your smart-assery? I never saw you leave the house?"

"Well, Miss Teine, I never. Whatever do you mean?" I quip innocently. "But yes, I graduated with a Masters in communication technology, minor in mechanical engineering. Did it online, coursework, live lectures, all of it. Which makes me sound like a hermit, I know. But with... my *gifts* and all, it just made it easier."

Shifting uneasily on top of the armrest, Darby smiles at me. "I totally get it. But what about this idea of yours?"

I shrug. "Nothing much. I guess necessity is the mother of invention indeed. You may have realised I kinda like movies?"

"Yeah, picked up on that," Darby agrees sarcastically. Points for delivery.

"Well, just an idea I had about making movies more accessible earlier from home, without people ripping off the people making them. Sort of Netflix for cinema premieres. Anyway, the production companies liked it enough to buy the idea from me and with each subscriber, I get a small fee. In addition, it more or less killed the illegal movie industry."

"You mean, you created CouchVision? But that is huge? And small fee? That must be..."

"Let's just say I get by, okay? Anyway, we are not here to talk about me. So, now that that's out of the way. We have someplace to be – so let's get this show on the road, shall we? Before we leave, as we are in my world now, it is your turn to follow my lead. Wouldn't want you smiling to people on the bus or pulsing anyone who does anything too Earthy for you, now would we?" I wink at her, knowing full well she can handle herself.

"You do know I lived here for like five years, right?" Her look seems almost wistful, not matching the edge in her tone.

"Sure thing, but still."

She frowns at me, and we exit the house. As I lock up, Callan comes striding up. "What a dump! You live here? And yeah, perimeter secure."

Darby shoots him a warning look, but I ignore him.

"Good. Now, let's Shift to our original destination," Darby says, turning towards me as I trot down the stairs.

"Oh no, you don't. I have somewhere to be, and lucky for you, you didn't make me miss my appointment. Now, jump in!"

I point to the car sitting in my driveway. A black '68 Camaro – my baby. It came with the house, as Lizzie had no use for it, though I had insisted on her selling it, she wouldn't hear of it.

Callan's jaw drops. "That is yours?"

Continuing to ignore him, I stride over and get in on the driver side. Darby stands where I left her, hands crossed. As I wake up all three hundred and fifty horses sleeping in their V8-stables, I smile. The radio is on, and I crank it up. I start backing out of the drive-way, but slam the brakes as Darby and Callan suddenly pop into the car.

"You know, sometimes it is possible to walk?"

I get stark silence, which I take as the best I could hope for, and back out. "I thought we could go through the city centre first, and perhaps I will pick up on something there?" I try a smile in Darby's direction, riding shotgun, hoping to placate her clearly fuming mood. She grunts, but I feel the waves of anger rolling off her dissipating a bit. Callan sits quietly, staring out of the window. I want to ask him how long it has been since he was on

Earth, but decide against it. We roll through the city, which is slow on a Friday morning. As we come into more crowded areas, I can definitely feel an uptake in energy, both dark and light, and it is almost deafening. I force myself to turn the energy valve intake way down. We drive by my sanctuary when I lived on the streets, the library. I slow down as we pass by, and I think back to all those mornings and afternoons I got to sit in the warmth, and get lost in thousands of different worlds. The smell, the escape, the sense of safety made it my safe haven, small books with big worlds to disappear into. Everyday items creating magic relief in a harsh reality. Which I can now feel. A strong wave of light energy hits me as we pass, but it feels great and makes total sense. I speed up and turn down the main street, and as I do, one of the rock classics comes on and I turn it up. Also a place where I find salvation, just like in-between the lines in a fantasy novel. Without these I wouldn't be me and it would be like… Like working on the disassembling line, eating a cold dog with ketchdown, chopping down life bringing oxygen factories, dreaming of being poor… you get it. Cancelling Christmas and electing that dumbass for president. Oh wait. Point is, living life without music, movies, and books… it just isn't right. Suddenly the music is turned down and I might've just imagined it, but I thought I heard a sniffle from the shotgun seat. Before I can react however, Darby shouts into my ear.

"Grey, are you listening to me? Where are you taking us?"

"I have a few errands to run. Just stay in the car, I'll be right back." I jump out after coming to a stop, before she can protest which seems to be a winning strategy with that one, or so I think as I run into her. "Seriously, you know you can use those things you call legs, right?"

"Very funny. Just as funny as you not using those things you call ears. Or are they just useless appendages?" I try popping past her, but she stands her ground.

"Fine. I just wanted to check on a few of my friends. If that is all right with you?" I lock eyes with her, and she seems to read from them what she needs to see, as she steps aside. "Thanks," I mutter. I hear the door slam, and see Callan leaning up against the car.

"What is this, your summer condo or something?"

"Shut up, Stone!" Darby growls and turns to me. "Be quick."

"I'll be right back." I jog down the alley we stopped next to. Along the walls are shopping trolleys filled with a variety of junk, cardboard boxes set up as shelter and a few barrels serving as heat sources as flames spout out. It is one of the more frequented alleys for the older homeless population, not one where junkies like to shoot up. Still good to get beat up, shot, or killed in though. The people look at me and I quickly turn away, avoiding their gazes, save for a few.

"Grey! I can't believe it is you!" An old man comes running over, giving me a bear hug.

"Hi, Parker. How are you?"

He takes a step back, grabbing my shoulders, smiling broadly. "You know me, a day outside is a day well spent! I am doing okay." I smile back, even though I know the tall, grey-haired old man is hiding joint pains and a bitter past, after living with him out here for several years.

"Good to hear. I just wanted to say hi, I know it has been a while. And here, take this." I hand him a bundle of cash that I grabbed from home, and press it into his hand.

"Grey, I told you, it's too much."

"Nonsense. Spread it out between you guys." He nods gratefully. A bulkier man wobbles over, with his hat pushed down into his eyes.

"Back again, huh? What, miss living on the streets, boy?"

I grunt. "Well, ain't this karma's way of reminding me she can be a bitch. You still alive, huh? Chad, you haven't changed a bit." We stare at each other before Chad starts laughing and gives me a hug. Before he can answer I hear people coming up behind me.

"On your left," Callan announces as he steps into view. "Well, isn't this the ugliest group of people I have seen."

"Yeah, welcome to the club. Meetings are on Tuesdays," Chad snarls, taking a step towards Callan. I stop him and turn to face Darby and Callan.

"I thought I told you to wait?"

"Sorry," Darby offers. "But we had to make sure you were okay."

I scowl. "Bodyguards of yours, boy?" Chad scoffs. "Some kind of hot shot, are we?" Before I can respond, a voice is heard from further down the alley.

"Mm, now that is what I call some real boobage!"

The man, who I have never seen before, gets up from his cardboard tent and takes a swig from his brown paper bag. He is staring at Darby, and not at her face. I can't really see why. Don't get me wrong, Darby is pretty, but at the moment she is wearing a regular white tee and a leather jacket over blue jeans and black boots, not exactly centre page material. It's as if he has x-ray vision. He lurches towards us and at one point he chucks his now empty bottle in our general direction, though misses and hits the wall. This results in a loud smack and several of the people start shouting insults at more or less everyone.

And with that I step into his line of sight before Darby can pick up on his all-creepiness.

198

"What did he say?" Darby asks, her tone dangerous.

"Oh, nothing. It is just Terry, always speaking nonsense," Parker says, trying to diffuse the situation.

"Well, if you don't control your friend, he will regret it." That sort of threat does not go over easy with this crowd, who all too often have had visits from a too aggressive police force, something I've had personal experience with, and the situation only gets more agitated. Callan just stands there, nodding approvingly.

"What did I say about following my lead?"

Darby scowls at me, putting her hands up. I close my eyes and reach out with my powers, trying to calm everyone down with some of my light energy. It has an immediate effect, and everyone simmers down.

Parker smiles. "Good to have you back, Grey." I squeeze his hand, taking some of his pain as I do and walk away.

"Wow, that was some crowd. Your family, is it?" Wow, why insult someone on one level when you can get a two-for-one?

"They are my friends. Would you like to repeat that?" I stare at Callan, and feels wisps of darkness billowing around my hands.

"Nah, bro. Chill. I was just messing around." He smirks at me. "You do smell like crap though."

I walk briskly out of the alley and jump into my car, Callan and Darby following close behind.

As they climb in, Darby asks, "So Callan, where did you live on Earth?" A dark shadow passes over Callan's face, and he starts fiddling with his silver bullet.

Shrugging, he mumbles, "Too young, don't remember."

The car ride back through the city is quiet and tense. Darby, however, tries to stay on point. "So, Grey. Have you noticed anything? Any… eh, vibes?" I turn onto Park Avenue, and glance at her.

"Yeah. I get what you said about there being power attached to objects. And there were a lot more happening as we entered town. But still working on that pattern."

"Oh," she says dejectedly, staring out the window.

"Can I ask you something?" I say, as I near our next destination. "You turned down the music earlier, and I thought I heard… Was there any reason for that?"

"Yeah, I guess it's my turn to spill the beans. I had a…" She hesitates. "A very good friend who loved the old rock classics. Used to listen to them with him all the time. Well, he died in the Great Battle, and…"

"…And they remind you of him. I get it." My tone is brusque, and I don't mean to sound so harsh, but it just comes out. "Music can do that, store memories, good and bad."

Darby nods. As we pass through the neighbourhood, the sunlight makes yellow brush strokes through the foliage of the large trees forming a tunnel as we drive down the road.

As I look at her, the light rays play across her face, and I realise how little I really know about this person, besides her sassy and bossy attitude, and the freaky size shifting thing. "I really admire what you did back there," Darby says.

"What, I just said hi to some friends, that's all." Even though I could and want to do more, there is just too much pride involved. But I keep it to myself.

"Oh stop it." She pounds me in the arm, and I stop. The car.

"We are here," I announce, and get out.

"We are where?" Darby enquires.

"Another friend. Feel free to, you know. Wait here."

"Callan, do another…"

"Perimeter sweep? Gladly." He scurries away, leaving us

alone on the curb. The street is gloomy in the midday light, with neat little one-storey houses on both sides of the street, framed by flowery gardens and porches.

"Okay. You have dragged me along on these errands of yours, you owe me some answers." Darby pulls me up outside the light blue house, with white roses blossoming even now in November. "You live modestly, when you clearly can afford not to, and you share your money with homeless people. Who are you?"

I laugh inwardly. Right back at you, I think to myself. "Fine," I sigh. "I just try to give what I can. I've been where they are, but they are proud people and won't accept much. So, I give them food, clothing, money. Bits and pieces. Things that are easier for them to accept. When I was alone on the streets, I was doing okay on my own, got to where I was without any help for a long time, and was not interested in anything anyone had to offer. But as the world can be dark, scary, cold – it is hard to find where you can be safe, and I may have settled for somewhere I felt safe and comfortable, but I was wrong. I was jumped one night by some thugs out to have some fun and they would have killed me, but Parker and Chad saved me. They are old military vets, so they gave the thugs a good scare. After that, we helped keep each other safe. It was what we had, and we made it work. It made it easy to disappear actually, as I didn't want to stand out. I was just one of the invisibles with them." As I speak, I am walking up and down the sidewalk and when I finish, I feel someone hugging me from behind.

"You are the most fearless, reckless and clever person I have met, Grey," she whispers before she releases me. I stand stunned for a second, before a familiar voice jolts me from my paralysis.

"You are late, young man!"

Chapter 23

Grey

"There is something to be said about not being early or late, simply arriving when you were meant to, though I might be stealing that," I say cheekily.

"And here I thought that only went for wizards," she quips. Standing there, hands on her sides, this woman is a sight for sore eyes. My heart swells and I start laughing as I run up the stairs and give Lizzie a huge hug. She squeezes me tight, and I feel myself relax, for the first time in weeks. I let her go and turn to Darby, feeling myself blush. She is standing there with a cocked head.

"Who is your friend, then honey? I thought I taught you better than this…" Lizzie catches her breath as Darby draws near, but smoothly continues, "Come on now, introduce your friend, honey."

"Oh, sorry. This is Miss Darby Teine, a friend from…"

Darby beats me to it. "I am one of his neighbours. It is nice to meet you, Miss…?"

"Oh, no, just call me Lizzie, sweetie." She gives Darby a quick hug too. "Now, both of you, come in from this chill. They say it will snow today even. My poor flowers!" She bustles inside, and I stop to hold the door for Darby. A strange expression is stuck on her face, but when she sees me looking at her, she smiles.

"What is it?"

"Nothing, just good to see you acting so…"

"Human?" I finish dryly. She just smiles and walks into the house. I follow her, enjoying the feeling of being back here.

I find Lizzie inside the kitchen leaning over one of her many cookbooks. "I thought I'd whip us up some lunch, before we leave?" She smiles, and pokes my side as I sit down on one of the barstools at the counter. Collecting pots and pans from her summer yellow cabinets to make us some omelettes, she hums on a light tune. Typical Lizzie. Darby seats herself next to me, studying the white drapes around the two windows to the backyard and the red tablecloth on the round table behind us.

"Looking for something?" I ask, but she just shakes her head.

"So, Miss Teine," Lizzie says, pronouncing Darby's last name as 'Tee-haine'. "Is that Scottish?"

"Yes, ma'am, it is."

Lizzie nods, stirring up some eggs in a bowl. I can't see her face with her back facing us, but I wonder how she knew that. Before I can ask, Lizzie spins around. "Anyway, you have grown so much, Grey." She puts down her whisk and leans over the counter. I jokingly lean towards her with my serious face on, but she scans me up and down with her eyes, like she is trying to see through me. "You really have changed a lot, little one," she says, almost as if she is talking to herself. She shakes her head and leans back, like she is snapping herself out of it. "Wow! And I am so proud of you. Today is the big day!" I feel a nudge in my back from Darby, but ignore it. "But, ah, you smell a bit dear. Have you been visiting your friends again? You are too generous, dear."

I blush again. "Just following your example, Lizzie."

"Oh, hush child."

"Child? Wait, so you're the generous friend Grey has been talking about."

Lizzie blushes. "Now, what have you been telling people, Grey? Another one of your stories I venture?" I shake my head innocently. "Well, Grey is like one of my own, not that there are no others." A wistful look crosses her face, but it quickly disappears as she looks back at me. "Actually, there are a few things we need to talk about, honey. But we will, okay?" I grin and am a bit mystified over what it is she has on her mind. To be honest, I have decided; I am leaving Eader after helping Darby sort out what it is she needs to know. This was never my fight. Not that it hasn't been cool and all, but I have my family here with whom I want to stay close.

Out in the hallway, the door bangs open and into the kitchen strides Callan. "Perimeter all clear, Gen…"

"That is great. Callan Stone, meet Lizzie, a friend of Grey's."

"Another friend? Well, at least this one smells a whole lot better! Good to meet ya, Miss Lizzie!" He bows his head, smiling cockily at her.

"Mr Stone, a pleasure to make your acquaintance. Now, would you be so kind to get those dirty shoes out of here, and please, wash up for lunch." Callan gapes at her, and I can't help but laugh. "Oh, that means you too, mister!" Lizzie chides. Damn. I never feel as much like a kid as when I visit Lizzie.

"Yes, ma'am," we mutter in unison.

When we return, I hear agitated murmurs coming from behind the kitchen door, but as it swings open, Darby is seated by the kitchen table, and Lizzie is serving up the omelettes from the stove. "There we are, now all of you. Eat up!" My stomach growls at the sight of the amazingly smelling food, and I dig in.

"I must say I love your house," Darby states over the scraping of forks on plates and loud chewing from Callan and me.

"Thank you, dear. The most wonderful thing happened last year – I won the lottery! So, the mortgage is paid off, and I have enough set aside to live more than comfortably. Even got myself a new stove." She smiles proudly, and I see Darby eyeing me knowingly. I forget how to swallow for a second and choke on a piece of egg.

"Wow, that *is* a coinci— So cool I mean, now isn't it!" Darby says, landing ever so smoothly. Nice, real subtle. I put down my glass of lemonade and search for a new topic.

"Yes, Lizzie was a nurse at the local hospital, and retired a few years ago, so that was really lucky." Right on man, I think, high fiving myself.

Callan snorts. "Bloody hell, this is some fine dining," he exclaims, after taking a sip of his coffee to flush down his eggs. "Even by Earth food standard!"

And that is my cue. I choke on another piece of egg and manage to knock over Callan's lemonade glass in the process. Callan looks at me in disdain.

"Good coffee, Mr Stone?"

"Hell no, not really my beverage anyway."

Lizzie doesn't seem to have heard Callan's alien comment, but she definitely hears this one and sends him a stern look. It is enough to scare the pelt off a bear, and Callan freezes as he is about to grab another serving of scones.

"I mean, yes ma'am, delicious."

Lizzie smiles approvingly. She was never one for swearing. "Wow, would you look at the time. You should get going," Lizzie announces, smiling at me now. "Don't worry, honey. I'll get that and meet you over there, okay?"

Callan looks sourly at me, and Darby is shooing him out of the room.

"Are you sure?"

"Absolutely, and after, we'll have that chat, and maybe you could look at that water heater again for me? It's been acting up."

I get up from the table and give her a last hug. "Just call me MacGyver."

From outside the kitchen door I hear Darby, "Who?"

Now, that is just sad. Lizzie laughs again. It sounds like warmth and Christmas hugs. "You need to introduce that girl to some of the classics it seems, dear."

Rolling my eyes, I grab her by the arm. "I reserved a seat for you, just talk to the…"

"Yes, yes, I know. It will all be fine. Just fine." The smiling wrinkles around her face makes her look like the nicest grandma, and I squeeze her hand tightly. "Now you go. And I will see you there. But before you go," she draws me to a stop in the hallway, which is now void of any Eadorians. She picks up my medallion from my chest, and strokes it gently. "Remember what I told you about this?"

I nod.

"Well, I want you to keep that with you, always. You have always been brave, but now more than ever… I mean on a day like this, it will be important to always look ahead. Dive, honey. The waters will be cold, the journey will be hard, and you will be a new person when you come up on the other shore, which is scary. But it will be worth it, I promise you." Her tone has grown serious, and her eyes look pleading, and it scares me. Something is definitely going on.

"Mind elaborating on that?"

"Yep, I do!" She nudges me out the door and waves me off. "See you in a jiffy, dear!" And with that, she is gone, slamming the door in my face. Gotta love that woman.

Callan and Darby are already in the car, which is weird, as I had locked it. Guess stealing a car is easy when you can Shift.

We arrive at the university with just a few minutes to spare. I manage to find a parking space and run to get ready, leaving Darby and Callan behind. This is something I have to do for me. For Lizzie. They can go Darkness-hunting without me. The campus is dressed up and crowded with people, my least favourite type of crowd, but I power through, getting my cap, hood, and gown.

"You do know we can easily Shift to catch up with you, right?" Darby and Callan are striding easily next to me, seemingly unencumbered by the surrounding herd of energy drains.

"Yeah, yeah. Whatever."

"Not 'whatever'. You should have told us it was your *graduation* today!"

We walk into the hall for the ceremony, which is packed with graduates and their family members. The stage is set with huge purple curtains hanging above it, the university colours of course, and the embroidered insignia of a harp-playing bear hanging on each side of a podium where the speakers will tell us how awesome we are. There are chairs set for the faculty on each side as well, in tiers. The seats for the students are set in increasing half circles as they move away from the stage, and made so you can walk all the way down to the podium through the middle. People are mingling and finding their seats, making it look like a buzzing beehive in here. I feel a nudge and remember that I am not here alone, trying to remember what Darby just asked.

"Eh, didn't deem it necessary really. I had more or less forgotten about it until I saw the invitation at home. Just lucky timing." Timing might have been luck, but I had been wanting to be home for this. As I look around for my seat, I hear whispers and snickering by people reminiscing from me attempting a few days of face-to-face lectures. Let us just say it didn't last.

"There he is…"

"The freak!"

"Remember what he did?"

"Why is he even here?"

I will them to go away.

"Mr Popularity right here," Callan says, smacking me on the back. I get a vile taste in my mouth.

To Darby I mutter, "I tried a few weeks here in the beginning of the course. It didn't really work out." She squeezes my arm reassuringly, but I shrug her off. Not the time.

I leave them behind again. At least I hope so, and find my seat just in time for the ceremony to start. My heart is pounding in my chest. I see families waving to their son or daughter, nervous laughter and people taking selfies with each other. For me it is enough that I am here. Finally, it's happening! There are several speeches, fulfilling my prediction of telling us we are awesome. Then it is time, they start calling names, working their way down from the top of the alphabet. When they reach the Cs, I start looking for Lizzie, but I can't spot her. Maybe I forgot where I reserved the seat. She is definitely here somewhere. They are just finishing with the Os when I spot her seat. It's empty. Why would it be empty? I start getting that familiar hollow pain in the pit of my stomach. But maybe she is just in the bathroom, or running late. But she wouldn't be late. Not for this. I get up from my seat to my classmates' disgruntlement, and sneak up the aisle to find Darby.

"Have you seen Lizzie?"

She shakes her head. "Isn't she here?" I explain the situation and she frowns. "She is probably just late, Grey."

"She would never miss this." My heart is pounding, but out of fear this time. I tear off the gown and throw down the cap as I storm past Darby and out of the hall. This time I take it in a little more, the mix of old and new architecture, how foreign it all seems to me. The granite versus the metal, the nice floral arrangements against the modern fountain sculpture supposedly of a bear in the middle of the courtyard outside the conference centre.

As the doors slides shut behind me, I hear 'Grey O'Shearan' being called over the speakers from inside the hall. The pit in my stomach intensifies. Tearing across the courtyard I try not to think, but my brain is running away from me as always. What if… I have to hurry. To stop… What?

As I get out of view of the crowds who have been staring after the pale, crazy-eyed man running past them, I Shift to Lizzie's house. Her car is still in the driveway. Damn! As I run up the stairs, I feel an extreme chill behind me, and I whirl around. Across the road, next to one of the giant oak trees, stands a shadow. It is humanoid but it is like the edges are smudged out. I swear it is smiling at me. Is this… an Eilne? As I think it, it melts into the tree and is gone. That can't be good! I spin around and burst through the door of the house shouting Lizzie's name. There is no answer. My hands are shaking, heart about to jump out of my chest and I can feel tears welling out of my eyes. No, not again. Not Lizzie.

I find her in her bedroom, all dressed up in her favourite blue dress. She is lying across the bed on her back and it looks like she is sleeping. I am frozen in the doorway, and I cannot seem to remember how to breathe. Her skin is grey and drained of light. I can't feel any energy emanating from her, but as I stumble towards her, I hear a sharp intake of breath.

"Grey... Grey is that you?" Lizzie's eyes flutters open. Her voice is like sandpaper and when I grab her hand, it is cold as ice. "I am so... sorry. I should've..." There is a fragile look in her eyes, which I have never seen there before. She is always so strong.

"Shh, it is okay." I want to sound braver than I feel; I want to comfort her, save her. I feel the tears streaming down my face.

"Oh, my beautiful boy. I am sorry. It wasn't supposed to... Should've brought you back sooner... to... Eader." Her breath rattles and she closes her eyes.

"No, Lizzie, don't leave me!"

I yell, and try to give her light energy, but there is a barrier of some kind pushing back. I can't help her! She squeezes my hand lightly and whispers, "I have loved you since the day you were born, my son. Always remember..."

How did she know about Eader? But how?

"Remember what? Lizzie?"

But she is gone. I stare at her. Lizzie is gone. My Lizzie. It's getting harder to breathe. Should I call someone? There is no one to call. I stare at this person in front of me. She is really dead. I slowly get up, backing away and I walk straight into Darby.

"Grey, are you... Oh, no." She looks past me at Lizzie, but I continue walking down the stairs and out of the house. Stuffing my hands in my pockets I feel the letter there, and I start feeling angry, only angry. I just cannot, will not, feel anything else right now. Ever again.

Outside, Callan is waiting. "Hey bro! Where have you

been?"

I walk past him and continue across the street. I stop next to the tree where I had seen the shadow figure. There is no trace.

"Grey!" Darby yells from Lizzie's front porch. She says something to Callan who looks shocked. They walk across the street to me. What a time to be an empath, as I can feel the pity rolling off them both, like a heavy fog rolling in from a sea on an unsuspecting village. It settles over me, in every fibre and pore, and it is pissing me off.

"Oh, bro. I am so sorry," Callan mutters.

While Darby takes the more direct approach. "We have all lost people, Grey, this is no different. This is what happens in war."

Callan's pity is the last thing I need. Now – Darby's cold brush off I can work with, so I feed off that instead. "They did this. I saw one."

Callan and Darby exchange looks. "A what, bro?"

"An Eilne. At least I think it was one. How did it know...? How did they know about Lizzie? Did they follow me here? Must've been Cox!" I am rambling and can feel my anger rising. "And you, you moron! You said you checked the perimeter, how did they get through, huh?" I step up to Callan, tears welling, and he takes a step back.

"Grey, we don't know, okay? Calm down, we will figu—" Darby tries.

"No, now you listen here. You knew Lizzie, didn't you?"

Darby shuffles uncomfortably. "I was going to..."

"It is too late now. Well, you wanted a warrior, so you got one!" A torrent rage is building, and I am seething. No more trying to be the nice guy, it's time to embrace my own darkness. Actually, I welcome it. Darby takes a step back...

211

"Grey, your eyes! They are… darkening."

I shove her aside, and send her flying onto the hood of my car, and as I look at my hands, tufts of darkness are billowing around them.

Callan shouts, "Oy!" But I don't care.

"Take care of Lizzie, if you can manage that." I should really do it myself, but I am too angry.

This just got personal, now this is my fight – I will kill every last ounce of Darkness if I have to, to find him. Find Cox. I scream with all my might, causing all the lightbulbs on the street to explode, raining glass down on the street in a symphony of misery. I Shift away to the only place I can think of. Where this all started. The reason for her being dead. The freaking clearing. I sink down to the ground, with my head between my knees, fuming. The trees quiet around me, as if mourning my loss with me. But no one is with me. Not anymore. I had started to think about it. A family. What Lizzie had given me, and with me now understanding my powers. Being able to be intimate with someone else, not being afraid to touch them, hold them, make love… Of course, it isn't like I never wanted a family before. A girlfriend. Children. For Lizzie to be a grandmother. She had said I was her son? What I do know is that it has to be better than what I had when I grew up.

But with my, eh, powers or whatnot, I had accepted the fact that it will be just me, me and my little bubble. And that was fine. But now, knowing what I know. Damn it. Wish they would have just left me alone. Oblivious to what I do not have. Still having Lizzie.

There is this gnawing in my chest, like a black hole growing, sucking everything into it and in some weird way, I like it. It reminds me of who I am, why I am here and what I never can have. Call me a martyr, I don't care. I will not put anyone through the hell that is me. And I cannot take this pain again, not after she... Not that my snoring and epic fail to ever choose what movie to watch are totally my charming sides. That is what I love about being me – when people say I have to do this, or have to do that, I just throw it right back, because you ain't gotta do anything. No matter how Insta-perfect everyone tries to be. Well, I wanted to have a family, I needed one. Now maybe the only thing you really have to do here in this world, is the only way for me to find redemption. Cox or me. So now – I will save the world. As long as it involves removing Cox from any plane of existence. For Lizzie. Then all of it can sod off. Or at least I will die trying, with no Instagramming in sight. Maybe that means it never happened?

Chapter 24

Grey

When it gets dark, I Shift back to Eader, pushing aside all thoughts of the day's events. A day which started out so blissfully ignorant. Well, those days are over. I end up by the fire pit by habit more than planning and bump into Lay.

"Grey!" she shouts and throws her arms around me. "Where have you been? We have been worried sick about you! When Darby and Callan came back without you… We didn't know…" She lets go and steps back. I can feel her holding something back, and then she bursts into tears, her sympathy rolling off her. "I heard what happened to your friend, Lizzie, she was a strong warrior… I mean, Darby told me. I didn't…"

"It's fine, Lay. Thanks. Wait, you knew her?" I try a smile, but I can't seem to make my face remember how it is done quite right. Turning away, I hear a sniffle coming from Lay. If I start talking about this, I will not be able to stop the flood of emotions crashing against the wall inside me.

"That is a little more complicated to explain." I notice Lay has been crying, her eyes red and cheeks still red. A small smile blooms on her face as she continues.

"Lizzie and I, we were close. Very close." She blushes and sniffles as she looks at me. "She chose to leave when they evacuated you, and it made me so proud. Even though it hurt to lose her. And now… she is gone all over again." I take a breath and ask the first question that pops into my mind. "But you are so young?" Lay laughs, which lights up her face, almost making her look like she always does, light and happy. "Dear Grey, after all your time here in Eader, you still have so much to learn." Still looking puzzled, she winks at me and grabs my hand. "Fairies are magic, remember. And just so you know, we have taken care of her and will lay her to rest as soon as we can."

"Thanks, Lay, and I am so sorry I didn't know you and Lizzie… were together. That must have been hard. But glad she had someone like you in her life, and that you shared her with me." I smile at her as warmly as I can, though I can feel it falling short of my eyes. "Likewise, Grey. And you know Lizzie, she was strong and always followed her heart. I would have never stood in the way of that. She was one of a kind! However, Darby told me if I found you, that it was time," she continues.

Taken by surprise by the quick change of subject, I pull my hand back. "Time for what?"

She smiles, wholeheartedly this time, seemingly relieved to talk about something else. "For you to see the Eader! She thought it might help you, how did she phrase it? 'See the patterns better,' or something like that. She would've shown you herself, but…" The happy expression on Lay's face turns to one of concern.

"Where is she?"

"She went back to Earth, to continue the mission. I heard you had some success with noticing the increased energy readings, but since you got… eh, side-tracked?"

"Yeah, I guess I wasn't much help." Damn. More things I messed up.

"Hey, none of this is your fault! And what happened…" She falters, and I can't blame her. It is all awful.

"Okay, so… I thought we were on Eader. What is it you want

215

to show me?" I pat her on the shoulder and try to look optimistic, which must look painful as she looks ready to start crying again. But it feels good, comforting someone else. After a few seconds, she lights up and flutters to the air.

"You just wait and see. Mind if you Shift there? You are a bit on the heavy side to fly all the way there." What these people have against walking, I will never know.

After giving me the coordinates, Lay flies off and I Shift away. To be honest, I would've have found it myself, if I had had a keener eye and noticed that particular nuance in the layers of Eader before. When I get closer, it is overwhelming, however. It pulsates with energy, spreading out through the ocean like a tidal wave of colours. All I have to do after that is just move to the source. As I pop out I almost slam into Lay, who is just landing.

"There you are," she says, as I topple out of what seems to be her shadow, greeting the ground with my face. "Elegant as always, I see." As I get up, I see the usual surroundings of unbelievably tall trees, moss, and rocks. But then Lay grabs me by the shoulders and turns me around. All I can do is gawk. There, in front of me is a tree almost ten times the width of any of the others, shooting up into the sky. Dust is floating around it, millions of them swirling in a dazzling pattern, and right at the bottom is an opening in the stem, just big enough to fit a fairy. "The Tree of Eader! What do you think?" When she doesn't receive an answer from me, she laughs. "I know. Pretty cool, huh? Well buster, you ain't seen nothing yet!"

Buster, really?

"Yes really. Now, follow me." She walks, actually walks this time, over to the doorway, and I move slowly over. There is a special vibe coming from this place, almost primal and it is intense, so intense that I turn down my intake valve. Need to give that a better name. As we enter the chamber what hits me first is the light. Literally. So, the Eader is hard to explain. It is there, but at the same time not. My confusion must be easy to read, or she just reads my mind, as Lay tries to clarify. "It's like a celestial body with no tangible form that is transforming into something tangible."

"Okay…" Not really okay, but sure. More specifically, the Eader is a beam of light stretching from below the floor and shooting off into the beyond where the eye can see up through the tree stem above. Fluttering, streaming, pulsating with all the colours imaginable in the middle of the circular room. I just stand and stare at the play of lights and colours bouncing off the walls, which is breathtaking to say the least. "So, this is the Eader. Cool enough," I say, leaning against a wall.

Lay raises an eyebrow. "Yeah, yeah, cool guy, remember I can read minds?"

How can I forget?

"Exactly. So yeah, this is the Eader. The source of all powers, the Dust and, well, you. It is also the source, or more like part of the Dán, the Flames of Eader, as you already know." She smiles at me and motions for me to come forward. I hesitate. It isn't like I haven't been itching to find out what the fuss is all about, but to see where I actually came from. No birds and bees, no mum and dad, but an illuminated beam of creation. Sure thing. "Don't be such a wuss, Grey. Just…"

Her voice dies as I start moving towards the Eader. My mind has gone blank, so maybe that worked as Lay's mute button, but all I can see now is the Eader. It is as if it is calling me, and I have no reservation from picking up the phone and answering. As I draw near, I lift my hand and move it closer to the light column. Lay moves to stop me but I casually use my powers to gently stop her. I can feel her objections, but she lets me pass. It is all working so naturally, my powers and senses. I reach out, feeling the beating pulse through my skin. When I touch the Eader, I almost scream. There is so much information that slams into me: faces, scenes of battles, numbers, pain, warmth. The strongest message is however clear – help. Without warning, the connection is broken and I fall back. Lay barely has time to catch me as I stumble into her.

"Grey, what happened? What did you do?"

"The Eader, it… it spoke to me. It's dying, Lay…" the words fall out of me as I get my balance I stand up and look at Lay, whose face now looks ashen.

"What do you mean, dying? I mean, I know the Eader is much weaker than it used to be. Used to be warm and brighter, but we all just thought it was part of the cycles. You know, like the seasons. But… dying? Are you sure? It couldn't have… Wait, it spoke?"

I put my hand on her shoulder and she stops her rambling.

"I am sure, Lay. There was more, so much more, but it was too much. I couldn't catch it all." She nods, and sniffles, and almost yelps as I reach out to it again, but this time nothing happens. My hand just grows a little warmer when it passes through the river of light.

I look past her and notice the drawings on the wall for the first time. Around the room are engravings of previous Fiors. I step past Lay to study them. Some are of humans performing magic, others are of fairies, trolls, elves and many more.

"The one right across from the door is of the First. The first Fior, I mean." Lay steps up behind me, and walks with me around the room. We stop at the drawing she indicated. "That is the first Fior, the first Conduit. Like you. They are all Fiors, and appear

218

here when they are given back to the Eader." I open my mouth to ask, but it falls shut just as fast. It feels like my hard drive is crashing and there is no way anything short of rebooting it will save it from being fried. "There are four categories, and we always have the same amount of each." I look at the First Fior. He had been an elf with kind eyes, wearing a headband over his long hair, which looks like it is dancing in the lights from the Eader.

"What are the categories?" I ask and continue along the room, shuffling my feet on the soft, earthy floor.

"The Conduit, The Healer, The Shapeshifter and The Clairvoyant, and within their range of power, they all excel. Though not all have the same powers."

"Yeah, Darby told me about the lack of an instruction manual for these things."

Lay nods. "Yeah, no wonder you screwed up so much and almost got yourself killed on numerous occasions."

"What? Is this your idea of a pep talk?"

"No – not really. We are beyond the point of pep talks now." Her bluntness takes me by surprise more than her harsh tone, but she smiles, touching my arm. "Grey. The Eader is the most powerful source of energy in all of creation, and the powers you have been gifted to control are linked to it, with the added benefit of being able to channel dark energy, which is very rare. A few, shall we say, bumps in the road were to be expected." Bumps. That is hilarious. But I decide to change the subject.

"Hey, is that why you can read minds, Fior powers?"

Lay draws herself up and nods. "Yes, my great-great-great-great-great grandfather was a Clairvoyant Fior, and inhabited the power of foresight and mindreading. So I inherited a speck of it." She looks proud and I smile.

"That is awesome."

Nodding, she skips ahead of me as we draw near to the exit. Then she stops. "Crap. I need to alert the council. About what you saw."

"Before you go," I interject, "how far can your powers reach exactly?"

"Why do you ask?"

"Well, something you said on the first day we met, about terms and conditions and all that?"

She gets that same wicked look in her eyes, and winks. "Oh, yes. I see. Well, I technically need to get permission before reading someone's mind, and let's just say for one of your updates on your computer, Ryder might've snuck something in there which you easily clicked 'Accept' on before reading. Meaning I have access. Not complete access, just enough to get you out of the house and keep an eye on you." I knew there had been something fishy with my sudden interest in forestry. She winks at me again and is almost out the door before she stops and looks at me one last time. "Grey, before, we only had Darby, now we have you, and that can tip the scale in our favour. Remember, we usually always have four Fiors to fight with us. Now we have only two. With your Conduit powers, the strongest of them all... we might have a chance to fight this. So don't worry, you got this." And with that she is gone.

Wow. Shit just got real. Like, for real. It was fun while it lasted. The magic, Eader, the Shifting. But now... people are relying on me to save them? Save the Eader? For fuck sakes. Me? How can I save anyone? Do they even know who they are entrusting with this? It is too much. Never realised how real it was until now. Like a dream gliding into a nightmare. It had been something free and abstract which is now solidifying into something tangible that I have no idea how to interpret, control, or in any way handle. I feel powerless, useless... scared, and a tad hungry to be honest. Not really hero material. And no pep-talk in the world is going to fix that. Overwhelming expectations to a recluse nerd... a nerd with no form of cheat codes. How did they all do it? The heroes I had grown up watching and reading about. Percy Jackson, William Wallace, Captain America, Iron Man, Batman, Deadpool, Kvothe and so many more. Some with masks or extraordinary power, with conviction or vengeance as motivation, all prevailing against impossible odds. Fighting for their cause. What do I have? I crouch down next to the wall, leaning under a troll lifting a boulder to throw at an enemy. Maybe he could just drop it on me and get it over with.

I wrack my brain, searching for any remnants of what the Eader showed me. There had been Light and Darkness, and it was overwhelming it. Can there be too much light energy? Has there ever been? Is that even a thing? And I know you need darkness, to balance out light. Lizzie always said that darkness was needed to inspire caution from fear. "Who d'you think invented spiders and angry mother in-laws?" she had said, half kidding. My heart clenches as her face pops into my mind, but I push it away. Not now. Now darkness is fighting light, not balancing it out. And I need to figure out why. As I understand it, the Darkness is growing in strength, while the Eader is losing the battle, without enough people or Light to defend it. I close my eyes and lean my head back onto the troll on the wall, balling up the fists resting on each knee of my jeans which look as put together as I feel.

Over the next three days I dive into training, brooding, and exploring the city, dodging the few people I know and who still talk to me. With all that has happened I don't even know how to start processing it all, let alone talk to other people about it, so I just don't. My training has consisted of doing the Ranger with increasing speed, practicing summoning energy while fighting with my silver knuckles and working on propelling myself in different directions using the force from the energy. The brooding needs no explanation, and I've got that bit down, easy. The exploration of Eader, and Manawa specifically, is interesting though. More details come into focus the more time I spend here, from the small differences of how people look and act, their accents, and the way they dress, to the big or small signs revealing their heritage. From elven ears to a hulder tail.

The scents are even better. The bakery and the florist smell awesome, but then I pick up on something more exotic and end up at the potion shop. How they have mixed technology with magic amazes me. The way they are welding swords, producing electricity through converting Light energy through a form of air-to-power osmosis. Or at least that is as close as I can describe it in terms I understand. When Ryder tried to explain it one day I just nodded, feeling my years at university were really well spent. I pass a building crew one day building a timber hut at the edge of Manawa, and it is truly a remarkable sight. In a matter of hours, the hut is complete by simply moving the materials around and fastening them, then fusing the materials together by letting the wood knit itself together. No wonder I never saw any traditional construction work. This could revolutionise the industry back on Earth. The best thing I see is however at the knick-knack store. The store owner, Dante, can create his knick-knacks from nothing, using Light energy. As he isn't a Fior, this means small objects, like glass figurines, bracelets and such, but they make the most beautiful pieces. Same power as Cox had, though much prettier. The most prominent discovery I make is

222

however the growing tension in the city. The uncertainty of what is happening and the rumours along with increased security is keeping everyone on edge. In a conversation with Dante, I find out that it has never been this bad, although the Darkness is always a threat. When I ask about how it all started, he shrugs and repeats what I already know – with the library and scholars gone, no one knows. Their history is lost. To keep myself from getting too depressed, I spend most of my free time at the cinema. Re-watching old classics and catching up on a few of my shows. I don't see Lay, as she's busy with the council, or Darby, but it doesn't bother me until the third day, when Lay almost lands on my head outside the cinema doors.

"There you are!" She looks flustered and has bags under her eyes, and her normally pointy ears have gone rogue, hanging sourly around her glittery face.

Before she can read my mind I say, "You look terrible!"

"Gee, thanks. But never mind that. Where have you been? I have been looking all over for you. Don't answer, it doesn't matter," she says. Stopping me before I can even form a thought. "Darby is in trouble. At least we think she is. We can't find her, and she hasn't reported in. She never does this. Grey, something must have happened to her!" Lay keeps fidgeting with her quarterstaff, almost knocking me down as she spins it around in front of her. I grab it as it makes another pass and fix my eyes on Lay.

"What do you know, Lay? Where was she going?" She takes a deep breath and jerks the staff out of my hand.

"That is just it, we don't know! Don't you think we would have found her by now, if we did?" she says defensively, planting the staff in the ground in front of her. "And it's not like she is defenceless. It's Darby. She is stronger than you think, with her shifter-powers, pulse, Lika, and Riley…" She looks up at me. "Sorry. Rambling again. But no, we don't really know anything, other than that she was going to continue the investigation of the attacks on Eader from Earth." I start pacing in front of her, between the columns of the cinema.

Suddenly I stop. "I can find her!" Quickly I explain to her about my emotional navigation system, which sounds stupid when you say it aloud, but Lay hangs on every word and does not doubt me for a second. Plus for the mindreading.

"Well, what are you waiting for? Get going, would you?"

"I haven't really done this before, other than finding home, which I know where it is. Give me a second."

I lean against the nearest column and close my eyes, trying to remember Darby. How she looks, smells, how she makes me feel, what she feels like. Her emotional signature, I guess. The more I think about it, I feel a memory itching to reveal itself from deep down somewhere and suddenly it bursts out. I gasp and throw open my eyes. That feeling. That touch. It was her!

"Grey, are you okay? Did you find her?" Before she can blink, I reach out for the feeling in the Ocean of Earth and Shift away.

I land in a dark room, or at least I think it is a room. There is nothing to see or hear, only my own breathing. Then suddenly I hear a creak in the floor above me and some low whimpering. Lika! I fire up my silver knuckles I have grabbed from my back pocket and get a view of my surroundings. In the shimmering light I see old, dusted living room furniture, windows covered up with sheets and to my right a staircase. I leap up it, taking three steps at a time, and as I reach the top step on the second floor, I see her. There is only one wall left standing on the otherwise shattered upper-storey room. Leaves are blowing in from the surrounding forest, mixing with the debris from the house, and the only light available is me and the faint glow of the moon. In it, next to the last wall, I see a shape.

"Darby!"

More whimpering, and as I draw closer, I see Lika lying next to Darby. She's a mess. Her clothes in tatters, arms and face bloody, and she is holding her stomach, wincing as she tries to get up.

"Grey, how did you…" she croaks.

"Never mind that, stay still." I lean down, trying to examine her wounds, and as I do, I pass her some of my energy, which seems to relax her.

"It was like they were waiting for me. Lika never had a chance, and Riley…" She catches her breath as she resumes her efforts of sitting up, succeeding this time, and leans against the wall. "They fought so bravely," she whispers, and a tear rolls down her cheek. Lika nuzzles Darby's hands, whimpering. "Riley… I don't know if I will get him back, he was badly hurt."

"Riley, that is your lynx, right?" I ask, crouching down in front of the pair.

"Yes, I had to recall him…" Darby sobs.

"I bet he will be just fine. Darby, what happened? Where have you been?"

Darby's features grow serious, and she stares at me. "I picked up where we left off, or barely started. Followed a few leads and reports on Darkness attacks, and it led me here. But it was a trap. How did you find me anyway?"

"Oh, I just followed your emotional homing beacon," I say, trying to sound nonchalant. But to be honest when I first saw Darby, there were butterflies. Then I see her injured, and a whole damn rampaging zoo replaces the butterflies.

"Always such an emotional lad," she mocks, wincing as she laughs.

"I repeat, who did this to you?" My voice more insistent now.

One word slips out of her lips, "Cox."

I nod. It is all I need to hear.

I take Darby's hands and help her stand. Then I grab her shoulders, letting my right hand slide down her arm to her wrist, while looking into her eyes. There is an intense, searching expression there, and it pulls me in. I start pulling her closer by the wrist, until we are standing almost chest to chest, still looking down at her, still supporting her. I let go of her wrist to put a few strands of hair behind her ear, not really understanding why I am doing it, but I do not want to control it either. There is a sweet tension in the air that seeps into me, and I embrace it.

Smiling my crooked smile, which lights up Darby's face, she whispers a quiet "Oh shut up," under her breath, and her forehead drops onto my shoulder. I wrap my arms around her and pull her into a tight hug which she timidly returns.

"I know it was you, that night in the alley."

She looks up at me, misty eyed. "Oh Grey, I should've been there sooner. I am so sorry."

I feel my heart swelling in my ribcage. I smile my best rebellious, lopsided grin. "And now I am returning the favour," I say with finality. I bend down and slip my arm under her knees, picking her up. She groans, but doesn't protest.

"Why did you help us, you didn't have to care... After Lizzie..." I shut her up with a look as I walk over to the staircase. Not knowing what to say, I decide on the truth.

"All my life I just wanted to be needed, to help, to feel wanted. I felt that in Eader. I have a purpose, at least I think so.

226

And I know I might be a crappy substitute for a hero, but I will do all I can to help. I am not giving up. Especially after what happened to…" My voice catches and as I enter the living room downstairs, I put Darby down on one of the couches. "There is always a way, and I will find it, I promise. What I can't promise is that I won't make a mess of things while doing it and I will probably be a pain in the ass, but… it's who I am."

Darby sits up on her elbows, smiling. "You are still a mystery to me, nerd. Thanks for the assist," she whispers the last few words and I nod, then lean down and activate her Beacon. Darby tries to stop me, but she's too weak to have any luck. "Hey, what are you…?" I set coordinates for the fire-pit, and with a smile, I push it.

Chapter 25

Grey

After Darby vanishes, I immediately Shift to my hometown, this time making no pit stops. After the last days' events, there is no longer any doubt in my mind – I need to figure this out. Until now it has been a confusing mix of rumours, overheard conversations, and scattered information. But after connecting with the Eader, it all is coming into focus. There is a war on two fronts happening, one that the Eader is fighting, and one that the Eadorians are fighting against minions of Darkness. I walk down through Main Street, trying to connect the dots. I know the trees in Eader are showing signs of decay, and I know about the increasing attacks on Eader. And now – Darby getting attacked. And Lizzie… Well, enough. The street is empty and all that moves is a newspaper tumbling across the square in front of me. The streetlights are golden yellow, creating a warm light in an otherwise cold winter night. I stop by the water fountain and look around at the previously all too familiar place, which now seems foreign, almost hostile.

Taking a deep breath of frosty air, I close my eyes, hold out my arms to each side and then reach out through my senses – in every direction, with all my might. As a Conduit I know I can sense the energy flows around me, but as it is a quiet night, there isn't much to pick up on, so I extend my search. Suddenly, there is a tingle in the air of a something. Nothing more than a murmur, a whisper of energy. When I concentrate on it, it suddenly turns the whimper into a screaming voice. I wince and pull back. It is something broken, something dying. Could it be...? I need more information, so I Shift to another time zone, and end up on a bustling street, in front of Caz Reitop's Dirty Secrets, a 1920s looking pub. Walking inside, I look around and no one pays any attention, as they are busy with their otherwise important day. I sit down at the first table by the door, looking around at the crowded bar, with laughing people, a blonde bartender chatting up this bloke she obviously has a crush on, in her Australian accent. The bar is quite cool and a place I would love to grab a beer, were it not for other pressing matters. I gaze out through the window at the foot traffic, refocus and try my luck again. This time I start easy, as there are so many people around, and sure enough, there are so many streams of energy, from each person, and there are millions of them. Darkness, Light and all the degrees in between. It is overwhelming, but I force myself to reach further, searching for I don't know what, but something. The flows of energy seem to have a direction, as if having a specific course plotted. The sources of light are hugs, smiles, happy tears, sarcastic laughs. And then it hits me how much power these humans have. I feel a girl smiling to an old man on the bus, a boy standing up for his friend who is being bullied. A man who is being harassed for the colour of his skin, laughs it off, and walks away. Hard workers at a paper mill, people letting a stressed person pass them in line to reach their flight. I reach further and further, and it is heart-warming. A young man leaving home for the first time, feeling excited and terrified, while a farmer is enjoying a cold beer after a long day's work, and appreciating the last rays of sunshine. It is simply the magic in the in-between of moments. Not just bright yellow light, no.

Also, the greyer tones – the twilight. Heartaches to feel the depths of love, blue Mondays to appreciate Fridays, losing, so to work harder to win. A perfect balance.

I pull back and feel a tear running down my cheek. I roughly brush it away, and feel my pulse racing. I rush out of the bar, past the now sulking blonde sipping her glass of red. Outside I pause, to think. Okay – so humans aren't so bad – weird how I have started to think of them as something different than I am. I have lived as a regular human for most of my life though, so I guess I should consider myself human behaviour-wise at least. Humans write the most thrilling and magical stories, create jaw dropping and awe-inspiring art through music, film, and paintings. They care about each other, survive in the toughest conditions, and can find strength in adversity. I Shift again, and again. Now focusing on the Darkness. Which is emanating from the littlest things. Fear of the unknown, pollution, hating change, and a lot is coming from cell phones, computers, and television. Probably a dispersal method, a catalyst even, for both light and dark, which isn't odd when I start to think about it. And underneath it all, a painful moan, like someone or something crumbling under a heavy burden.

I stop for a minute and consider my findings. There are different forces, and sources. The world isn't just black or white; it is a world of in-betweens. Nothing big – but together it is plenty. It is choosing the lighter nuance in an ocean of black, rising above and not letting oneself being dragged down by self-pity, anger or hate. This is what I see here on Earth. Problem is, it looks like the Darkness is winning. It is everywhere! Slamming of doors, neighbourhood brawls, fuming on the subway over irritating people, stressing about deadlines, building up under hate, insecurities, and anger – both people and places. Hating people you have never met. Warring for territory and for contempt and hate for another's religion. It is overwhelming. As I continue to Shift, I start to see the pattern – all the darkness and light energy streams all have the same directionality, outwards, almost as if they are racing each other. The Light trying to overtake the Dark, but it is like putting out a fire with a single drop of water. That is when it hits me – it is drawn to the Eader! The barrier! As I get the thought it is as if a door opens and in between the layers I see darkness pouring into the ocean of Eader, with small drops of Light blending in, fighting it along with the Eader. It isn't hard to see that the Eader is losing. Wait. Something about a shield. No, Darby had said barrier. It was the Eader that had shown me a crumbling three-edged shield. That must be the Eader.

I Shift faster and faster, each place is the same, the Darkness overwhelming the Light. I end up back home and collapse outside in my backyard, panting. How can humans be so dumb? How can they not see it? It's right there in front of them, clear as day... But it was Mark Twain who said "You should never argue with stupid people, they will drag you down to their level and then beat you with experience." It seems like the Darkness is everywhere, with the humans feeding the wrong wolf. I get it, really. People fear terrorism, angry over losing jobs, bitter and stressed trying to live up to impossible standards. As I lie there, I stare up at the brightening of the sky and the last stars of the night are barely visible, being hidden by the rays of the morning sun. My body aches from the exposure to so much emotion, and I just rest here, breathing. I wish it wasn't all so complicated. I'm used to science, and math, which is infallible – right or wrong. While this, this is more like the infinitely intricate perception of science. Which is subjective, meaning it is messy, hard to control and predict and most of all, it is dangerous. An idea can spread like wildfire – whether it is good or bad, right or wrong. It is infectious and no matter how hard you work to prove what is going on, it is counteracted by popular opinion. People might think it is a hoax, corruption, a scheme, or the best thing ever. And they have the right to their own opinions – but when that stands in the way of seeing what is happening right in front of them, and they justify it by twisting it to fit their own agenda? Not good. Getting up, I brush off the leaves and dirt from my jeans and hoodie, and start to think how divided the world is, where wars are waged, lives lost. Also, it is too easy nowadays to step on other people's toes. Walking up the stairs to the house, I stumble and swear. Damn it. There are too many considerations to be made, being politically correct about every little detail. When did the world become so fragile? And complicated. Wow. Because *that* line of thought makes me feel better. Inside, I switch on the light, trying to keep in mind all the good things being done – aid work, technological advancements, renewables, sustainability, fantasy movies, chill Sundays in coffee shops and so on. The odds are just so overwhelming, depressing even. God damn. Stop it, brain. Anyway, it seems like humans are choosing between two options, either hope and perseverance, or just foolishly ignoring defeat. Gotta give it to them – they are at least not giving up on themselves. Mental high five. I can work with that! It is almost reassuring to know that there is a reason for all the horrible things going down in the world. How the Darkness is influencing humans, and it isn't all self-inflicted destruction. As I enter the kitchen, an idea hits me. Humans are light bringers who have lost their way. It is almost like humanity lost an inherent part of their brain, unable to see the big picture, to understand or to grasp what they are doing. An inability to fathom how their actions are basically cutting their own and everybody else's lifeline. Damn. My old mantra 'People only cause pain' is out, new mantra from now on – 'People always have potential'. Humans are still a young species, with so much to learn. And as they are so desensitized to their own surroundings, it breeds more darkness, which is how the Darkness is winning. Humans are the biggest source of darkness, and with them just piling it on, Eader won't stand a chance. Let's be fair though, Cox has been involved here, so the humans need help.

My stomach growls for attention and I grab an apple from the counter, before Shifting back to Eader.

Chapter 26

Grey

Or so I think. As I pass through the layers and cross into the Ocean of Eader, I feel a chill creeping up my spine and then something grabbing my ankle, yanking me off course and down through a cold obsidian veil, beyond the Oceans I know, where darkness swallows me and my apple.

I smack down on solid ground and hit my head hard. As I try to get up, my vision swims, and I roll over, trying to make the room stop spinning. When it finally does, I see I am not in a room at all. I am outside, but there is no sky, there is only pitch black, lit up by four large pyres surrounding me, and in between these are large stone columns, connected with stone arches between them. Beyond this, I see nothing. I sit up, feeling my head, where a trickle of blood has started its way down from my left temple. My apple lies next to me, no worse for wear.

"Awrite, Grey. Fàilte, tae me humble abode. Sorry fur interrupting yer meal thare, son," a familiar voice snarls from the darkness. I can't seem to pinpoint quite where it is coming from. It is bouncing off the columns, and is echoing in my ears.

"I ain't your son, you traitor. I know what you are up to." I don't know why I say it, but I can't stop myself. This guy is pissing me off.

"Weel, weel, weel, wee boy. Thare ye go again, getting in th' wey. Juist lik' yer wee baby sitter. Ah cannae hae ye running around, interfering wi' mah script, now can ah?" Suddenly he is standing there, Shifted right in front of me, in the archway. Dark wisps of energy are billowing around him, as if the darkness behind him is yearning to be with him. He steps towards me, dragging the dark tendrils after him. I get up, swaying on my feet. This is the first time I can get a really good look at him. He looks like a black, shaggy dog, but not the kind you want to take home, more the kind who will chase you all the way home and haunt your nightmares. He has long, black hair, piercing green eyes and a scraggy beard. His clothes are a different story. A sharp black and white pinstriped suit, with shiny black shoes, and a cane to go along with it. He stops in front of me, smiling his most creepy smile. "Sae, Grey, it has come tae this." He flicks his cane in my direction, and suddenly there is a chair behind me, which an unseen force pushes me into. Another one pops up behind Cox and he sits down facing me, elegantly crossing his legs, and lays his cane neatly across his lap, held with both hands. We sit on opposite sides of the circle, with flames dancing around us.

"Sorry, I seem to be a bit underdressed for the occasion. I would've dressed up, but I wasn't informed of this meeting."

Cox grips his cane firmly, smiling at me. "Yae know, th' plan wis so simple, so elegant," he starts, ignoring my previous statement. "Finally, bein' able tae extinguish ours and tip th' scales, disturbing th' balance. Ah could've just leant back and gawked at it all unravel, terminate Eader and folk on Earth th' same time. But *nae*," he exclaims, smacking his cane into his hand. "Ye have bin lurking around, messing up mah script," he sneers.

"Me? Lurk? Never. Scout's honour." The last sentiments are conveyed by showing him my middle finger.

"Oh, make fun all yae want, Grey. Actually, ah welcome it.

Sae ah can snuff out that which ye call humour and watch it die along wi' ye." Again, with attacking my humour. Seriously, my sarcasm is wasted on dumb people. "Ah almost had ye when mah scouts spotted ye finally goin' out of that shack ye call a home."

I look around me, "At least I had walls, dude."

"Silence, I'll give ye a skelpit lug!" Cox's voice is high-pitched, and I feel the air around me drop a few degrees. He gets up from his seat and starts pacing in a circle around me, his path emphasised with the pounding of his cane on the granite floor. "Ye were untouchable inside them walls, thare were wards up by the numpties or sae called guardians, which ah couldn't penetrate. Bit finally, ye just went for a stroll in the woods. Mah spy told me ye were bein' extracted and it should have been like shooting fish in a barrel. But yer annoying burd and her posse showed up…"

"Keep Darby out of this!" I start to get up, but I can't. I am pinned to the seat and as Cox passes in front of me, he waves his hand and a black knife appears from nowhere, hovering just over my heart.

"Please, Grey. Ye will die soon enough, dinnae rush this." All I can do is scowl, and he continues his walk. "Where was ah? Oh aye, yer precious Madam General. She whisked ye away, and ah had to go find ye in Eader, nae that ye made it tough, as it seems ye have a habit of taking off alone in tae the woods. After losing ye again, well, mah wee spy kept me well informed on yer progress, not willingly of course, but ah have mae ways. Seemed like ye were talking up some auld lang syne." As he says it, he smacks his cane into the back of my chair, making me jump, almost causing me to cut myself on the knife. "Canny thare, son, ah wouldn't dae that if ah were ye. Shadow blade and all."

I have no idea what that means, so I blurt out something else.

236

"Your spy, who is it?"

"Ah think ye know that already, or ye should, if ye only could remember the training sessions with me and…"

"No, it can't be. Callan…"

"Aye, Callan. He has done his job and ah dinnae need him anymore. Me good-for-nothing *son*…" He says the last word like it is leaving a sour taste in his mouth. "He could nae even keep a close enough look on ye tae keep ye from sniffing around too much. Sae ah had tae step in. Yet again."

My thoughts are racing through all the conversations I had with Callan, and my memories from when we were younger. How defensive Callan had been about Cox. Our Swordmaster. His father. Damn.

Cox just rambles on from behind me. "He wasn't even that solid tae convince, nae efter whit happened afore th' battle he was easy to influence… anyway, here ye ur. The Conduit. Ye see, ah want tae break it all down, and yer spirit." He stops in front of me and gestures towards me, poking me with the knife. "Is th' ainlie thing that stands in me way. Ye hae na idea what power ye wield, what ye can do with enough energy… it's such a waste, really." He sighs and sits back down in his chair. I try to Shift, but something is blocking me, so I wrack my brain for something to keep him talking.

"What about the humans? Why did you have to pull them into this?"

Cox scoffs. "Ah haven't pulled anybody intae anything. Thay just needed a wee nudge, the rest they did on their own. 'Twas sae easy, just feed their ignorance, ego, hate, anger, bitterness, thirst fur power and revenge, even love with a wee bit of darkness, the rest they did on thare own, and it spread like wildfire. Folk of the light indeed." Leaning back, he looks at me with a smug expression. I kinda agree with him on some weird level. Things are screwed up, but clearly this isn't fair play. It would be easy to just start over, without them. Let animals and nature live in peace? Then again – this guy is a megalomaniac, and a psychopath such as this tends to give effective, though destructive advice.

"You know what, you need to shut the hell up." My voice cuts through the silence created by Cox finally taking a break. "You talk too much. Same as every villain in every story – yapping away and wasting time. Shut the hell up would you and get on with it?"

Cox raises an eyebrow and I feel the knife pushing harder against my chest, but I ignore it.

"I get that you are proud and all of your little plan, you said so yourself. And basically what you are saying is that you are scared of me. I get it. I can be pretty intimidating, but don't worry. No one is perfect, I will not hold it against you."

"Ye wee scabby rocket!" Cox jumps up, but before he can do more, I send a pulse of Light and a little bit extra straight at Cox and he flies backwards. The force holding me down disappears, along with the knife.

"What did ye…?" I hear Cox roar as he clambers to his feet, and I hear a distinct sob. Tears are streaming down his face, then transitioning into anger and confusion, and I smile.

"I call it the Emo-Attack. You like?" I have no plans to stick around to find out if I should trademark it or not, and try to Shift. It is harder this time, and is taking too long, as I can't immediately locate the layers. Cox has almost shaken off the emotional bomb I dropped on him, but it is like… Can't be. I am outside both Eader and Earth. But as I think of home, I feel the familiar tug and step through, leaving Cox behind.

"Ah will find ye, and we will end this, Grey."

238

Deep down I know he is right, but it will not be today. He does however send me a parting gift, the black knife come sailing after me, but luckily only nicks me in my side and I leave this hellhole behind.

For a guy who hadn't been home in forever, I'm certainly making up for it now. I end up Shifting out of a shadow behind my house, cast by the light on my back porch. A pain in my side reminds me of the close encounter with Cox's knife, but on closer inspection, it is just a shallow cut. It is raining and it makes me feel better straight away. I am soaked in seconds and my Chucks are now a dark red again. I am relishing the feeling. Rain has always been my favourite type of weather. The simplicity and purity of rain is what does it for me. It is really coming down hard, but I take my time walking up to my house. The wind is whisking around my ears, dancing through the newly rain-washed blades of grass. The rolling cotton hills in the distant sky are bathing in a soft silver glow from the rising moon, mixing with the grey skies above. Wow, so glad it is only me inside my head. I close my eyes. Home. It must be around eight o'clock as dusk has settled. Feels like the day is giving me a hug with its lingering darkness, though a wet and cold one. And it makes me smile. That fresh, petrichor smell that follows, like nature's personal exclusive fragrance. The sound of rain is even better. How it taps just the right places on different surfaces in what sounds like the ultimate soundtrack. No matter where you are, in a car, inside an apartment, outside in the park or walking through downtown, you always have the perfect backdrop. That is why I always wear headphones when it isn't raining – to block out the ugliness and disruptive noise, which will be drowned out by rain ordinarily. It is like rain is trying to wash away this ugliness, wash away the mistakes and replace it with something pure. I stand outside for a few more minutes, savouring all the impressions. This is definitely something Earth does better than Eader. I

239

decide to sit down on the porch, and I cradle my head in my hands. What just happened? The revelations about Callan, the Eader dying, and Earth being tainted by Darkness. What is even happening anymore? I was trained by this guy too, and I can wield darkness. And just like the rain, I feel like everything is crashing down, and there is nothing I can do to stop it. The power Cox talked about, the one I am supposed to have. Which one? Darkness or Light? And what did I do to Callan to make him hate me so much, and make him want to help someone like Cox?

Whatever the answer is, I need to warn Eader. Fast.

Chapter 27

Darby

Grey pops out in front of me, as I sit nursing my coffee cup by the fire, making me spill hot liquid down my shirt. The man is soaked and looks like he is between freaking out, ready to thrash someone, and passing out. He staggers over to one of the logs and drops down. Lay comes running over from the training grounds, and she does not look happy. "First Darby goes missing, then you. Explain yourself! Where in the world have you been?" she rants, as she hovers distressed in front of him.

Grey leans on his elbows resting on each knee, staring at her. "Don't you mean 'which world'? And hey, Darby is here. So am I. Calm down." His voice is gravelly and void of emotion. Almost scary. I could have told him that that was no way to calm Lay down. She had been worried sick, even when I returned, falling headlong into the med tent. She had been screaming, more terrified than anything else, but Thiam fixed me right up. After that she wanted to go after Grey, but I stopped her. I knew Grey had a plan. At least, I hoped he did. And here he is. More or less in one piece, though by the looks of it, there may be a few fragments missing.

"That isn't the point, Darby!" Lay yells, making me jump and spilling half my cup of coffee. Grey looks half-amused, half-distracted, holding his head in his hands.

"Lay, most important thing is that he is back. Also, by the

looks of it, he needs a cup of coffee, too." I let my words hang in the air until finally she takes the hint, and flies off, annoyed and teary-eyed.

"Thanks," Grey mutters, looking up at me. His face reveals only a blank stare as if he is far away. I notice him wincing as he sits up.

"Are you hurt?"

"Nah, it's nothing. Just had a chat with Cox, is all." This time I drop my whole cup onto the ground.

"What do you mean 'chat with Cox'? What happened?"

Grey sighs despondently, and dives into the story of his discoveries on Earth.

I catch myself shivering when he finishes. His whole demeanour is so detached, which scares me even more. And him being caught while Shifting makes it all more distressing. What place had he been taken to? And what did Cox want? I feel myself freaking out. "Do you remember anything else?"

Grey sits up, again wincing, and grabs his side with his right hand. "What? From the fight or from… way back when?"

I realise I don't know. Both would help. "I guess both? Seriously, I wish we could jumpstart your memories."

"Well, I don't!" Grey shouts, standing up. "All of this. This world. What is happening to me, all of it! I've had enough of it. It was all so safe and familiar in the beginning, but now it is all pain. I wish you would've just left me out if it!"

He turns his back on me and storms off towards the forest. I see him crouching down next to a tree, half devoured by the shadows.

Lay comes back with a cup of coffee, and I gesture for her to leave it where Grey had been sitting. She does as I ask and flies off, not saying a word. I guess she doesn't have to. Usually, we have a deal on the mindreading, and I keep a few safeguards up, but right now I am too raw to care, and she probably picked up on my thoughts easily enough.

Thinking back to when we met Lizzie, and on how Grey had been so relaxed, and looked so young. Talking animatedly with her, smiling and unguarded. Maybe it is my fault, turning a carefree nerd into a brooding reluctant warrior. Smiling morosely to myself I get up, and kick the ground. "Always fucking shit up…" I mutter, and make my way over to where Grey is hidden in shadow.

As I draw near, I hear Grey's voice. "You know how ideas can be good, right?"

I nod, and stop a few metres away from him, trying to find his eyes in the darkness cast by the tree.

"I think so too. Ideas help define a person, make them who they are, give them guidance and direction. Make them feel like they have meaning and a purpose. This idea can be initially good, but interpreted into something bad, which is how subjective thought is the most powerful weapon in the world and how the Darkness is gaining such a strong foothold on Earth. I'm not saying freedom of thought is a bad thing, because it is a beautiful thing. Just look at the world of books. What I am saying is that what is the largest force of energy is humans and they are currently on the dark side, for the most part – whether they realise it or not. I for one did not know when I lived there. If we do not act fast, the Darkness will overwhelm the Eader, and I have no idea how to stop it." As he finishes, he straightens up, letting light find his eyes, and I see a deep well of frustration and anger there, making me miss Nerdy-Grey more than ever. Again, I notice him wincing as he starts over towards me and the fire pit.

"Hey, let me have a look at that. You might need healing."

"We can do that later. Right now, there are more important things to do." I let it go, seeing how determined he is.

"Fine, so what you are saying is that darkness is being drawn to the Eader, overloading its defences?" We sit back down at the fire, and Grey dives into his coffee cup, nodding as he goes. "Well, at least some of the pieces are falling into place. If we are reading the signs right, with the build-up of darkness, increase in attacks and now Cox trying to stop you, we are definitely on to something. He must really fear what you can do if he'd go to such lengths to get to you."

"He said my spirit has the power, but I have no idea what he meant by that," Grey grumbles. I frown. All of this is making my head hurt. I look back at Grey where there is no smile and no sarcasm. He is totally changed, which scares me, though it is a bit more charming than creepy. He does seem stronger now, more confident. "Anyway," he says, catching me off guard with his piercing blue and purple speckled eyes. "How are you? I mean," he pauses, scratching his neck with his coffee-free hand. "After what happened with Cox and all."

"Oh, I am fine. Riley and Lika took the worst off it, though they are healing up fine, Callan is looking after them now."

I try a smile, but all I get is a nod, as he continues his staring-match with his coffee cup. Clearly, he isn't up for much of a conversation, and I start picking up the broken pieces of my cup next to my feet. I really want to find out what that man is thinking right now, but as I inhale to ask, I suddenly hear something shattering and look up to see a broken coffee cup where Grey had been sitting. Who is now running across the field towards the lieutenants' quarters.

"Have you lost it?" I yell, ready to run after him.

"No, actually I think I found it!" he replies darkly as he

disappears around the corner of the first row of tents. Whatever that means. I decide he has earned the benefit of the doubt, and wander over to my tent. Inside I wade through my jungle of stuff and lie down on my cot.

What a mess everything has become. Cox and his encompassing Darkness looming. The horrors inflicted upon Grey, who never asked for any of this. Who now more than ever needs to be protected. I send an irritated pulse out and hear a muffled yell outside my wall.

"Damn, Darby, was that necessary?"

Lay opens one of the tent flaps and peers inside. I gesture for her to enter, and she throws herself into the chair next to my desk, making sheets of paper fly in every direction.

"Sorry," she mumbles.

I sit up and shrug. "No worries, I think you made it better actually," I say with a flourishing gesture, grinning, which finally brings back that infectious smile of hers and we both laugh. As the sound of our moment of cheer dies down, a gloom is cast over our faces.

"It is happening again, isn't it?" I do not need to reply, because she knows. "I don't know if I can do this again, Darby. So many lives lost, all our history gone and so much misery…"

I get up and start pacing, hands to my side. Stopping, I stare out into the forest. She is right. After last time… We have spent so much time rebuilding. Trying to gain our footing again. I never thought I could envision a future after losing them… losing him. I close my eyes and suddenly he is right there, smiling his annoying smile. "Hey, baby, you got this, do your little shimmy for me and go kick some ass." I reach out for him, and he wraps me up tight in his arms, and the whole world melts away. "I missed you," he whispers.

"Really?"

"Really, really, baby. You belong here in my arms."

"You been gone too long, babe."

He pushes me away softly and laughs. "You reckon? Better watch that attitude, or else I might come and kiss ya." He winks, and I feel my insides crumbling as I try to shake the memory. But I can't. Instead I shimmy and snuggle up into the nook of his arm. "Excellent, perfect fit as always," he murmurs into my hair. "Now, go do me proud." I feel the tears streaming down my cheeks as the vision melts away and I am left standing alone. He was the first and last person who ever saw me, understood, and could melt through the tough armour down to the soft core with one of his hugs. Then he went and got himself killed in battle, leaving me all alone, all hardness, no love left. He was the reckless to my calm, the comfort to my wild, and the strong to my wavering.

Even after training my whole life to fight the Darkness, I lost. And now, here again, without him… It is happening all over again. I will not lose another.

"Sweet as, girl," Lay cheers half-heartedly, and my face lights up from her making an effort. Lay is feeling this as much as I am.

"Thanks, hon'."

When I served as the Guardian watching over Grey, I had a few friends at my part-time job, but never anything like the companionship I have forged here in Eader. It didn't take me long to figure out that the colour of the grass doesn't matter, you need to take care of what you have, not long for something that might be better. Sometimes what seems greener is yellow and dead. I was actually happy when news came of Grey being in danger and he needed to be extracted. As it meant I got to go home. A home

I now will defend against our enemies, though there are many unknown elements to be figured out on the board still. I wipe my tears and turn back around to Lay.

"So, Lay, are you ready?"

"Ready for what?"

"I think it is time to break a few rules."

A smile spreads across Lay's face as I explain what I have planned.

"Lead the way, General!"

Chapter 28

Grey

I make my way through the camp, where I am more or less ignored by Guardians busy with their training and assignments. As I turn the corner I spot him, sitting next to the wall of his tent, cleaning his sword. It is like I am seeing him for the first time, and I do not like what I see. Before, all I had remembered from our time training together and hanging out now had up until this moment added up to a cool dude who had my back. Now, all I can see is a treacherous spy, only caring about one person. I hang back for a while, waiting for a few people to pass. Before getting snatched up by Cox, I had felt like I was being pulled in all different directions, but now however... Now I know what I must do. From wanting to be left alone, to thinking I had a home, which Cox is now threatening. Thinking I had a family, before Cox took it away. Thinking I had a best friend, a friendship now poisoned by Cox. I can't just walk away. Neither will he.

When the coast is clear, I walk over and without further ado I grab Callan by the shirt, pulling him to his feet. He is so startled; he doesn't have time to react before I Shift us away to my house back on Earth, not considering I had not really Shifted someone else before. In my living room, I slam him into the wall.

"You're just a low level, wannabe Keyser Söze, ain't you, Callan?" I glare at him. "You played your part perfectly too." The shock of the grab-and-Shift is starting to wear off, and he scowls right back.

"What the hell are you on about, bro?" I release my grip and he leans down to pick up a picture, which fell off the wall after he so rudely knocked into it. "Nice pic by the way. Really liked Lizzie."

I grab the picture out of his hands and toss it onto the couch. "Don't you talk about her."

Callan steps towards me and slides into the chair. "Fine. Can you just tell me what the hell is going on, you little twerp?" he says calmly, locking eyes with me.

"Like you don't know. Sure thing." I spit in his face.

"Dude, drop the sarcasm."

"I wouldn't have to be so sarcastic if people weren't so stupid. But fine. I will spell it out for you, or rather, maybe we can call your dear old dad and have him do it for you?" Dead silence. Callan suddenly grows pale and sinks back in the chair. The look on his face jogs something in the back of my memory. Callan running away from our Swordmaster, hiding in my house. Begging me not to tell anyone, about… something.

"Bro…"

"There are no 'bros' here, Callan. Just you and me, having a chat."

I walk around the coffee table, facing Callan, who is now tapping his foot, avoiding my gaze.

"This is when you tell me everything and I try my very best not to kill you." I hold my right fist in my left hand to keep them both from shaking, waiting for Callan to try and redeem himself.

"I won't apologise for anything." Fine, not redeem, more like bury. "You would remember this if your memory weren't all muddled, but our childhoods weren't exactly the same." His posture alters with the topic change, and he leans forward.

"Remember I told you I lived on Earth till I was five? Well, let's just say moving to Eader was a real improvement, even with Cox."

"Wait, you mean..."

Callan gets up, making me do the same as a reflex. We stand there, chest to chest, both scowling. He steps off and starts pacing.

"Anyway, after escaping my literal hell on Earth, dear old Dad revealed to me what he was. An Eilne. Living in hiding."

"And you stayed with him?" I say accusingly.

"Dude, I was five years old. What do you want from me?"

I'll give him that one. But still. "Well, you aren't five any more, are you?"

Callan stops pacing and looks at me. "It is complicated. You don't know how he... what he is capable of..."

Kicking aside the living room table I get up in his face. "Say that again! How I don't know! How I don't understand? Excuse you, but I think you forget who you are talking to."

Stepping back, Callan trips over the rug, falling back into the wall.

"Nice one, nitwit, real smooth. They teach you that at spy school?"

Sitting up against the wall, Callan rubs the back of his head. "Damn it, Grey, I wanted to tell you. When you came back, I didn't want to..."

"But you still did. Cox told me about your lovely rendezvous and updates. Stabbing us all in the back to suck up to that cretin. I always wondered what it would be like if Luke had just said 'Sure thing, Vader, let's check out the dark side!' Guess now I know."

At this Callan jumps up. "Shut up, you ignorant bastard.

Always so pampered and protected. Never known what real hardships…"

Before he finishes my fist has decided to greet his left chin rather violently.

Again, Callan is caught off guard, and reunited with the wall for a third time. This time he needs no more invitation and flies at me. He hits me hard in the stomach and I hear my silver knuckles hitting the floor, disappearing out of sight as I crumple at Callan's feet. Damn. I hit him with an Emo-Attack, and he stumbles, but catches himself.

"Really? That won't work on me, dude. Already a wreck." He towers above me, smiling a hollow smile. "We're bloody emo twins, you loser!" He chuckles, but before he can gloat too much, I gather up dark energy behind him and ram it into his back. He topples over me, and I shove a foot into his sternum and kick him over myself, Simba style. My aim is true, and he crashes into the bookcase, bringing down my whole library over him, rewarding me with a sound groan. Not that I want to kill this guy. Not yet anyway. But he deserves what is coming to him.

"This is what is going to happen," I state clearly, as the pile of books starts moving, cascading off a now panting Callan. "Where you are now, besides in one of the finest book collections this side of the city, is between a rock and a hard place. Me being the rock, the council being the hard place. You choose."

Callan's shoulders sag, and he disappears. Really? He's willing to risk the council? I feel myself feeling sorry for him for about half a second, before I hear a crunch from behind me. "This requires snacks," Callan says from the same chair he started in, which is more or less the only thing still standing in the now messed up living room. He holds a bag of crisps, same brand I always have stashed in my kitchen cupboard. As he eats a crisp, I see his tattoo more clearly – a fox. The trickster. Fitting. I move towards him, but suddenly I am overwhelmed by a wave of dizziness, and I feel super tired. Halfway to the couch, I stumble into the wall next to the door and slide down the wall. Callan notices my bloody side. "Did I do that, bro?"

"What? No, just a scratch I got earlier."

"And it is still bleeding that much?"

"You know, me being such a weakling and all." I wink, a gesture that comes automatically despite us just having a brawl in my house. I try to get up, but the room is spinning so I sink back down. The side of my shirt is soaked in blood. Which shouldn't be possible from such a small cut.

"Nah, man. That ain't it. Cox gave you that, didn't he?"

I frown. "How did you know that?" I ask. He walks over and crouches beside me.

"Ain't it obvious by now? I mean, I am smarter than you, but damn, dude. You're the Fior and all."

"Whatever man, I am fine."

"Yup, you will be fine, until you won't be, 'cause the poison is keeping that wound from closing up and pulling more and more blood out. Except for that, you are golden. Kinda amazed you aren't dead yet, to be honest." He reaches for something inside his shirt and pulls out the chain he always has hanging around his neck. Still on it is the silver bullet. Yanking the chain from his neck, he holds the bullet in his hand.

"Cox, he... he gave me this, in case something went wrong during training when I was younger." Holding up the bullet, he twists off the top of it and pulls out a small vial with a black liquid inside.

"So, I'm just supposed to trust you now? Think I'll take my chance with the healers, thanks." I manage to get to my feet, walking away from Callan, still crouching on the ground.

"They can't heal it, you moron. It is Dark Poison, from an Eilne. It will incapacitate people like me, but it will kill Fiors.

Without the antidote, you will eventually die. It is how... how Jared..."

Touching my injured side, I wince. It isn't like it has been bothering me, just a small cut. Inconveniently bloodying my shirt, but other than that... "Sorry, Callan, I just can't trust you." Which really sucks, especially if he is telling the truth. But after all that has happened...

"Look, I understand. I would not trust me either. I never meant to or intentionally betrayed you..." I roll my eyes as loudly as I can.

"I am trying to apologise here. Would you just stop being such a righteous dumbass?"

I spin back around and step right up in Callan's face, a threat that is heavily undermined by me struggling to stay on my feet. "We wouldn't be in this situation if you hadn't been Cox's lackey, spying on and sabotaging us!" Callan looks hurt.

"I didn't... What do you know? You never even had a parent to lose!" I take a step back, feeling like he punched me in the gut. Callan's shoulders drop.

"Sorry, low blow. I didn't mean it like..."

"No, you are right. But at least I do not go around stabbing my friends in the back because my daddy told me to." The room is spinning again, and everything gets a little fuzzier, before I can focus again on Callan's angry features.

"You have no idea what he did to me, or what he is capable of. I have tried telling you... I don't even know why I bothered trying. It is like arguing with a teenage brat."

I am about to give him a bratty comeback, but before I can I lose my balance and fall sideways. Just as I am about to hit the ground, I am saved by Callan's lightning reflexes, and he drags me over to the wall again. I shut my eyes, willing the room to stop moving and my breaths come in quick, raspy succession.

"You see? You need to trust me, Shady. Please! I will not

stand by and let you die." Before I can argue, his hand is on my face, forcing my mouth open, and a cold liquid is poured down my throat. I try to spit, but Callan's hand is clamped over mine, which I am too weak to remove. When he is sure I have swallowed, he backs away, with me left coughing and cursing.

"Damn it! Would you just…" But before I can finish, I feel a warm sensation in my side, and as I lift up my shirt, the wound is closing before my eyes.

"Told you it would work."

"Aren't you the gift that keeps on giving? No gloating needed, thanks."

I eye him daringly, but he saunters over and helps me up.

"This doesn't mean I trust you," I mumble.

"I know, Shady, I know."

We sit in my living room, and Callan tells me everything. Well, not everything. I notice him pausing now and then, almost like words are escaping him. But it is okay. At least I got him talking, making a mental note to double check the information somehow later. He is always to the point, no fuss, and gives me the facts. The target for the last Great Battle was information, to gather it and destroy it. He doesn't know why; it was need-to-know. What is more interesting however is his information on Cox. He is an Eilne, but was found when he was young, and taken care of in Eader by a local family. None other than Decipiér's family. Meaning they are kind of brothers.

"Well, they are equally as charming," I say dryly, not even bothering to feign surprise. I knew there was something up with that guy. "What is his plan now?"

At this, Callan looks away. "I should've come to you sooner. I was a coward." Looking into the wall, he takes a deep breath. "It all changed when you came back, bro. I mean…" He turns to look at me, and he looks pleadingly at me. "Please, forgive me, Grey. I promise to help you make this right. Cox, Dad, he made sure Lay couldn't read my mind, while he… gave me this mission to keep an eye on you and…" He stops, a pained expression on his face and stops talking.

This is a no-brainer for me. Where would the world be without second chances, and I have never been good at holding grudges. When it boils down to it, it isn't Callan's fault anyway. It is all Cox. And now, it seems, he has lost his spy. Or at least, I am willing to play along with Callan for now. He is not off the hook, and it will take time for all this to be sorted out. And I know I will just have to assume everything I say will find its way to Cox.

When Callan doesn't say anything else I take a deep breath. "I'll think about it, and Darby needs to be looped in as well," I say, pounding his back and getting up. The relief is palpable and rolls off Callan in waves. We have both been through tough childhoods, him with Cox, me on the streets. I don't know which is worse. What matters is that we got through it. Suddenly, with a pang, I remember something. Callan pleading with me to not tell Cox where he is hiding. We had done something wrong, stolen something? I don't remember. But I had ratted him out and Cox had punished him. That was right before the Great Battle. The last time I saw him. Damn.

"Bro. I am sorry for not having your back way back then."

Callan gets up. Smiling. "All forgiven. Now, we need to get going. We don't have much time to get our defences ready. They are coming."

Chapter 29

Grey

First of all, let's just start with how much I absolutely hate bureaucracy. Two people can get so much more done without all the red tape and egos involved. But alas, I have gathered the council, minus Darby, who is M.I.A. again. We are gathered in the Castle, in a round meeting room, and Bob, Bethany, Ryder, Thiam and Decipiér are sitting at the top of a round table. Also in attendance is Ren, the supervisor from the Academy, and Haines from my class who is an excellent strategist. As we are in the midst of a crisis and have a looming deadline, needless to say, we are focusing on anything but. Right now, they are focusing on how audacious it is that I of all people have the nerve to gather the council. Callan is lurking in the back, looking like he is ready to bolt. I wink at him, and he shrugs.

"You all have to chill out, and listen to me right now." I hold my hands up, trying to calm them down as they talk over each other, Ryder and Thiam saying they should hear me out, while Bethany and Decipiér say they have better things to do. Bob is just sitting there smiling. I like Bob.

"Excuse me, son," Bethany starts, "you need to take a step back and let us handle this." Getting real tired of people calling me that. Even though some of these people are way older than really possible.

"With all due respect, ma'am, handle what? Bickering

amongst yourselves when I have important information that might, you know, *save* Eader? By all means, carry on. We can all just leave you to it until Cox comes knocking." I stride over to Callan and start dragging him out the door.

"Grey, hold up. No need for the theatrics. Tell us what you have found out. We will *all* listen." It is Ryder who has gotten up and is now staring sternly at the members of the council, who grudgingly nod.

After I finish telling them about my findings on Earth and my encounter with Cox, Callan is halfway through his story, leaving out the more damning information, while the council is staring at us both, speechless. As Callan draws breath to explain about the imminent attack, he gives a perfect opening for Darby and Lay to come storming in.

"Sorry we are late! What did we…?" Her voice dies out as she sees the shocked looks on everyone's faces.

"Impeccable timing, girls. Please take a seat." My commanding tone mixed with the tension in the room is enough to stop them both from arguing and make them go to sit next to Haines and Ren by the door, Darby with her eyebrow raised. I gesture for Callan to continue.

"Yeah, so, as I was saying," he stumbles through the words, "Cox and his minions will do anything to get to Grey. To prevent him and us from saving the Eader. They will attack at dusk. Tonight."

Again, you could probably hear a quark fall in here. Everyone looks stunned, me included, even though I already know how deep the shitpool we are currently swimming in is. I clap my hands, making everyone jump.

"Yes, do you get it now? Time is over for waiting and seeing. For planning and scouting. We need to act. Now."

When no one speaks up, I start to get angry. Do they need a flowchart? Seriously. "Calm down, Grey," Lay pipes up from the corner. "They all get it. More than you know." I glance back at her, and she smiles sadly. Beside her Darby shakes her head as if popping out of a trance.

"Right. Thanks guys, for that dazzling presentation. What we need now is a fix." She strides up to the tables, putting both her palms on the table. "Just so happens, I have an idea…"

"Seriously, Darby, can we just get the information without the drama?"

She turns slowly towards me. "'Seriously,'" she says mockingly, "can I get you without the nerdiness? No, and still I endure. Now, where was I?"

I stick my tongue out at her, making Lay giggle, but Darby ignores us. "The reason for my tardiness is that I have been concocting a little, shall we say, 'welcome present', to our gate crashers. But I am getting ahead of myself. First of all, I resign as General."

The stunned silence that follows is trailed by shouts of utter disbelief, but no explanation is given.

"All in due time. I will be busy with this plan, and more, so as my last act, I appoint Daryuen as my successor, and Haines as his first lieutenant."

No one interjects this time, though as Daryuen is not here, the only one to accept is Haines. All he can do is make an inaudible response with a dumbfounded expression. The rest of us just want to hear what is going on.

"Okay, I got the idea from Grey and his Emo-Attack which rattled Cox." I arch an eyebrow and Darby grins at me, before continuing. "He infused an energy attack with emotions, the kind the enemy is not used to handling, which gave him the chance to escape. What I suggest is to…"

"Oh! I say we serve them up some real *The Notebook* head-trips, or…"

"Grey…"

"But what about just a little PMS…"

"Grey, no."

I see her smile though and I feel a little part of me flutter, forgetting all the heavy, horrible hate creating turmoil in my inners. It is like a small world inside a world fighting for survival. For now, it holds its ground. "Anyway, if there are no more helpful suggestions… Good. So, me and Lay have been working on this for all of two hours, so it is a bit crude, but it should do the job." She picks up her Beacon and puts it on. "Now, brace yourself." She looks around the room, closes her eyes and pushes the Beacon. At first nothing happens. That is, she doesn't Shift. After about three seconds however, a wave of anger, bitterness, and sadness washes over me. I shake my head, and let it seep in, embracing it. Looking over at Callan, he has more or less the same reaction. The rest of the room has a more severe response. Some are crying, while others are grabbing their heads, and some are just hugging themselves. I must admit it is fun seeing Decipiér in the foetal position on the floor. After a few more seconds, people start regaining control. "For us it gives around ten to fifteen seconds of disorientation, for our friends of Darkness… Well, even Cox can't withstand it."

Darby beams at the council, clearly proud. Ryder clears his throat, still wiping away a few tears. "No doubt it will make an impact, but what about the impacts on our Guardians? Will it not also affect us?"

"Ah, I am glad you asked. I have a plan for a protective shield built into the Beacon, to help with that. And also, the

Shifting capabilities are maintained." She holds up the Beacon showing the extra button implanted. "Just be careful of which one you use."

Ryder nods, as does the rest of the council. Well, except Decipiér. "Are we just going to ignore the obvious infractions done by Darby and Callan?" It is Decipiér who now feels he hasn't heard his own voice in far too long, as that can be the only reason for him to interrupt now. Though I must say it is almost weird not being the only wrongdoer for once. "Conspiring with the enemy and tampering with the Beacon. They need to be punished."

"This is not the time, Decipiér," Darby grumbles. "It is more like the time for you to pick your battles, and there are quite a few to choose from. So sit back down. Or maybe we should rather talk about your affiliation to Cox, and how you have failed to mention this earlier?" At this, I get a high pitch squeak, and a certain pair of black wings turning not so glossy.

The rest of the room gives me appreciative nods and smiles, along with a few confused frowns, and Darby steps up to me.

"We are planning the defence of Eader, which is good, but how do we save the Eader? From what you told me, Grey, it sounded like you meant we are in between. I know something was up the last time I Shifted. You mean…"

"Yes, seems like there are more than two layers, at least three." I turn to Ryder, who must know something. He clears his throat again.

"We know very little of the plain of Darkness, or as it is named, Dorchadas. What we do know is that Darkness breeds Darkness, as it is all part of the same substance and all connected. They are trying to find each other – say opposites attract, well… not true for light and dark… as more dark energy fills Earth, the bigger the draw is for the Darkness. To sum it up, it looks like we will be overrun here in Eader, if I am reading the signs right."

"Why didn't you say anything about this earlier?" Darby demands, but I feel like I know the answer.

"My dear," Ryder starts wistfully, "we didn't have all the pieces until now, only clues from the remnants of our history. These secrets were once well guarded as the dearest treasures, in our archives and libraries, which were so brutally erased by fire. The signs were subtle. The shorter and colder days, the dimming of the Eader, the increase in attacks. We are unable to learn from our history as we have lost it, and may now be condemned to repeat it. I should have seen the signs earlier. I am sorry." Ryder looks ready to cry again.

Darby sighs. "No, I am sorry. This is by no means your fault."

The silence drags on, everyone lost in thought, or memory more likely. I don't want to trespass onto people's memory lane, but we don't have time for this. "To sum up," I start, and no one argues. "Basically there is now too much evil on Earth – and the effects are that the Eader can't withstand the pressure any longer. The barrier is crumbling, and it is only making people feel less hope. With no support, the humans are giving up, and are looking for ways to disconnect, kind of jacking into the Matrix. Using video games, playing out the death tolls that are actually happening in real life. Hiding behind screens and online profiles. Feeling like you are accomplishing something, but nobody will care about the level of your video game or how many likes you have when you don't…"

"Grey."

"Oh sorry. Went rogue there for a bit. My bad."

Callan nods.

"Anyway, the Eader is weakening, too much pressure – too much stupidity, darkness, ignorance, passiveness, carelessness…"

"Grey," Darby interrupts.

"Yeah, the Eader is crumbling, both physically and mentally, and it needs help. Meaning, we need to stop Cox, and also strengthen the Eader or alleviate the pressure. As it isn't that easy to cure idiocy…"

"Grey!"

"What? I am being serious. We can't stop the flow of darkness, at least not right now. We need to boost the Eader. But first we need to stop Cox."

I don't expect people to rush to volunteer to fight impossible odds. But I do however hope for more than what I get. A few nods, non-committal shrugs and examining of fingernails.

"People, we cannot wait. We need to act now. I suggest we take the fight to them. Surprise them. They will never see it coming. I assume they have a base of operation? A hold up? A lair?" I have clearly overestimated my audience. "I mean, somewhere we can strike to weaken them?" More blank stares. Sighing, I take a step closer, meeting each of their gazes. "Where can we go to hit *them* before they attack *us*?"

"Grey, we can't do that." It is Bob who has now decided to leave his nails and join the conversation. Oh, Bob. I used to like him. "We do not have enough people to defend Eader and attack Dorchadas. It would be suicide. We have no intelligence on the targets or escape routes, as you could hear from Ryder, we know very little about where the Darkness reside. It would be a better strategy to have the best defences here and pick them off as they come through."

Haines is nodding in agreement. I must say, it makes sense.

Even Luke had the plans to the Death Star before being able to destroy it. I nod and go to sit down next to Lay by the door. But before I do, I turn and address the council.

"We…" I hesitate for a second before I try again. "I mean, we won't be able to do anything if we let fear overwhelm us, fear is the hindrance of action. The solution is to act first, then worry about being afraid. If fear leads to inaction, then your light will not be allowed to spread. My… a friend used to tell me this when I was younger. Thought it was fitting." I go to sit down and feel all eyes in the room follow me to my seat.

Then, the most unlikely of things happens. "You are right, Grey." It is the day for impossibilities, as it is Decipiér who speaks up. He stands up and walks around the table and leans against it, looking at me. "It is time we act and act we will. I have been a pain in the ass, and I am sorry." Lay giggles. "It has always been a burden having grown up with Cox, treating him like a brother and to have him betray us all. It is easy to become a little cranky. I apologise, I shouldn't have let my bitterness affect you. It is just…" he pauses and rubs his eyes. "Your twilight powers scared me. Both how they might impact us, but also you. Too much of anything will kill you, and I did not know how so much power would treat you, which side you would identify with. And that more than anything made me treat you with caution. We did not realise Cox was an Eilne, not before it was too late." Decipiér's voice sounded melancholic uttering Cox's name, not angry. If he only knew. I don't know what to say, but I nod to him once and he seems to relax a little, then returns to his seat. "Still doesn't mean I like you," he states as he sits down.

"Yeah, you are also, shall we say, an acquired taste?"

Decipiér scowls. "Is that that sarcasm again?"

"Me? Sarcastic? Never! We are having a love fest right here;

I would never mess with that!"

He frowns, and nods. Lay stifles a laugh and Callan rolls his eyes.

Suddenly the door opens again, and Daryuen enters. "Sorry for the intrusion, I was just briefed on an attack and needed to report to…"

"Ah, perfect timing, Daryuen. Please take a seat at the table. No need to brief anyone, you are General now," Darby says smoothly, gesturing for Daryuen to sit down at her regular seat. If this surprises Daryuen, it doesn't show. He walks over to the table and sits. Darby quickly brings him up to speed, and Daryuen then tells the council about a demon attack at the edge of Manawa. A young Guardian girl, a combat fairy, was jumped.

"Sawyer?" I say, forgetting my place. As I often do.

Daryuen nods. "She fought it off and sent it packing, but sustained several injuries. They are getting bolder."

Poor Sawyer. That shy little girl I had met on my first day at the Academy. But hey, she fought off a demon by herself.

As the meeting draws to an end, the strategy is taking shape. Lay is in charge of the aerial troops, setting up a perimeter with darts and Dust. These darts will have a fiercer bite than the one I encountered earlier. Daryuen is in charge of the Guardians, with teams of scouts and setting up the ground troops, with the help of Haines. I will work with Darby and Ryder to fit the Beacons with shield and the Emo-Button, plus helping Daryuen teach the troops how to operate it. Just as we are about to adjourn, Haines clears his throat from his seat on the opposite side of the door from me.

"What about Callan? He is after all a spy, and should be treated as such." Callan shrinks a bit in his seat, and the council looks uncertain.

At this I start a coughing fit. "Oh, sorry. Just choking a bit on your shocking unoriginality there, Hainsy. It is actually deeply disturbing; you should have that looked at."

Haines's face darkens to a lively shade of red, but I smile at him. Oh, yes, default setting is definitely on.

"Callan is not only our best fighter, but also our inside man when it comes to Cox and their plans. He stays."

I lock eyes with each person in the room and no one argues. Except Darby, of course.

"I agree with you, Grey. However…"

I roll my eyes at her.

"You vouch for him, so he will be your responsibility," she says with finality.

With only twelve hours to nightfall the meeting ends, and everyone runs to start their preparations.

I decide to get changed, as I am still wearing my now half-dry and still bloody clothes from my trip to Earth. On my way to the mansion I already see signs of battle arrangements happening. Everything working like a well-oiled machine. In teams, the bakers, blacksmiths, and medics alike. Everyone is stepping up. I hear steps behind me as I turn into the little avenue to the mansion. It's Darby.

"Hey! Wait up." She catches up and we walk together to the house. "You were great in there. Really pulled it all together."

I shrug and put my palm on the door, letting it pull me in. Darby pops in after me. As I start up the stairs, she puts her hand on my shoulder. A jet of energy fires up where she touches me and creates a little firework display. She jumps back, while I get busy with putting out the little fire on my shoulder.

"What was that?" I yell, but as I turn to look at her, she is crying.

"I... I am sorry. So sorry!" She sinks down on the lowest step and hides her face in her hands. With the fire put out, I decide to avoid starting a new one, and crouch down in front her at a safe distance.

"What is wrong?"

"Everything! It is all happening again."

"What is happening?" I reach for her, but she jerks away and walks over to the only room I haven't been in yet. Gently she touches the door, then opens it and disappears down the stairs inside. I follow her in silence, and we enter a small circular room with a tall ceiling and in the middle, a pyre, burning hot in dark blue flames, reminding me of the Flames at the Academy.

"We burned him here, my Jared." She says his name with such tenderness, I can't believe it is the same Darby I know who is speaking. "All Fiors are burned here, and thereby returned to the Eader, signalling the need for a new one. Though no new ones have come after..." She wipes her tears away. Anger having replaced the sorrow. "I will not lose any more friends. I will not send any more loved ones back to the Eader." She says it like it is a promise, and I believe her. The room feels sombre, almost like it is forgotten. The flames barely give off any light onto the wooden walls. As I turn to ask about the flames, I notice Darby has gone, and I follow her back to the foyer, thinking how this place seem to be bound by flames of birth, rebirth and death. I shiver.

"So, as we are preparing for the worst fight ever, any pointers? Is fighting the Darkness like in the bad Green Lantern reboot, with him fighting Parallax? Imagining weapons with his mind and so on?" It was a stupid thing to say, but I needed to cheer her up, and shake the chill from the trip to the basement.

"Sure, minus the artillery tanks and fighter jets. More energy bombs and hand-to-hand combat."

"And Emo-Attacks!" I chime in. She smiles, and we walk to our rooms to mentally prepare for what is coming.

First thing I do is to put on a good fight soundtrack, and only thing that comes to mind is Queen. After showering and changing into a pair of black jeans, black boots, and a long dark blue sweater, I go through the motions with my silver knuckles, striking an imaginary opponent in a shadow-boxing fight and I am only seeing one person – Cox. I lunge and strike Shadow-Cox through his chest, and just keep on going as he smiles at me. I knock him down again and again with my fists, sweat dripping down my face and in the end, I am struggling for breath. Would he be this hard to kill in real life? Of course he would. Pulling off my now sweaty sweater, I wish I had more power or at least had had time to learn more at the Academy. All I have managed to learn from basic magic at the Academy are small gravity tricks, small solid energy blocks, and shooting people with my wacked out feelings... much power, less discipline. There has been something bothering me for a while, as if there is something messing up my focus. But every time I approach the thought, it is as if everything else fills up my brain at the same time, burying it. I know there is something lurking in me, Cox had said as much. I need to figure out what it is and embrace it in time to win. It is all so frustrating. When I open my eyes, I am staring at a wet-haired Darby. Through the door. Which I just put my fist through.

"Make it as cheap as possible, would you?" she quips, then returns to her room. I pull back my fists, and the door patches itself up as I go. Neat. But seriously. Sitting down on the bed I start thinking. What if I can't do this? Somehow, I am the main event of this fight, and that is one role I have never liked.

Shouting, I roll out of bed and hit the floor. Damn! I must've fallen asleep. That was one freaky dream. Flashing lights in darkness, me balancing on the edge of a knife, cutting me as I started to lose balance, tipping between light and dark. How poetic. A knock on my door brings me to my senses and I run to the door, grabbing my silver knuckles, and pull on another blue sweater.

"I see you fixed it," Darby states nervously.

"You know me, handy-man." I try a smile, but fail. Together we walk downstairs, me in my already sweaty clothing, her in her leather fighting gear. Neither of us prepared. I stop, with my hand on the doorknob.

"Shit is about to hit the proverbial fan – you ready?"

"No, wait, don't sa—"

"Because I was born ready!"

"…You said it. Well, let's see you prove it, young padawan."

Darby purses her lips and I ball up my fists as we leave the Fior Mansion, neither of us knowing if we will return to our rooms or will be offered to the dark blue flames of Eader.

The night has come with a haunting whisper through the branches and a trembling cry echoes through the black blanket of night, muffling the sound. The first hour of darkness is upon us, and it is like the resolution of the world is turned down. A quiet before the storm, as if feeling the whole world inhale before the inevitable screaming exhale.

Chapter 30

Grey

It feels like I blink the world I know away, and when I open my eyes again, the world is on fire. We have just gotten to the camp and are amid preparing the troops when chaos erupts. From the shadows around the fire, dark creatures crawl out, ambushing the outer perimeter, sounding the alarm.

"Form ranks!" Darby yells, which rallies the Guardians and suddenly I am in the middle of the fray. There's no sounding of a horn to mark an attack. No war cry. No first move. It's just upon us all at once, turning the world into chaos, like a wave of action hitting us from all sides. As the Eader is so weak, there is no way to fortify a position, other than in Manawa and the Academy. We are the first wave, a wave that is now being evaporated by fire.

I am fighting shadows, literally, and they are hitting back. Using my silver knuckles infused with light or dark, I force them back, darkness exploding and dissolving around me. Callan is right next to me, a whirlwind scattering the creatures. I try to get a look at my opponents, the Majin and their lackeys, but they move in and out of focus. Despite being so intangible, they pack quite a punch, with claws and teeth to spare. I feel my chest burn and return the favour by blazing my way through the curling shade's chest, or at least what I think is his chest. No matter, it bursts into a thousand flakes of dark ash. We are starting to make headway, though I have no way of knowing the extent of the battle. Darby is keeping track of Manawa and the Academy, and she is nowhere to be seen. I work my way over to Callan, who is now knee-deep in ash and laughing.

"Maximum effort!" I nod to Callan and smile. He totally gets the joke. He winks. I lunge at him, and he dodges me as I go through a horde of what looks like singed and fuming creepy crawlies, giving them a hit of my emotional luggage. I turn back to Callan who is smirking at me.

"I've missed this."

"I don't think we've done this before."

At this he rolls his eyes dramatically. "No, funny guy. This. Us. Hanging out."

"Sure, me too, man."

"Aw, aren't you guys adorable! Well, you can get a room when we are done. Now get your bromancing asses back in the fight!" Darby thunders past, hunting down an enormous shadow troll, leaving Callan and me behind, gawking.

"She is certifiable," Callan states.

"Dude, did she just have that troll on the run?" We both shake our heads, pretty impressed. It isn't hard to understand why the troll was running; Darby is the size of a small skyscraper, and with her black helmet and silver sword she looks worthy of a seat in Valhalla.

After what seems like an eternity, a silence settles around me. The clearing is now, well, cleared, and I move into the forest. Not my favourite of places with my track record, but the Dust is helping, lighting up and peppering the shadows all around. The darkness is still thick around me, and I can feel the enemy creeping. I can't understand the endgame of this fight. Where is Cox and what does he want?

Behind me I hear Darby return, the sound of her steps

lessening, and when I see her, she is her normal size again.

"Guardians, assemble," she yells, drawing the fighters to her. I have to stifle a laugh. Darby raises an eyebrow, but turns to her warriors. "Good work; we have them on the retreat. Secure the perimeter and let's start a sweep. Fortify a safe zone between Manawa, the Academy and here." The Guardians nod, and get to it. Then a thought hits me, and I start making my way towards the forest. If I am right... Darby is conferring with Callan on the injured and I see Thiam in the distance, healing as he goes. Not too many serious injuries which is a relief. As I fade into one of the shadows, my heart skips a beat. In the distance I see him, and I have a small fangasm. It is bloody demon Deadpool skipping towards me like only Deadpool can. Figures he would be on the darker side of things. It breaks my heart but as he twirls his swords at me, I send a light wave at him, disintegrating him mid-skip. Hopefully, he appreciates me thinking of unicorns to get some extra light put into the attack. But where have the rest of them gone?

I move towards my goal, being careful not to trip this time. Sounds of fighting can be heard in the distance, and the guilt of not helping gnaws at me. But if I am right, this is where I will be able to make the most difference.

"Nice try, nerd."

Crap.

"Hi, Lay." She lands in front of me, with a sour look on her face, fire in dancing in her eyes.

"Did you really think that was going to work again? Sneaking off like that?"

I roll my eyes, which she can't really see as I am standing with my back to her.

"Don't you roll your eyes at me, Fior."

"What? You can hear what I do now?" I turn around, smiling my best smile.

"Don't you change the subject. What are you up to?"

I sigh and tell her my suspicions. Nodding slowly as I talk, she starts to look convinced.

"You are right, there must be more to this. Fine, but I am…"

"No, you are not."

Looking slightly offended. "You're the mind reader now, are you?" She steps back, but before she can stop me I rush into it.

"This is for me to sort out, and it might not even be real. Please, Lay, you are needed in the battle, and you know it. I don't need you here." She winces at the harshness of my words. I am kind of surprised myself, but I feel that I am right. Colour drains out of her face, and she sighs heavily.

"Okay. I will leave you to it. But I will alert Darby to your stupidity." With that she flies off.

If she reads my mind before she leaves or not, I don't know. I hope not.

I turn around and walk the last hundred metres to the edge. Here it is quiet, almost too silent as if a muffler has been added to the fight going on around. A dead zone. Hopefully not too literal. I forge ahead and down into the gorge, a bit more gracefully this time. Lucky for me someone has fastened a rope at the top, which makes the descent much easier. The bottom is covered in darkness, with no Dust in sight. I would Shift down but I don't know what is awaiting me down there, if anything. Nearing the bottom, I let go of the rope and disappear into darkness. It is like it envelops me, like thick, black fog, and I stop.

I reach out with my senses, but the moment I do, I feel a flood coming at me. A flood of hurt, darkness, and pain, and I fly backwards, hitting a pile of rocks. My vision swims, or is it the black mist around me, as I see the shadows shifting.

"Yer in quite th' quagmire here, laddie." He steps out right in front of me, sharply dressed as always, glaring at me. I get to my feet and run at him, fists raised. As I hit him, he parries my strike easily with a swift sidestep, only using his hand. I scream in frustration and come at him again, but with the same result. I stumble to a halt, shaking my head. He's so fast; I hadn't even seen him move. It's like he's even more powerful than the last time I met him.

"Give it up, Grey, there is nae more ye can dae. She is almost dead."

"Who is dead? What do you mean?" My voice sounds fragile at best, and I stumble. Not Darby. I go through the whole nine yards of scenarios of how I would kill this guy.

"'Twas never a question of ye beating me, son. Ye could have joined me, but ye are nae worthy, as the moment ye reached the bottom of stupid ye were mine!" He laughs his scratchy, hollow laugh and I shiver.

"Never say never, old man," I croak, not making much impact. Instead of thinking of a better comeback, I run at him, but this time Cox is not having it. He waves his hand and the mist around me thickens into dark ropes which trap me and tighten as I struggle to get out.

"Cheers fur saving me the trouble of getting ye here. Ye just sped up yer dear Eader's demise."

I stop struggling. "So Darby is okay?"

"Who the hell cares aboot Darby or anybody else. This was never aboot them. It's aboot ye and me, finishing what we started. Now, beg for me, if ye would."

I squirm in my dark prison, but to no avail. Cox holds up his hand against my chest and pushes against me. Then stops.

"Hauld yer horses. What is this? Ah sense a chaynge in ye, son. Is that hope? Love?"

He shakes his head. I keep following him with my eyes, as he is all I can make out in this swirly obsidian mist.

"My good-for-nothing son used his bullet oan ye, but at least that left me tae finish ye off myself. Just like ah did yer Lizzie."

"Don't you talk about her, you bastard!"

I strain and try to wiggle out my hands, but they are not budging.

"Ah, thare it's, the anger, the pain! Aye!"

Before I can think I feel that same cold all over again, but it is not draining this time, it is more like filling me up, no, passing through me.

"Aye, laddie, that is it." Looking up I see a funnel of the black fog forming right over me and a black jet of shadow shooting up. "She will nae have enough power tae fight this. It's over."

"What the hell are you talking about?" I am actually getting annoyed now.

"Well, ye see, with yer powers mine are amplified, and will cut this battle short. Sae thank ye fur that."

"The hell you will!" I hear Darby shout and a blast of Dust hits Cox in the chest.

"That one is for Lizzie, Coxie!" Lay yells.

I am freed from my bonds as Cox is distracted and I hit the ground running, punching Cox as he tries to get up. Holding my powered-up silver knuckles against Cox's throat, I glare at him.

"I can, and am required to tell you to *fuck* off."

I don't recognise my own voice, with all the menace and gravel fed by my hate and pain. Cox looks wildly around and tries to get up.

"Yer minions?" I mock, staring daggers into the asshole on the ground. "They are dead and spread all over the place, good luck with finding back up. It's over."

"Grey, wait."

I hear steps behind me and Cox smiles cruelly.

"My friend here is questioning my actions, two seconds!"

I turn to see Lay, Callan, and Darby standing there, arms crossed, posing like a judgy new age modelling crew.

But before they can lay down their judgement, Darby gasps.

"No, Darby," Lay interrupts, "he is messing with you!"

I turn back and see I am no longer holding Cox, but someone with a sandy blonde mane, boyishly blue-green eyes, and a crooked smile. His clothes are those of a Guardian, green and all fit with silver details, with a large sword at his hips.

"Jared…"

I feel a hand on my shoulder.

"Grey, don't…"

I turn around and the pain on Darby's face is evident. This is the guy. Using the distraction and my loosened grip, Cox shoves me off into Darby and jumps up, back to his old self.

"Tae easy, lassie. Shouldn't let yer guard down like that. Aye, Jared's essence has bin handy tae have in mah arsenal."

He holds his hands up before Darby can run at him.

"You are the vilest creature…!" Darby starts, but chokes on her words through her tears.

"Ah, refreshingly honest feedback, nae easy tae come by, indeed."

We all move towards Cox, but a wall of darkness pushes my friends back, blocking my view of them. I whip around to Cox, trying to reach him, but he only laughs.

"Aye, it's ye and me again laddie."

As if on cue, I hear faint shouts from behind the shadow wall.

"Oh, they can't help ye now. Just look." He opens a small window in the wall, and I see them there, sprawled on the ground, choking on the dark mist.

"Stop it! What are you doing to them?" I try yet again to get to him, but he waves his hand, and the dark strands of mist are once again holding me in their clutch.

"All ye need tae do is surrender tae me, Grey. I am nae interested in these creatures…" I glance through the small opening again, as it closes. Darby on the ground, gasping. Lay unmoving.

"Fine! But I have a counterproposal."

"What dae ye have tae offer me, puny Fior?"

"Wow, how original, old man. *Sure* you think you have won this. Why wouldn't you? But you are wrong." I try wiggling, but nowhere to go this time.

Cox laughs. "How are ye sae intolerably arrogant? This is yer and yer world's demise we are talking aboot." He laughs, and as if to underline this he tightens my restraints.

"Whatever man, that is what you think."

"Oh aye? Where is yer buddy Callan, huh? Ah remember him sae well. Have ye seen his back? Some of mah best work."

I ball my fists, shaking. "I will win every time, as it all depends on what you are fighting for. So you listen here," I growl at Cox. And move on to whisper my terms to which Cox quickly agrees. The fog dissipates, leaving me standing alone in the clearing. Darby comes running at me, looking no worse for wear.

"What happened, we couldn't break through the wall, you dumbass! Why do you always have to be such a…?" Darby stops herself, punctuating her rant by smacking me on the head.

"Wait... you are okay?"

"Of course we are!"

When they look at me, I feel naked. "I... I thought..." My stuttering comes out all feeble, but Lay cuts me off.

"Yes, yes, yes, we know, you are sorry, we are angry, this is getting old. No time for any more blah blah blah." She puts her hands on her hips, looking defiant. We all look shocked. Nice Lay, all bossy and annoyed.

I think about my deal with Cox and look at the two girls in front of me. "Lay is right. We need to end this." As if to prove my point, I send out a light burst, clearing the darkness.

Darby smiles. "Well aren't you just the light in the centre of this tornado of darkness? I am in, let's do this, for humans and Eadorians alike." I roll my eyes, but nod, as Lay whoops, and flies ahead.

Chapter 31

Darby

Well, this is great. Cox is gone, and we are no closer to solving this. I survey the camp, where the amount of injured is staggering. Thiam looks exhausted as he runs between the cots scattered around the fire, healing the worst injuries, ensuring people aren't bleeding to death. Note to self – we really need more healers.

The whole thing was weird. One moment we are fighting the dark minions at every turn, even Cox came out of hiding, then this. Nothing. Quiet. It is like they decided to go for lunch mid-battle. Grey seems to be none the wiser as well, though I feel like something happened when he was captured by Cox. The whole explanation of him fighting him off, making Cox retreat, sounds a little too good to be true. Like having an interlude in a horror movie. I take a page out of Grey's book and roll my eyes. I need to take it for what it is, a breather. Walking towards my tent I make my way between the cots spread out everywhere, smiling to the Guardians. My Guardians. I round the corner and escape into the safety of my tent. Looking around, I half expect Cox to jump out at me from under my desk. My nerves are frayed – I would seriously punch a butterfly if it snuck up on me right now. And on that note, Grey crashes into the room.

"There you are, great, we need to talk, you busy?" he rambles, and seats himself on the edge of my cot.

"Hi to you too, Grey. You all right?" He blows raspberries derisively, and nods as he goes, seeming flustered. Walking up to him I sit down opposite him on my desk. I grab his hand, which is now shaking in mine. He looks so vulnerable. Suddenly his eyes harden, and he jerks his hand back.

"I was just checking if everything is ready. You know, for the second wave?"

I frown. "Yes, or, we are as prepared as we can be, still don't know what Cox wants, other than to keep fighting us. Have you…?"

He jumps up, edging towards the tent entrance. "Good. That is good." He doesn't look at me, and it is pissing me off. Before I can say anything however, he pushes his way through the tent flaps and walks off.

"Hey! Nerd! I wasn't done with you."

When I get outside, he is already at the edge of the clearing, but he waits for me.

"What is your problem? We have planning to do! Get back to my tent, now!"

Grey turns around and winks at me, with his annoying crooked smile. "I am afraid that I cannot, even though your invitation to join you in your quarters is quite enticing, madam."

I roll my eyes. "Oh yeah? Well, I happen to know that you have to get your puny ass over here before I make you!"

"Ah. You make a convincing argument there, and I could heed your warning to avoid the consequences you so eloquently put forward, but I do not have to. Didn't you know, Darby, there is only one thing in life you absolutely have to do, and that isn't it." The amused light in his eyes flickers and dies. What is he talking about? Grey turns back around and walks halfway around the nearest tree trunk, stepping into the shadow it casts on the

279

ground. I take a step towards him, but it is too late. "Don't worry about me, Darby, I'll be fine. I'm Deadpool, remember?" His image flickers in the shadows of the large tree trunks and he is gone.

Crap. Why did he do that? Did he just use my name? "Grey! Get your ass back here or I swear…" Nothing. Not that I am surprised at all. This is all my fault. Damn it! I pushed him to this. Should have just locked him in the mansion forever. Okay, maybe not. I jog back to the fire pit, searching for Lay. Shouting out in my mind I soon see her, floating down, followed by a murder of Dust.

"You rang?"

"Have you seen Grey? He was just here, acting all dumb and mysterious."

She shakes her head, touching down on top of the nearest log. "He did seem weird after the ravine though. Couldn't read his mind, too much interference. What are you thinking?"

I start pacing in circles, surveying the injured, the fire, the forest and then Lay. "Lay, crap. You don't think…"

"No, he wouldn't have. Wait, yes, he would. Crap. You're right!"

"Yes, that martyring nitwit." I'm running out of things to call that boy. But before I can do anything I hear the last thing I need right now, a war cry.

They come from every angle, and the injured are sitting ducks.

"The hell you will," I shout as I grow ten feet and start running in circles around the clearing, stomping, and swinging my sword as I go. Lay follows suit, blasting out with her Dusties, chasing them off. How dare they? Have they no honour? Of course they don't. The Dust does its job and holds the perimeter as I storm off into the forest, cutting them down as I go. I hear her before I see her, growling as she goes. "Lika!" She bounds in from the shadows crushing the shadow demon coming up behind me.

"Couldn't let you have all the fun. Riley is coming too!" I laugh as I slice down two creepy ass twin shadow girls holding hands and run into the fray. Grey or no Grey, I have a job to do.

Chapter 32

Grey

The distraction is working like Cox planned it, it is unmissable. That he hit so close to the camp was not part of the plan, but it is too late now. Darby and Lay are probably all over it. Callan, however, I have not seen since the ravine and I lost him in the fray. Most likely pissed he is missing all the fun. Speaking of fun, I am back in the ravine, again.

"Took ye long enough, laddie. Ye had tae kiss yer wee lassie farewell now, did ye?" He chuckles, and it sounds like a cat's dying whine.

"Okay, I am here," I say as I touch down in the middle of the now dusky rock bowl, walking up to Cox. "Call off your attack and we can go."

Cox looks me up and down as I draw closer, smiling. "Ah don't know son, seems like this is going real well, mah minions are havin' sae much fun. Wouldn't wantae take that from them."

Don't get me wrong, it isn't like I am surprised, but still confused. One piece of the puzzle is still missing. "Tell me, why the hell would you go through all the trouble… Or no. I do not really care, man. You are a sorry ass old man, and ain't nobody got time for this." I whip out my silver knuckles and draw energy from my surroundings. As I do, I get an overload of dark energy, coming from Cox.

"Oh no ye do nae!" It all goes dark, and I feel the energy

coming at me before I know what it is.

The darkness flashes off his sword as it comes down towards me in a wide arc. It barely nicks me, but where it does, it feels like a terrorist attack on my body – the first initial hello, like I just got shot full of bullets poisoned with Darkness. But then there is the internal recoil. More or less like searing hot barbed wire is running through every vein in my body with three-inch spikes. All I can think is that I never got to tell Darby... How I still owe Callan a broken nose or a kick in the nuts, and how I still have all those TV shows to finish. All valid reasons to not croak right now. I am panting and sink to the ground, hugging myself.

"There 'tis, give up, Grey, and give in. Ah have enjoyed following yer metamorphosis, but ye know ah am right. Ye will lose and ah will have what's mine." He reaches out to me, as I feel the cold creeping in like water in a sponge, and suddenly I am right back where I started. But at the same time I am not, something has changed, and I feel it click into place inside of me.

"You might be right. The Grey that once was might have lost. Unfortunately for you however, there is a new monster in town." I duck under his hand and roll to the side, coming up next to the dead tree I so gracefully met last time. Bracing myself, I do as Cox suggested. I give in. Which is usually tragically easy. This isn't one of those times. It feels like running through a wall of molten lava. The wall set up between light and dark, always keeping me on the side of light but allowing me to tap into darkness. I tear it down and feel something ripping through me, stripping me of myself. I hear someone screaming and realise it is me.

"What did ye dae? Yer eyes!" Cox demands. The Eilne sounds uncertain, almost scared. The power surging through me feels unbelievable – it is intoxicating and drowning me at the same time. Light and dark are rippling through my body, clashing, fighting. Taking a deep breath, I struggle to my feet.

"I did exactly what you tried to do, old man. Only difference is that I did it on my own terms." A shudder runs through me, and I double over, as the war inside my body gets harder to contain.

"Yer a wee scunner and a fool! Ye will have tae surrender tae the darkness, Grey, it always wins. Meaning, ye just lost."

I straighten up, glaring at him.

Too much talk. I close my eyes and focus on the magic battle raging inside me. The darkness is trying to extinguish the light, and the light is trying to chase away the darkness. It is a no-win scenario, just as Cox said. Something will have to give – so I concentrate on them calming down. I feel the wind whipping up around me, like a tornado of light and dark. Darby had been right there. Trying to meld them together – making an emulsion of twilight, like yin and yang. Never been much of a meditator, but feel like this just makes sense. Feeling like time just slowed down, Cox seems miles away. I sense it, the balance. Everything will have its counterpoint, but sometimes fusing them together just makes something new and magical. Salt and sweet, fire and water, black and white. You cannot have light without dark. I feel the forces resisting, but I put all my willpower into it, envisioning the dusk, grey areas of life, thinking of me. Seriously, it seems like I've been fighting this battle forever, between who I was and who I thought I should be. I am just me, Grey, and suddenly it all falls into place. I see it, the Eader, the three Shields coming into one, working in unison, between all that is. It has no direction, yet it is perfectly placed. It has no start or end, yet it is perfectly timed. Opening my eyes, Cox is staring at me in utter disbelief.

"How did you…? That should nae be possible!" I look down

at my hands and see swirling clouds of energy. Not purple dark ones, not golden light ones, but a blue-greyish colour.

"Didn't you know you can't destroy energy, light or dark?" I ball up my fists, thrust my chin out and say, "Bring it on, asshole."

"Okay now son, let's nae make this harder than it needs tae be." Sounding uncertain, Cox is circling me in the gloom, keeping his distance.

"No please, let's." I hold my ground, and wait.

"The twilight warrior ay? How utterly quaint."

I can feel him stalling, biding his time.

"Ye have tae know how entertaining this has been for me. Watchin' ye searching fur answers. Must be terribly frustrating bein' kept in the dark, pardon the pun, nae knowing what's going on or how come 'tis happening." He stops circling and stares at me.

"Why don't you enlighten me then, pardon the pun."

"Nae, ah am just nae that kind of body, sorry, laddie." He seems hesitant, almost reluctant to engage. Eyes shifting from side to side as he sidesteps over the rocky ground.

"That is quaint. You thinking you are a person." I fire up my knuckles and lay it on him. Which nothing could prepare me for. It seems like time slows down and I have no problem connecting with his face. He looks as surprised as I feel and flies back, hitting the side of the ravine. Shaking his head, he gets up, no humour left on his features.

"Ye don't know how right ye are, Grey," he growls, as he starts to change. He morphs into a shadowy beast, with no distinct shape, more like a shifting mist of darkness, only recognisable by his eyes.

"Oh, look at you! Who is a pretty little cloud?" I tease, and

285

he attacks. But I am ready for him. Gathering up energy around me, I feel the temperature sink, the remaining light flickering. He lunges at me, like a barrelling thunder cloud, and I focus all my newly found emulsion powers on him, his essence and being. Just as he is within reach, I hit him with all I've got, which is good, because so does he. He slams me to the ground, a cold laugh echoing over the wind whipping up around us. Then it sounds like the laugh chokes on something, most likely my fist which is thrust through its master's chest, where the light is now spreading, multiplying, and killing off the dark tufts that is Cox. As a last attempt, he raises his hand and bears down on me but instead of hitting me, he disappears in a whirlwind of black light. I jump up, feeling the temperature returning, my hands still shaking. I whip around as I can hear coughing behind me.

"How did ye do that?" Cox is lying on the ground, pin stripe suit in tatters, hair in disarray. The most alarming part is however his face, which looks to be shrivelling up. "Aye, look all ye want. This is what happens when the dark gets overcome by light."

He dazedly struggles to sit himself up, but can't, which only makes him look more pathetic.

Creakingly he starts laughing. "Now who would've thought that we would end up here, ay? Ye stopping mah misanthropic mission. And 'twas sae easy tae, pushing the folk towards the edge. Their wee bomb weapons, terrorists, starting global warming, bureaucracy. It's like they wantae end themselves. Almost had 'em in the cold war, and now with that oaf as president, it would've bin sae easy. Bit 'ere ye are... weel, na maiter, the domino effect has started, the sources will die and the balance reset..."

"Whoa, whoa, whoa... Let me just stop you there, man."

Cox rambles, coughing, and it looks like he is shrivelling.

"This isn't going tae be bonny, ye wee fool. Only shame is that ah won't be around tae see it. She is almost gone, and then there is nothing ye can do tae stop the last one from failin'. Ye are tae late."

"What do you mean? Who is dying?" I am bending down, shaking his torn suit, but all I get his hoarse laughter.

"Who would have thought, the bairn born from the two sources, from twilight, would be the one tae end me, ah should be honoured ah think…"

And with that he disperses into the gloom – like he was never there. As I crouch down, still holding his pinstripes, I see wafts of light melting away into nothing. More confused and tired than ever, I Shift to the only person who can help make sense of this. Lucky for me, I dexterously Shift into her lap at the fire pit, tipping her and her coffee onto her back.

"You got three seconds to get off me or I'll send you flying." She snarls and without further ado, sends me flying. Not cool.

As I get up, brushing off my ripped and yet again bloody clothes, she comes stomping towards me, ready to pound me no doubt. Before she can, I grab her and hug her tight. She freezes and stands there, until I can feel her relaxing.

"Did you get him? Is he gone?" she whispers. I nod into her shoulder, and she hugs me back. Suddenly I feel how tired I am and how it just got really quiet. Looking up, I see everyone in the clearing staring from their cots and conversations, and in the flickers from the fire I see coffee. Ignoring everyone, I gently escape Darby's arms with a smile and make a beeline for the coffee pot next to the main fire. Darby follows and we sit down next to Lay, who has her broken wing in a sling after falling during the attack. According to Darby, Callan was last seen fighting over at Manawa, but no one has seen him in a while. I feel my heart sink, but try to stay focused. I have tried to narrow down his location using my emotional navigation system so to speak, but every time I try, I come up empty, and it is starting to freak me out.

"It's over." Lay sighs happily. She looks beaten up and strung out, but still she manages a smile. I really don't want to burst her bubble, but sadly I have to.

"No, it isn't. Far from it. But before we try and fix it, there is something we have to do."

Chapter 33

Grey

Leaves dance across the clearing, being chased by the wind howling through the trees. It looks like the ground itself is a river, flowing under our feet. I ask about the leaves, but no one knows. The trees usually never shed their greens.

In preparation for the ceremony the day following the attack, the fallen are placed on pyres around the clearing, and the injured healed or moved into the med tent. Lay told me earlier that Lizzie has been preserved and will be burned along with the other warriors. I feel ashamed I did not think of her earlier, though grateful she will be honoured today with the rest. The atmosphere here in Eader is sombre. After walking around I can see why. We have lost one hundred and forty-six Eadorians, this including Bob and Bethany. We still haven't located Callan, or his body. And seeing the destruction in Manawa, burnt down houses, the Grasshopper's Feast smashed, all the injured people, it pisses me off. But worst of all, the cinema was sat upon by a troll. A troll! Seriously, the Darkness will perish! My broken nerd heart tries to stay occupied by looking for Callan and helping Thiam out in the med tent. Since the battle with Cox, I have much better control of my powers and can now take the dark energy and transform it into light, such as pain for instance. I am no healer, but at least I can relieve some of the discomfort for the patients, and take away any inflicted Darkness where required. Seems like the battle ended ages ago, not just a few measly hours, as I sit next to the fire, drained from working in the med tent.

"Not flat on your back for once – how refreshing," Darby mocks as she approaches from her tent. Before I can retort or ask, she shakes her head. "No, we haven't found him yet, but don't wor…" And that is as far as she gets, before I hear a familiar jeering voice.

"How many battles does a guy have to win to get a beer around here?"

Needless to say I freak out. "Where the hell have you been, you twat? Why couldn't we sense you anywhere?"

"Whoa, whoa, whoa, calm yer tits," he says calmly.

This of course catches Darby's attention, in a bad way. "Excuse you, moron?" She sends pulse – sending Callan reeling.

"Wow, no need for name calling. Am I late?" By the looks me and Darby are sending him, Callan sighs, realising a more thorough explanation is needed. "Fine, so, I fought six of these angry Valkyries yesterday and of course, won," he states brazenly. When all he gets is an annoyed eyebrow lift from Darby he goes on. "Um, yeah. So after heroically fighting these mean-ass women, I tried fighting a giant. Let's just say, when a giant goes down, get out of the way. Been trying to get out from under that thing for the last ten hours, probably why you couldn't sense me too."

I roll my eyes. He seems fine, though a little off maybe. I ease back down on the log, nursing my cold coffee.

"So, how has it been going here?" Callan asks. Before we answer however, he looks around the clearing, and mutters under his breath, "Damn… How many?"

Darby looks solemnly around. "One hundred and forty-six brave warriors. Almost added you to that list. Good to have you back, Lieutenant."

He nods firmly, looking almost defiant, murmuring that he

will go see if he can help in the preparations. Darby turns to me, smiling, crinkling nose and all. "Today's win, ay?"

Later that night, Lay, Darby and I are all standing in the middle of the clearing, looking around at the one hundred and forty-six pyres spread around, mourning friends and family gathered around each. Decipiér, dressed all in black, is standing next to Bob's pyre, comforting his wife, while Ryder is up on a little platform, getting ready to speak. The Dán is even up there, floating next to Ryder, dark blue and fiery. Addison, the seamstress, is sitting on the other side of the stage, strumming a guitar. The clearing quiets down, until all you can hear is the crackling of the main fire.

Ryder then speaks up. "My dear Eadorians, tonight is for our brave warriors, our fallen loved ones, our lost friends." He nods to Addison who strums a few chords before she starts singing. The pyres all around the clearing are lit, and the first notes are hummed in a low, eerie tone, before people join in and they all starts singing a requiem for the fallen ones, making chills run down my spine.

> *The balance must be kept*
> *On the edge of a knife*
> *For our comrades, we have wept*
> *Their sacrifices for life*
> *Conquered by death's spell*
> *We salute in bittersweet farewell*
> *Deó, Dorchadas, Eader*
> *Strong we stand tall*
> *Deó, Dorchadas, Eader*
> *Slàinte mhath, to all!*
> *The tainted and the pure*
> *Our Guardian Forces*

Bring twilight forever more
Our Shield of Sources
Forged in darkness and light
This is why we all fight
Deó, Dorchadas, Eader
Strong we stand tall
Deó, Dorchadas, Eader
Slàinte mhath, to all!

As it ends, everyone claps three times, with a second between each, before sounding off in a deep 'Hooh', reverberating deep in my core long after the voices and final flames have faded into the night.

Darby sighs heavily. "Curse this war. Too many people have been lost." She glances apologetically up at me. We are in the living room at the mansion. Darby sprawled on the couch, and me pacing the length of the windows on the opposite wall. "Sorry, it's just…" She is right, and I can't help but feel guilty. Though this has always been the state of things, Guardians fought for Eader, and I will not taint their memories. I smile, remembering a quote from my favourite author.

"No worries. You know how they say that it is better to light a candle than to curse the darkness?" Darby nods wistfully. "Well," I continue, "someone very smart once said that the truth is, sometimes it's better to do both. That the darkness needs a good cussing out sometimes."

Darby crinkles her nose at me. "Smart guy. Who was this smart man?" I pull her up from the couch.

"A certain Mr Patrick Rothfuss. So, what do you say? Want to go cuss out some darkness with me?"

Darby raises her eyebrow and smiles wickedly. "Lead the way." That is what I like about this place, we move forward – there is always a way, a solution to every problem, we just need to change our perspective, think of something we haven't before. No bureaucracy, because why go around when you can power through? We head outside and are met with bursts of wind streaming between the tree trunks, which are creating wind corridors and chimes, whirling Dust around and making the night pulsate with its own music and light show. I don't know how I will pull this off, all I know is I need to start somewhere, and starting in the dark after fighting the darkness is poetic in a way. I actually always liked the dark. Darkness adds softer edges to the world, brings some mysteries, and is more forgiving than the harsh daylight. Where everything is bare and revealed. We walk down towards the council castle, Darby asking questions all the way. I try my best to deter her from what the real plan is.

"That song, at the funeral, where is it from? Those words seem so familiar to me." Darby says she doesn't know. No matter. I know what I must do, and I actually feel great about it. I have known since I got the rest of my memories back during the fight with Cox, to be honest. Opening that door, unleashing that power, it changed everything and connected all the dots. Especially when Cox was so kind as to more or less spell it out, at least the most imminent issue. First, we needed to defeat Cox and his minions, but the Eader is too weak after degrading for so long, and now it is almost gone. The leaves, the wind, the increasing darkness in Eader is proof of that. It is making Earth extremely vulnerable. Lay will be an issue, hopefully she will be distracted by her duties and injury, so she won't hone-in on my thought frequency. Damn those terms and conditions. Thing is, I have a theory, but need help, however. And all of Eader will have to pitch in. Which means, I need to talk to a crowd. Damn it.

Chapter 34

Darby

"Okay everyone. I realise that not all of you may know who I am, or you may just have heard bad things about me. Or in general, you just know I am a Fior. It does not matter now. All that matters is that I have a plan to restore the Eader, but it will require all of us." Grey is standing on the top of the stairs outside the Castle with most of the people of Eader gathered in front of him, or within earshot anyway. His voice is being magically enhanced so everyone can hear him. "I know that you are all scared, you have just lost someone close to you, and many of you are injured after fighting so bravely in the battle, but we need to pull together for one last effort." The way he says 'last', with a long pause before and after makes him sound so sad, but I don't think anyone other than me picks up on it. "The Eader, as you all know, is what protects us and the Earth from the Darkness, and makes it possible to live safely here, and there. It is now so weak that it can no longer sustain itself, and needs a boost, so to speak." He smiles reassuringly and goes on to explain how it can be compared to pressure dispersion on a plate. When hit in one location, the point of impact might break the plate. But if hit all over at the same time it would equally spread the pressure. When he gets curious looks, he tries by comparing it to heat transfer theory, where the Eader is not able to dispel the darkness equally any more, and needs to be hit all over at the same time with Light to boost it. I smile when he does his nerd talk, feeling proud more than anything else. He gesticulates with his hands, trying to make everyone understand what is happening. As only a few more are nodding, I decide to step in. I Shift up on the rock, put a hand on Grey's shoulder.

"People, we need to give the Eader some light, to help it battle the dark before it breaks down, okay?" Everyone nods and smiles.

Grey gives me an annoyed look, but nods gratefully, nonetheless. "What Darby said, and the most important thing is that we all do this together!"

Ryder now steps up. "As we all know, our trees are what channels the energy for the Eader, and they are dying. We will use them as conduits to infuse the Eader. This means we need to spread out appropriately." Grey looks stunned, but nods as if it all suddenly makes sense. To be honest, he looks drained, as if he is bracing himself for something. The black hair all over the place, his navy-blue sweater torn and his eyes somewhere far away. I feel annoyed. We just won the battle, but we are still losing the war. At least we have a chance. How did we not know about this? At least Grey has a plan. Even though he still hasn't told us what he is planning, other than everyone doing something at the same time.

"Okay guys, the plan is simple – we arrange a chain of people, all walking out from the firepit clearing together, and when in position, everyone will blast the surroundings with light, specifically focusing on the trees. Those with training and without it, it is all about the intention." Grey is shouting out instructions, and the rest of the council is implementing it. Callan, Daryuen and Haines are running around, making sure we are covering as much ground as we can.

Seeing all these people come together, although similar to what we do on a daily basis to fight the Darkness, it was nothing like this. Never this visually unified in one effort. I can feel my tears well up. I organise a half-circle to start stretching out into the woods, leaving both ends of the chains here, which will result in a circle. Now that it is all underway, I manage to lose track of Grey in the chaos of it all – but he is probably just off somewhere helping with the communication, as we need a countdown to synchronise everyone. I spot Lay, Ryder, and Decipiér, who are all working on getting people into the line, and Thiam telling a few of the Guardians to spread out in between the commoners, to help them channel their light when the show starts. My Guardians, or I guess Daryuen's Guardians now, have all been briefed, so it is really superfluous, but I am glad Thiam is joining us after the tough battle he had.

Again, I look for Grey, and ask a few of the Guardians and surrounding people if they have seen him, but no one has since he rallied everyone to the plan. I don't have time to find him, but I hope he is close by.

After about an hour and a half, the circle is starting to take shape. Around sixty thousand people in increasing circles around the Tree of Eader. Quite impressive to be honest. I can see Lay approaching, grinning. "I am so excited for this! The Dust – which is now an official title by the way, change approved by the council – is ready!"

I nod, I heard this from the new General the other day, who is now recuperating from a broken arm and darkness burns in the med tent, and I am glad.

"The Dust have spread out along the circle and will signal a countdown in the form of a dim on-off feature. When you and Grey say the word, they will blink three times rapidly, signalling the start. Okay?" I nod once more, smiling. She walks off again. The circle is now complete, and I too take my place, alongside Ryder and Thiam. We are ready. With no Grey in sight, I decide to give the signal. We are running out of time. Glancing at Thiam, who looks tired, but excited, I smile.

"On the light signal, people! Dust – now!" The Dust holds for a while, hovering a metre above us, in a line curving off in both directions and then it blinks three times in rapid succession. I fire off my light attacks straight ahead of me, and I see my fellow Eadorians doing the same. Others are standing with eyes closed, smiling, sending off positive auras by thinking of loved ones, good music, or good times. The experience is amazing, and I feel happy. I only wish I could share it with Grey.

Chapter 35

Grey

I wish I could be there. Seeing them all. Lay, Callan, Darby. I've never been much of a believer in people. In general I have felt that people let you down too often. Think too much of themselves, and their own social network appearance. But since coming to Eader, things have started to change. I really believe now that it is possible to change something, to reach out. This is something I can actually do to help, so why not, right? It isn't like I had anything else planned for today.

I have slipped away from the circles of Eadorians and Shifted to the Tree of Eader, standing outside, contemplating what the hell I do now. It isn't like this part comes with a manual. Cox was the one who gave me the answer, saying I had the power, how my power was the only thing that could stop him. Which is what I am now prepared to give, to the Eader. It wasn't really a hard decision to make, even though I know that everyone has a daily struggle between light or dark, different shades of decisions – candy or healthy snack, walking or taking the bus, giving to charity or saving the money, having that last drink or not, calling your mum or continue binge watching Netflix. It is what makes us human – the decisions we make which make up who we are, and our lives. It doesn't make you evil or a bad person necessarily – we all have areas of improvement – and we can never be one hundred per cent in everything. We all have our strengths and weaknesses, which are just as important. I have just decided that all of that doesn't matter. It isn't really my decision. This is what I was meant to do, and if I don't do this, well… There will be no more decisions to make. So, by that logic, I am doing this. Deciding to not decide, so others can make more decisions. Seems legit.

As I walk towards the Tree's entrance, I think about what I am really trying to save. The magic in it all. In the small things, such as snow ladened trees in a frosty forest, the colourful sunrise over a smog-filled city, the smile of a mischievous little sister bugging her older sister just because she can, the dancing, green lights in the dark chilly sky, a coffee cup in the unforgiving hours of the day, the light sparkling in a mother's eyes when reuniting with her child. The creaking sound of dried leaves under your boots on a golden autumn afternoon. The tornado of rainbows competing for space in your chest when you meet the love of your life, or the smell of a new book. Or simply that sinful pleasure of tasting that one piece of chocolate you've been dreaming of, after a long day at work. It is all part of what makes life worth living. That is what I want to save.

Inside the Tree a lot has changed. Her colours have faded into almost nothing, and instead of a river there is more like drops flowing from the floor, light coming as infrequent as the flashes of lighting across a thundering black sky. It is like she is crying in reverse. Man, it pisses me off. Walking over to her, I feel like the world is now more divided than ever, barely held together by a string of events, people, and natural forces, and will at any moment be ripped apart. A fragile balance that will easily be tipped in the favour of darkness, pouring light out of the pools of life. Shaking my head, I resist the urge to smack myself. You are trying to save your home. Home. Hadn't expected that. But I now have one. And have to lose it to save it. At least I finally know now who I am, and where I belong…

I am also ready. Always been searching for that purpose, that direction, and here it is. So it wasn't Comic Con. I'll take it. I reach out to her, and suddenly, as a drop touches me, my powers make so much more sense. This is what she needed; she had planned for it. The Eader gives four Fior – adapting each with powers needed. My Phoenix, her rebirth. Smart girl, I'll give her that.

Now, how do I go about this? It did make sense a second ago. Crouching down next to the drops of light, I see the pulsating lights on the figures of prior Fiors on the wall. How they are drawn in by the light, and then extinguished. Opposites attract and opposites can kill, light is allergic to dark – and vice versa, lays to waste all the darkness in its wake – except in twilight, where the two melds together. Suddenly it comes to me. My power is the one prior Fiors didn't have, the power of Twilight, using the one for the other. I need to use it all. Embracing both sides. Time to embrace my inner demons. Which is fine, as I never chase them too far away. Being a gatekeeper never made more sense. Between Earth and Dorchadas, keeping the peace. It's like Leonard Cohen said about how the crack in all things will let the light in. Well I will add to that, as where there is light, there will always be shadows, just like my twilight. Man, it is all so complicated, so many factors and complicated matrices of power and opinions – sometimes there is only black and white, right or wrong, no loop holes, no grey areas, no financial gain, no bureaucracy, and no quick getaway. Just you and what needs to be done. It is mind blowing how many pieces of a puzzle that absolutely have no connecting edges, but are forced together when needed. Or, the opposite, when something should be done, but is not cost efficient enough, and therefore falls apart. Enough thinking – let's just do this. I see three flashing lights through the doorway as I am reaching into the Eader's fading pulses, I think of home, Lizzie, Darby, Callan. I give it all I have, absorbing her burden, transforming it into what she needs, light. I can't believe how much is weighing down on the Eader, what she has been fighting for us all, but I am taking it, all of it, and it is all pain, burning through me. As each pulse takes a little bit more, I hear myself screaming.

I liked me better before. Before I knew this part of myself. Blissfully ignorant of how dark and martyr-like I could go. I am forever changed, and I don't know if it is for the better. I miss me. Yet, this is the right thing to do. As I am fading and insides burning, I see streams of light joining mine, the Eader drinking it up. It is working, they are doing it. Smiling, I drop down on knee, then to my side, letting her take it all. With one last effort I grab my amulet. Lizzie's night watchman, just like she had predicted.

Chapter 36

Darby

A power wave surges through Eader, rippling through the air, the ground, and everything on it. Everything burns bright with light and colour, and it is as if the air suddenly is a bit clearer. "We did it!" The cheer explodes through the ranks of people, who jump and hug each other. I smile and Thiam claps me on the back.

"Way to go, Madam General." I smile back, accepting my old full title. Still feels weird, not being Madam General any more. Something feels off, however. The pulse was one directional, and it should've come from the barrier itself, meaning from everywhere. Somehow, I know Grey has gone and done something stupid again. So typical him. Adrenaline and fear surges inside me, and I run to the only place I can think of – the Tree of Eader. I hear Ryder shouting after me, but I do not care.

"No, no, no!" I mutter to myself as I leap over rocks and speed through the forest towards my destination. I hear people following me, but I increase my size and stride, leaving them behind. I skid to a halt outside the tree and look on in shock. It looks like the explosion went off here. The ground is singed, and in some places still giving off smoke. My pulse is pounding as I walk into the tree. Catching my breath, my mouth falls open. The walls are full of soot, but remarkably enough, the room looks intact. The Eader is now a radiant, dazzling beam of pulsating light, giving off heat and colour. It makes my heart swell, but it breaks just as fast when I see that right next to it lies a less intact Grey. He is lying face down on the ground, also singed and giving off smoke. His clothes are in tatters. His jeans are now ripped all over and his shirt is almost burnt off him, so I can see his phoenix tattoo clearly. It practically looks like it is glowing. I sigh, and my heart starts pounding hard in my chest. I know it is serious, as I start to understand what he has done.

"Here you are again, nerd. Sleeping on the job." Smiling sadly to myself, I crouch down beside him, running my fingers over the glowing phoenix on his singed back. It is warm to the touch, while the rest of him feels cold. I roll him over, so his head rests in my lap. He looks so peaceful, almost like he is sleeping, but his chest is still. I slowly brush his jet-black hair out of his eyes, picking out a stray leaf. Stroking his sooty cheek, I can feel a warm tear escaping the corner of my eye and it falls into his hair and his hand feels cold as I put my fingers around it and pull it up to my cheek, closing my eyes. "Oh, Grey, you bastard. You shouldn't have done this alone." I sit there, silently crying. He saved us all without hesitation. The sarcastic, annoying geek saved the world. Time floats by, and I have no idea how long I am sitting there, but I hear footsteps and then a careful cough from the doorway.

"I am so sorry, Darby." It is Decipiér, of all people. "He was… he was a brave man."

Looking up at him, I smile. "Yes, yes, he was."

He steps back out, leaving me alone with Grey. The tree, which is now alive and thriving, seems cold and void of any colour.

We just sit there. Alone. For what seems like hours. My nerd of a neighbour. The involuntary warrior who stumbled in and saved the day. Who would've guessed? I almost laugh. My Grey, who is now not so cold any more. Actually, he feels like he is thawing. No, like he is burning up! A glow is coming from his chest, and it is growing. I am frozen in place, just staring. The orange glow seems to spread throughout his body, glowing through his tattered clothes. Suddenly, it starts to pulsate over his heart and with each beat it seems to lift out of him. It grows larger and larger, until I see what it is. It is a phoenix, stretching out its wings and taking flight. Once, twice, three times, it beats its growing wings down, before it takes off, soaring around the room once, lighting the pictures along the walls as it goes, and exits though the doorway. Decipiér comes running in, followed by Callan, Ryder, and Thiam.

"Darby, what was that?" But I am too preoccupied to answer. My attention is focused on Grey's chest, which is now moving. In infinitesimal flutters I can see him drawing breath. His forehead is on fire and small groans are escaping him.

"Thiam!" Thiam gets the message, and runs over, checking Grey.

"How is this possible? With this amount of Darkness. He should be…"

"He was, but not anymore. We need to help him!"

Decipiér frowns. "We will use Grey's idea." With that he runs outside, and I can hear his sharp commanding voice in the distance. Only ten seconds pass before he returns. "We are ready," he states matter-of-factly.

Callan is standing in the back, eyeing Grey, but looks away when he notices me watching him. Grey twitches in my arms, squeezing my hand tightly, which I just now realise I am still holding. Raising my eyebrows as I get what Decipiér is up to, I nod, and Decipiér steps up, as the first one. He takes Thiam's hand, who is holding Grey's other hand, and gives whatever light he can. Then he steps away, letting Ryder take his place, who repeats the process. One by one, the people of Eader step into the Tree of Eader to help Grey fight the Darkness now tormenting his body and soul, trying to overcome him, yet again. I feel his breathing evening out with each surge of light he gets. His fever breaks sometime during the night and in the end, he is sleeping soundly in my lap. I lose count of how many people step in to help, but I am so grateful, and it seems like they are too. Being able to pay back the man who saved their home and their world. Sometime during the night I summon Lika, a bit for comfort and also for her to run and get some food and water. She gently licks Grey's ashen Converse and runs off. There are Dust flying all around us, and also outside, making the setting all the more magical.

We are alone when I can feel him stirring a bit, jarring me from my slumber. I sit up straighter, looking down on him as he slowly opens his eyes. It is like I have been without oxygen and can finally breathe as I see those stormy purple and blues again, and I smile. At the same time, I can feel my anger bubbling forth. He had been such an idiot for leaving me like that. All alone after just having... I stare at him.

"Hi sleepy head, had a good nap?" I try, but my voice breaks halfway through. "Oh Grey... You didn't have to do this." He smiles his crooked smile, and closes his eyes for a second.

"I know – but I wanted to, because I preferred these consequences, to you know, everyone dying," he croaks and coughs. As he is lying there, eyes closed, smiling, I roll my eyes, grinning.

"Wow, humble much?" I feel tears running down my cheeks, but I don't care.

"There is the Darby I know and love. No wonder your name

means fire." He winces as he reaches for me, and wipes the tears from my eyes. "Never want to see that fire go out, so it was worth it. And the Eader says hi, by the way. She made a poem for me." I frown down at him, trying to stay on point, but his purple tinged blues are making it hard to focus. "I hope I am reading that adorable frown wrong. Did we do it? Did it work?" Grey croaks again, giving me his incredibly annoying crooked smile. I feel my anger melting and I stroke him carefully on the cheek. He has got a bit of the colour back in them now.

"Yes, you nerd, you did it. You saved everyone." I give him some water, which makes him cough.

"Thanks," he manages. He closes his eyes, his smile lingering on his lips. I feel him squeezing my hand which I am still holding, and he whispers, "For you, Darby, all for you." I squeeze his hand, and I lean forward and gently kiss him. A kiss he softly returns. My lips only gently brush his, but it sends tingles all the way down my spine. The light in the room flickers and I see the Eader intensifying into a terrifying red, which just as fast dies down as I pull away. "Upside-down action, just like Peter Parker," Grey whispers, and I smile, as the Grey I know and love is back.

"Right you are, but I always preferred DC to be honest. And what poem?" I receive no sarcastic comeback, only Grey's steady breathing, and I realise he has fallen asleep again. Here in my arms, just where he belongs.

Chapter 37

Grey

Light never looked so good. Honestly. Standing outside that med tent is just what the doctor ordered. Thiam however wants me on bedrest for the next century. I refused. Walking around the fire pit I ponder what has passed and roll my eyes for wording it like that. Ponder!

Anyway, a lot has happened, like dying and saving the world. But I know better. I didn't really save the world. I postponed its demise. There is a difference. Only Darby knows this, who is the only person I told after waking up. The Eader told me all of it, after my powers woke me from the ashes of my sacrifice. She told me she is the third part of the Mana-Tali, the Shield of Power. The Eader itself is energy, or Malosi, which fuels the shield as one out of three. The second is the Dorchadas and the third is the Deó, which is on Earth. The point of intersection, or orthocentre between each point is the centre of power. This, along with the requiem at the funeral it started to all make sense. We have tried to explain this to the council, but they aren't buying it. It is just too much. But to hell with them. We got three numbers and a mission – save the Shield. The numbers are burnt into my memory, and I couldn't wash them out if I tried. As far as I am concerned this is the only thing that matters, and Darby is in. We have deducted that the numbers are coordinates, but that is where it gets tricky. The Eader shared that the first numbers was her location, 68theta.76phi in Eader polar coordinates. As for the second, we are guessing it is for Deó, Earth. 20theta.30phi. Which by my calculations leads to the coordinates 57°15'01.4"N 6°16'21.7"W – a rocky archway entrance, tumbling down with clear, magical water of the Fairy Pools in Scotland. Darby did her research, and tells me it has history of protective powers, with Gaelic legends of the selkies, spirits of those who drowned and lived on as seals, but in the full moon they become mortal again for one night. This should be our next stop, as the third set of numbers would be the Dorchadas, the third Source. Which according to Cox is already extinguished, at −89theta −06phi. Lay is still healing, but is eager to help when we leave, it is only Callan that seems reluctant. He has been different since it all went down, keeping to himself. Which I can't really blame him for. Standing outside he is watching me, as I pace around the fireplace.

"There you are, Grey, good to see you up and about. It was close as a split chest hair on a house fly, you almost dying, I mean," Callan says, eloquent as always.

"Yeah, I guess you're right."

Darby walks by in the distance, waves at us and turns down towards Manawa. I smile and continue my pacing, as Callan continues his staring. "Why the shade, Stinky?"

"What? I am just happy you found your Lumia Lark."

"Say what now?"

"Oh, old Eadorian joke. Never mind." He winks at me and slips around the med tent corner, into the shadows. There is something alluring and friendly about the darkness, keeping you company, but I am getting tired of Callan's darkness, always following me around. Curious of what he meant, I walk down to the newly-restored library with its limited content, looking up

Lumia Lark. Turns out it is a children's story called '*Shade and Lumia Lark meet in the In-between*' and I sit down to read it.

Once Upon a Time… There was this fellow named Shade. He was not like you and me. Because when you turned the light on, he would fade.

Shade was a Shadow, and a lonely one at that. All he wanted was a friend, to play with, and maybe have a chat.

There was also this funny girl, whose name was Lumia Lark. She was lonely too, and she had a secret. She was afraid of the Dark.

Lumia Lark was made of Light. She was pretty and danced all day. But when the evening came, she was chased away.

What she did not know, was that Shade only wanted to say hi. But every time he tried, she ran away, and every night he would cry.

As the morning returned, so would Lumia Lark. She did not know she chased Shade away, along with the dark.

One evening, as the light was suddenly switched on, Shade tripped and fell under the bed. He marvelled that he was not gone!

Lumia Lark was back, and saw the dark under the bed. Although she was scared, she saw a smile. And said hi instead!

They laughed and talked about how silly they had been. They agreed that next time, they would meet in the In-between.

Lumia Lark and Shade could finally be friends. May the story continue in your dreams. Because this is where it ends.

Reading the story, suddenly the poem from the Eader made much more sense:

Your journey has begun, here in the in-between,
The effects of which will soon be seen.

You must start at the end, in the third layer.
There in the dark, you must free the betrayer.
Travel to the north for ninety, where you will lose one,
Then retrace in reverse for six you must the Sun.
For the last destination
You must defy all creation.
Travel you must south and then reverse
To the difference between the layers,
And climb the nearest shore you find
What has been given, and give then in kind.

The fight is still between light and dark, but this time it is across time and space, and it is not about one beating the other. More like all of them balancing out. And it needs to happen fast. All of this seems like a storm in a teacup to be honest, and all happening on rhyme to boot. All I know is that it is real; we need to protect and reignite the Sources, but don't ask me how. And we will need help. I wish the Eader could help. She told me without the Dorchadas Source burning and with the Deó Source this weak, she couldn't produce another Fior. This is why the returning of the previous Fior hadn't helped and it had broken her heart.

I continue my circling, fiddling with the bullet around my neck, the very same that Callan used to save my life. My once best bro who is now just acting weird. Ever since the initial battle something has been off. What else is new to be honest, he'll come around. I walk out from the library and come face to face with Darby. She smiles and punches me in the shoulder as we walk together up the main street towards the camp.

"So nerd, you ready for this?"

I roll my eyes and walk by her, poking her side. "This nerd

just figured out Eader's message, thank you very much."

She rolls her eyes and picks up the pace. "Doesn't matter, you need more training, you won using pure will and a good dose of luck, that won't cut it next time!"

"Next time? Now who's the pessimist?"

"Trust me – you need more training." I see a small smile out of the edge of my eye, and I laugh.

"Sure, okay. But pretty sure I just died a little, though I wouldn't shuffle off my mortal coil that easily, right now I need to chill with some Netflix. Good with you?"

"Netflix and chill? Sure, let's do it."

"No, that isn't what I…"

Darby cocks her head innocently, looking ready to burst.

"Ha-ha, very funny."

Epilogue

Grey

So there you have it. We are royally screwed. And now relying on a handful of people to help us out. The Eader is good, but for how long? It is like Charles Bukowski said, 'The problem with the world is that the intelligent people are full of doubts, while the stupid ones are full of confidence.' I am somewhere in between – taking stupid risks to save someone else, maybe not the ideal hero for this story, but at least I am trying. You should be too. Don't let the Darkness's poison block your mind of what can be. It is easy to think everything is set in stone, just look at the politicians, different religions, terrorists – all blocked from seeing the opportunities, only creating hindrances. Be the change. Okay, sorry. I just threw up a little. I am no Hallmark card, but please, be a pal. Help a guy out. Anyway, there you go – people are stupid, like I told you. I do however need to amend my viewpoint a bit, because as you can tell, the real picture is a bit more complicated, and against the forces of darkness, most people have stood up very well under pressure. There will be more challenges ahead, but hopefully the Eader has been given some respite as it is back to full force. There is light in the dark – and many people have started to see it more clearly already.

As mentioned, I finally remember. Growing up in Eader, the battle, being thrust out into the world of foster care. Not all great. Also, I remember Lizzie. My Lizzie. On Eader. She was always there. She was my mum, my real mum. As real as a Fior can have. She had moved with me to Earth without waiting for the council's permission to keep an eye on me, but lost track of me during the Shift due to the raging battle, and had been looking for me until I showed up at the hospital, and in public medical records. Also, small changes have been seen on Earth. As the Eader is thriving and blossoming, Earth's conditions have been improving a bit, but not much. Certain people are still in power, people are still scared, but it seems like people have gained some gumption.

Here in Eader, I have been given a new name, Grey, the Twilight Phoenix of Eader. Which makes me feel like a total poser. They treat me like a saviour when I really didn't save them at all. But I will try, which is all you can do. Now, I'll give you some pointers.

What is your favourite feel good song? You know that feeling you get? Or from taking a ride in your car on a sunny afternoon? Or receiving a smile from the person you love? Hang on to that! It will take you through, every time. Nothing can change that. It will also help you to see the best in what this world has to offer.

Which is what I am trying to do right now. Me and Darby are at the cemetery on Earth, for Lizzie's funeral. The service is over and they put her in the ground, or at least they think they did as we gave her a proper Eader funeral. Her colleagues and friends are all here, and it feels so very final, all over again. I can feel the anger welling up, and tufts of twilight wisp around my clenched fists. Darby gently grabs my hand and the anger seeps away.

"Thanks," I whisper, as we walk over to the gravestone. We haven't talked about it, what happened in the Tree of Eader, it is more like we have a general understanding of it. We are in this together and we have each other's back. No need to make it complicated or name things. Crouching down, I lay my diploma

313

next to her grave, along with her favourite flowers, peonies. "We did it, Mum, we did it."

I feel Darby squeezing my hand as she whispers, "O'Shearan. Oh Grey, I didn't know." Turning to her, I look into her wide-eyed face.

"What do you mean?"

"Your name, you took her name."

"Of course, she was the closest thing I had to family. And now it turns out we were family. So are you. I forgot to thank you."

She looks at me confused. "Whatever for?"

"For that night, in the alley." She blushes and I tell her about my regained memories, and after she hugs me. I never asked about her upbringing or her story, as I know for us it is a touchy subject. We have to start somewhere though. I draw a deep breath and hand her the letter.

Dear Grey,

I know this is a tough time for you, love, but don't you fret. You have been through hard times and have come out all the stronger for it. There will however be tougher times ahead, and just know you have someone on your side. More than you know. You need to find people to trust, people to love, people to have your back. You have a destiny set out for you which will be filled with darkness and light, and it is up to you to find a balance between it all. This might not be much to hang on to right now but please take it and make a start for yourself. I will be there every step of the way. And Grey, you might not know where you are supposed to be yet, or what your purpose is, but this can help.

Love,

Lizzie

P.S. Remember to keep this medallion with you always, it will keep you safe.